Rodman The Boatsteerer
And Other Stories

by

Louis Becke

Double 9
BOOKS

Rodman The Boatsteerer
And Other Stories
by Louis Becke

ISBN: 978-93-61154-20-1

Published by

DOUBLE 9 BOOKS

2/13-B, Ansari Road
Daryaganj, New Delhi – 110002
info@double9books.com
www.double9books.com
Tel. 011-40042856

ABOUT THE AUTHOR

Louise Becke was an Australian author well known for his adventure collection and evocative tales that took a deep corner in people's hearts. He was born in Port Macquarie, New South Wales where he worked as a trader and Blackbirder in Pacific island which significantly helped him to overcome his literary career. During his career most of the time he co-authored with Walter Jeffrey through which he explored various themes of cultural clashes and challenges faced by both European and indigenous islanders. Most of his books, he always marked by vivid descriptions and provide the best efforts to contribute to his popularity in observation of various topics. However, some of his works faced criticism for not being able to address the cultural representation appropriately and faced financial difficulties that led him to return to Australia in later years. Still, he was able to make enough contribution towards Pacific literature and gain the attention of vivid readers those having an interest in cultural studies and gain valuable insights historical dynamics South Pacific region.

CONTENTS

IN THE KING'S SERVICE, SOME EPISODES IN THE LIFE OF A BEACH-COMBER

OXLEY, THE PRIVATEERSMAN

EMA, THE HALF-BLOOD

RODMAN THE BOATSTEERER

I

With her white cotton canvas swelling gently out and then softly drooping flat against her cordage, the *Shawnee*, sperm whaler of New Bedford, with the dying breath of the south-east trade, was sailing lazily over a sea whose waters were as calm as those of a mountain lake. Twenty miles astern the lofty peaks of Tutuila, one of the islands of the Samoan group, stood out clearly in the dazzling sunshine, and, almost ahead, what at dawn had been the purple loom of Upolu was changing to a cloud-capped dome of vivid green as the ship closed with the land.

The *Shawnee* was "a five-boat ship," and, judging from the appearance of her decks, which were very clean, an unlucky one. She had been out for over a year, and three months had passed since the last fish had been killed. That was off the coast of Chile, and she was now cruising westward and northward towards the eastern coast of New Guinea, where Captain Harvey Lucy, the master, expected to make up for the persistent ill-luck that had attended him so far. Naturally a man of most violent and ungovernable temper, his behaviour to his men on the present voyage had led to disastrous consequences, and the crew, much as they admired their captain as one of the most skilful whalemen who had ever trod a deck, were now worked up into a state of exasperation bordering on mutiny. Shortly before the Samoan Islands were sighted, the ship's cooper, a man who took the cue for his conduct to the hands from the example set by the captain, had had a fierce quarrel with a young boat-steerer, named Gerald Rodman, who, in a moment of passion, struck the cooper such a terrific blow that the man lay between life and death for some hours. An attempt to put Rodman in irons was fiercely resisted by a number of his shipmates, who were led by his younger brother. But the after-guard were too strong for the men, and after a savage conflict the two Rodmans and three other seamen were overpowered by Captain Lucy, his four mates and the carpenter and stewards. As was common enough in those days on American whaleships, nearly all the officers were relatives or connections by marriage, and were always ready to stand by the captain; in this instance the cooper was a brother of the second mate. Six days had passed since this affair had occurred, and when Upolu was sighted the five men were still in irons and confined in the hot and stifling atmosphere of the sail-locker, having been given only just enough food and water to keep body and soul together.

Four bells struck, and Captain Lucy made his appearance from below. The watch on deck, who had hitherto been talking among themselves as they went about their work, at once became silent, and muttered curses escaped from their lips as they eyed the tall figure of the captain standing at the break of the poop. For some minutes he apparently took no notice of any one about him; then he turned to the mate, who stood near him, and said:

"Have you had a look at those fellows this morning, Brant?"

"Yes," answered the officer. "They want to know if you're going to let them have a smoke."

A savage oath preceded Captain Lucy's reply—

"They can lie there till they die before any one of them shall put a pipe in his mouth."

"Just as you please, captain," said the mate, nonchalantly. "I guess you know best what you're doing. But there's going to be more trouble aboard this ship if you don't ease up a bit on those five men; and if I were you I wouldn't go too far. One of 'em—that youngest Rodman boy—can't stand much more of that sail locker in such weather as this. And I guess I don't want to go before a grand jury if he or any of 'em dies."

"I tell you, Brant, that rather than ease up on those fellows, I'd lose the ship. I'm going to keep them there till we strike another fish, and then I'll haze what life is left in them clean out of them."

Rough and harsh as he was with the crew of the *Shawnee*, Brant was no vindictive tyrant, and was about to again remonstrate with the savage Lucy, when, suddenly, the thrilling cry of "There she blows!" came from the look-out in the crow's nest; and in a few minutes the barque's decks were bustling with excitement. A small "pod" or school of sperm whales were in sight. Four boats were at once lowered and started in pursuit.

When first sighted from the ship the whales were not more than two miles distant, and moving towards her. The mate's boat was first away, and in a very short time fastened to the leader of the "pod"—a huge bull over sixty feet in length. In less than five seconds after the keen-edged harpoon had plunged deep into his body, the mighty fish "sounded" (dived) at a terrific speed; the other whales at once disappeared and Brant's boat shot away from the other three. The remaining boats were those of the captain and the second and third mates. For some ten or fifteen minutes their crews lay upon their oars watching the swift progress of the mate's boat, and scanning the sea from every point around them, to discern where the vanished and unstricken whales would rise to breathe again. At last they saw the great bull, to which the mate's boat was fast, burst out upon the surface of the water, two miles away. For a minute the mighty creature lay exposed to view, beating the sea into a white seeth of foam as he struck the water tremendous blows with his tail, and sought to free himself from the cruel steel in his body. As he thrashed from side to side, two of his convoy rose suddenly near him as if in sympathy with their wounded leader. Then, in an instant, they all disappeared together, the stricken whale still dragging the mate's boat after him at an incredible speed.

Knowing that in all probability the two whales which had just appeared would accompany the great bull to the last—when he would receive the stroke of the death-dealing lance from Brant—the captain of the *Shawnee* at once started off in pursuit, accompanied by the second and third mates' boats. The crews bent to their tough ash oars with strength and determination. There was no need for the dreadful oaths and blasphemies with which Captain Lucy and his officers assailed their ears, or his threats of punishment should they fail to catch up the mate's boat and miss killing the two "loose" whales; the prospect of such a prize was all the incentive the seamen needed. With set teeth and panting bosoms they urged the boats along, and presently they were encouraged by a cry from the third mate, who called out to the captain and second mate that the wounded whale was slackening his speed, and Mr. Brant was "hauling up alongside to give him the lance." In another fifty strokes the captain and the two officers saw the great head of the creature that was dragging the mate's boat along again appear on the surface, and on each side were his devoted cetacean companions, who were almost of as monstrous a size as the bull himself.

With savage oaths the captain urged his crew to fresh exertions, for just then he saw the mate go for'ard in his boat and plunge his keen lance of shining steel into his prize, then back his boat off as the agonised whale again sounded into the blue depths below, with his life-blood pouring from him in a bubbling stream.

II

On board the *Shawnee* the progress of the boats was watched amid the most intense excitement; and even the imprisoned seamen, in their foul and horrible prison, stretched their wearied and manacled limbs and sought to learn by the sounds on deck whether any or all of the boats were "fast" — that is, had harpooned a whale. Broken-spirited and exhausted as they were by long days of cruel and undeserved punishment, they would have forgotten their miseries in an instant had the fourth mate ordered them on deck to lower his boat—the only one remaining on board—and join their shipmates in the other boats in the chase. But of this they knew there was little prospect, for this remaining boat had been seriously injured by a heavy sea, which had washed her inboard a few days before the fight between the officers and crew. Presently, however, they heard the hurried stamping of feet on deck, and then the voices of the fourth mate and cooper giving orders to take in sail.

"Jerry," said a young English lad named Wray, to the elder Rodman, "do you hear that? One of the boats must have got 'fast' and killed. We'll be out of this in another half-hour, cutting-in. The captain won't let us lie here when there is work to be done on deck; he's too mean a Yankee to satisfy his revenge at the expense of his pocket."

But their pleasant belief that a whale had been killed, and that the ship was shortening sail while the carcass was being cut-in, was rudely disturbed a few minutes later, when the *Shawnee* took a sudden list over to port, and they were all pitched to the lee side of the sail locker in a heap. A squall had struck the barque.

Bruised and lacerated by the force with which they had been hurled together, the five prisoners sat up, and were soon enlightened as to the condition of affairs by the carpenter making his appearance, taking off their galling irons, and ordering them on deck.

The squall was a very heavy one, accompanied by savage gusts of stinging rain, and the old ship, with her canvas in great disorder, was every now and then thrown almost on her beam ends with its fury. After considerable trouble the officers and crew succeeded in saving her canvas from being blown to ribbons, and got the barque snug again. A quarter of an hour later the squall began to lose its force, but the rain descended in torrents, and obscured the view of the now agitated ocean to such an extent that the look-outs from aloft could not discern its surface a cable length away. All those on board the barque felt intense anxiety as to whether the mate had succeeded in killing his whale before the squall burst upon him, for they knew that had he not done so he would have been compelled to cut the line and let his prize escape; no boat could live in such a sea as had arisen when "fast" to a sperm whale which was travelling at such a speed, even though fatally wounded and weak from loss of blood.

An hour passed, and then, to the joy of all on board, the rain ceased, a faint air came from the westward and blew away the thick clouds of tropic mist which enveloped the ship. Ten miles distant the verdant hills and valleys of Upolu glistened in the sunshine, and then one of the look-outs hailed the deck:

"I can see a boat, Mr. Newman—it is Mr. Brant's. He has killed his whale, sir."

In an instant the fourth mate was running aloft, but before he had ascended to the fore-top the lookout cried:

"I can see the other three boats now, sir, and they are all 'fast,' too."

A cheer broke from the *Shawnee's* hands, and, disregarding for the time all discipline, they sprang aloft one after another to gaze upon the thrilling scene. Three miles away, and plainly discernible in the now clear atmosphere, was the mate's boat lying alongside the big bull, which had just been killed, and at about the same distance were the boats of the captain and second and third mates, all "fast" to whales, and racing swiftly to windward toward the horizon.

The fourth mate at once came down from aloft and held a hurried consultation with the cooper—an old and experienced whaler. It was evident to them that the three boats had only just succeeded in getting "fast," and that, as darkness was so near, the officers in them would have great difficulty in killing the whales to which they were "fast," as the sea was still very lumpy from the violence of the squall. None of the boats were provided with bomb-guns, the use of which would have killed the whales in a very short time; and the wind having again died away it was impossible for the ship to work up to them. Nothing, it was evident, could be done to assist the three boats, but it was decided to send the one remaining on board the barque to help the mate to tow his whale to the ship before the hordes of sharks, which would be attracted to the carcass by the smell of blood, began to devour it.

The carpenter was at once set to work to make her temporarily water-tight. By this time the sun had set, and only the position of the mate's boat was made known to the ship by a light displayed by Mr. Brant.

Standing on the port side of the poop, Martin Newman, the fourth mate, was gazing anxiously out into the darkness, hoping to see the other three boats show lights to denote that they had succeeded in killing their fish, and were waiting for a breeze to spring up to enable the barque to sail towards them. Although Newman was the youngest officer on board, he was an experienced one, and the fact that his boat had not been fit to lower with the other four had filled him with sullen rage; for he was of an intensely jealous nature, and would rather have seen the boats return unsuccessful from the chase than that he alone should have missed his chance of killing a fish.

Presently the younger of the two Rodmans, who was his (Newman's) own boatsteerer, ventured, in the fulness of his anxiety for his shipmates, to step up to the officer and speak:

"Do you think, sir, that the captain and Mr. Ford and Mr. Manning have had to cut their lines?"

The officer made no reply; and could the young boatsteerer have seen the dark, forbidding scowl upon his face, he would never have addressed him at such an unpropitious moment. But imagining that his question had not been heard, the youth repeated it.

Newman turned, and seeing the lad standing in an attitude of expectancy, asked him in savage tones what he was doing there.

"Nothing, sir; I only ——"

"I'll teach you that a man doing nothing doesn't suit me when I'm in charge of the deck of this ship!" and he struck the boatsteerer a terrific blow in the mouth, which knocked him off the poop on to the main deck.

When Ned Rodman came to, he found his head supported by his brother and young Wray, and the rest of the hands on deck standing around him in sympathetic silence. Newman was the most liked of all the officers, and the lad whom he had struck down had been rather a favourite of his, principally, it was supposed, because the two Rodmans came from the same town as himself; and when the disturbance had arisen with the cooper, and the two brothers had been put in irons, Newman had several times expressed his sorrow to them when he had visited them in their prison. His sudden outburst of violence to Ned Rodman was therefore a surprise to the men generally; and several of them glanced threateningly at the figure of the fourth mate, who was now striding to and fro on the poop, occasionally hailing the look-outs in angry tones, and asking if any more boat-lights were visible.

Gerald Rodman, though no words escaped his lips as he wiped away the blood which welled from a terrible cut on his brother's temple, had in his eyes a red light of passion that boded ill for the fourth mate when the time came. He was five years older than his brother, and, although both were boatsteerers, and had made many cruises in the Pacific, this was the first time they had been shipmates. Unlike Ned, he was a man of a passionate and revengeful nature, and the second mate, to whose boat he belonged, had warned the cooper of the *Shawnee* never to meet Gerald Rodman ashore alone.

"He is a man who will never forgive an injury, and I would not care to be in your shoes if he gets you by yourself one day."

And, as a matter of fact, Gerald Rodman had sworn to himself, when he lay in irons, in the sail-locker, to have his revenge upon both the cooper and Captain Lucy, should he ever meet either of them ashore at any of the islands the barque was likely to touch at during her cruise. He was a man of great physical strength, and, for his position, fairly well educated. Both his parents were dead, and he and his brother Ned, and a delicate sister of nineteen, were the sole survivors of a once numerous family. The care of this sister was the one motive that animated the elder brother in his adventurous career; and while his reserved and morose nature seemed incapable of yielding to any tender sentiment or emotion, it yet concealed a wealth of the deepest affection for his weakly sister, of which the younger one had no conception. And yet, strangely enough, it was to Ned that Nellie Rodman was most attached; it was to *his* return that she most looked forward, never knowing that it was Gerald's money alone that maintained the old family home in the quiet little New England village in which her simple life was spent. Little did she think that when money was sent to her by Gerald, saying it came "from Ned and myself," that Ned had never had a dollar to send. For he was too careless and too fond of his own pleasure to ever think of sending her money. "Jerry," he thought, "was a mighty stingy fellow, and never spent a cent on himself—and could easily send Nell all she wanted." And yet Gerald Rodman, knowing his brother's weak and mercurial nature, and knowing that he took no care in the welfare of any living soul but himself, would have laid his life down for him, because happy, careless Ned had Nellie's eyes and Nellie's mouth, and in the tones of his voice he heard hers. So as he sat on the deck, with his brother's head upon his knees, he swore to "get even" with Martin Newman, as well as with Captain Lucy and cooper Burr, for as he watched the pale face of the lad it seemed to him to grow strangely like that of his far-off sister.

He had just completed sewing up the gaping wound in his brother's temple, when the cooper came up to the group:

"Here, lay along, you fellows; the carpenter has finished Mr. Newman's boat, and some of you loafing 'soldiers' have to man her and help Mr. Brant to tow his whale alongside. Leave that man there, and look spry, or you'll feel mighty sorry."

III

As the cooper turned away the younger Rodman, assisted by his brother, staggered to his feet. The fall from the poop had, in addition to the cut in his temple, severely injured his right knee, and he begged his brother to let him lie down again.

"Yes, yes," whispered Gerald Rodman, hurriedly; "lie down, Ned," and then the lad heard him speaking to Wray in eager, excited tones.

"I'm with you, Jerry," said the young Englishman, quickly, in answer to something that Rodman had said; "where is he now?"

"In the cabin, getting some Bourbon for Mr. Brant's boat. There is only the Dago steward with him, and if Porter and Tom Harrod will join us we shall manage the thing right enough."

"What is the matter, Jerry—what are you talking about?" asked Ned from where he lay.

"Keep still, Ned, and ask us nothing just now; there's a chance of our getting clear of this floating hell. I needn't ask *you* if you'll join us. Come on, Wray."

The fourth mate and the Portuguese steward were in the main cabin filling some bottles from a large jar of Bourbon whisky. Their backs were turned to the door, and both were so intent upon their task that they neither heard nor saw the four figures steal softly upon them. Suddenly they were seized from behind by Wray and Gerald Rodman, and then quickly gagged by Harrod and Porter before either had time to utter a cry. In a few minutes the four men had armed themselves with cutlasses from the rack around the mizzen-mast, which came through the cabin at the for'ard end of the table, Rodman also taking the captain's and chief mate's loaded revolvers out of their berths.

The fourth mate and steward were then carried into the captain's cabin, and Gerald Rodman spoke:

"Newman," he said, "we are going to take charge of this ship for a while. If you make an attempt to give an alarm you are a dead man. Wray, stand here and run them both through if they make the ghost of a sound."

Again entering the captain's cabin, he returned with two or three charts, a sextant and the ship's chronometer, which he placed on the table just as a heavy footfall sounded on the companion steps. It was the cooper.

"The boat is all ready, Newman," he said, as he entered the somewhat darkened cabin; "who is going in her?"

"We are," said Rodman, dealing him a blow with the butt of his pistol and felling him. "Leave him there, Wray—he'll give us no trouble. Now take every one of those rifles out of the rack and put them on the table. There's two kegs of powder and a bag of bullets in Mr. Brant's cabin—get those as well."

This was quickly done, and, calling to the others to follow him, Rodman sprang up the companion. No one but the man at the wheel was on the poop, and the leader of the mutineers, looking over the rail, saw that the boat was alongside with only one hand in her. Besides this man there were but eight other persons besides the mutineers on the ship, including the fourth mate, cooper, steward, and carpenter.

Calling the carpenter to him, Rodman covered him with his pistol, and told him and the rest of the startled men to keep quiet or it would be worse for them.

"Two of you help my brother into the boat," he ordered. He was at once obeyed, and Ned Rodman was passed over the side into the hands of the man in the boat.

"Put out every light on deck and aloft," was his next command, and this was done by the watch without delay; for there was in Rodman's face such a look of savage determination that they dared not think of refusing. Then he ordered them into the sail-locker.

"Now, Mr. Waller," he said, addressing the carpenter, "we don't want to hurt you and these three men with you. But we are desperate, and bent on a desperate course. Still, if you don't want to get shot, do as I tell you. Get into that sail-locker and lie low. Mr. Newman and the cooper and the steward are already disposed of. And I'm going to put it out of the power of Captain 'Brute' Lucy to get me and those with me into his hands again."

"You won't shut us up in the sail-locker and scuttle the ship and let us drown, will you?" asked the carpenter.

"No; I'm no murderer, unless you make me one. If there is any one I have a grudge against it is Mr. Newman and the cooper; but I won't do more to the cooper than I have already done. Still I'm not going to leave the ship in your hands until I have messed her up a bit. So away with you into the locker, and let us get to work."

Then, with the man from the boat, the carpenter and his companions were pushed into the sail-locker and the door securely fastened. Looking down from the skylight into the cabin Rodman saw that the cooper had not yet come to, and therefore no danger need be apprehended from him. Sending Wray below, the rifles, ammunition, and nautical instruments were passed up on deck and handed down into the boat. Then, leaving Porter on guard to watch the cooper, Rodman and the others went for'ard with a couple of axes and slashed away at the standing fore-rigging on both sides; they then cut half-way through the foremast, so that the slightest puff of wind, when it came, would send it over the side. Then, going for'ard, they cut through the head stays.

"That will do," said the boat-steerer, flinging down his axe; and then walking to the waist he hailed the boat:

"Are you all right, Ned?"

"Yes," answered the youth, "but hurry up, Jerry, I think a breeze is coming."

Running aft, the elder brother sprang up the poop ladder and looked down through the skylight into the cabin. "Cut Mr. Newman and the steward adrift," he said to Wray.

Wray disappeared into Captain Lucy's cabin, and at once liberated the two men, who followed him out into the main cabin.

"Martin Newman," said Rodman, bending down, "just a word with you. You, I thought, were a shade better than the rest of the bullying scoundrels who officer this ship. But now, I find, you are no better than Bully Lucy and the others. If I did justice to my brother, and *another person* I would shoot you, like the cowardly dog you are. But stand up on that table—and I'll tell you why I don't."

The dark features of the fourth mate blanched to a deathly white, but not with fear. Standing upon the table he grasped the edge of the skylight, under the flap of which Gerald Rodman bent his head and whispered to him:

"Do you know why I don't want to hurt you, Martin Newman? When I came home last year I found out my sister's love for you; I found your letters to her, and saw her eating her heart out for you day by day, and waiting for your return. And because I know that she is a dying woman, and will die happy in the belief that you love her, I said nothing. What I have now done will prevent my ever seeing her again, though I would lay my life down for her. But listen to me. Ned will, must, return to her, and beware, if ever you accuse him of having taken a hand in this mutiny— —"

The hands of the fourth mate gripped the skylight ledge convulsively, and his black eyes shone luridly with passion. Then his better nature asserted itself, and he spoke quietly:

"Jerry, I did not know it was Ned whom I struck to-night. I was not myself.... I never meant to harm *him*. And for Nell's sake, and yours and Ned's, give up this madness."

"Too late, too late, Newman. I would rather die to-night than spend another hour on board this ship. But at least, for Nell's sake, you and I must part in peace," and the mutineer held out his hand. It was grasped warmly, and then with a simple "goodbye" Rodman turned away, walked to the poop ladder and called out:

"Into the boat, men!"

Five minutes later they shoved off from the *Shawnee*, whose lofty spars and drooping canvas towered darkly up in the starless night. At the last moment Gerald Rodman had hoisted a light on the mizzen-rigging as a guide to the four absent boats. As the mutineers pulled quickly away its rays shone dimly over the barque's deserted decks.

When daylight came the *Shawnee* was still drifting about on a sea as smooth as glass, and the four boats reached her just before the dawn. The boat with the mutineers could not be discerned even from aloft, and Captain Harvey Lucy, in a state of mind bordering on frenzy, looked first at his tottering foremast and then at the four whales which had been towed alongside, waiting to be cut-in. With the rising sun came another rain-squall, and the foremast went over the side, although Martin Newman with his men had done their best to save it. But Lucy, being a man of energy, soon rigged a jury-mast out of its wreck, and set to work to cut-in his whales. Three days later the *Shawnee* stood away for Apia Harbour in Samoa.

"Those fellows have gone to Apia," he said to mate Brant, "and I'll go there and get them if it takes me a month of Sundays."

But when the *Shawnee* dropped anchor in the reef-bound harbour, Captain Lucy found that he had come on a vain quest—the mutineers' boat had not been seen.

For seven years nothing was ever heard of the missing boat, till one day a tall, muscular-looking man, in the uniform of a sergeant of the New South Wales Artillery, came on board the American whaleship *Heloise*, as she lay in Sydney harbour, refitting. He asked for Captain Newman, and was shown into the cabin.

The captain of the *Heloise* was sitting at the cabin table reading a book, and rose to meet his visitor.

"What can I do for you, sir? Good God! is it you, Gerald Rodman!"

The soldier put out his hand. "Is my sister alive, Newman?"

"She died three years ago in my arms, hoping and praying to the last that she might see you and Ned before she died. And Ned?"

"Dead, Newman; he and Wray and Porter died of thirst. Harrod and I alone survived that awful voyage, and reached New Zealand at last. Was Nell buried with the old folks, Martin?"

"Yes," answered the captain of the *Heloise*, passing his hand quickly over his eyes, "it was her wish to lie with them. We had only been married two years."

The sergeant rose, and took Newman's hand in his, "Goodbye, Martin. Some day I may stand with you beside her grave."

And then, ere the captain of the whaleship could stay him, he went on deck, descended the gangway, and was rowed ashore to the glittering lights of the southern city.

A POINT OF THEOLOGY ON MÂDURÔ

The *Palestine* Tom de Wolf's South Sea trading brig, of Sydney, had just dropped anchor off a native village on Mâdurô in the North Pacific, when Macpherson the trader came alongside in his boat and jumped on board. He was a young but serious-faced man with a red beard, was thirty years of age, and had achieved no little distinction for having once attempted to convert Captain "Bully" Hayes, when that irreligious mariner was suffering from a fractured skull, superinduced by a bullet, fired at him by a trader whose connubial happiness he had unwarrantably upset. The natives thought no end of Macpherson, because in his spare time he taught a class in the Mission Church, and neither drank nor smoked. This was quite enough to make him famous from one end of Polynesia to the other; but he bore his honours quietly, the only signs of superiority he showed over the rest of his fellow traders being the display on the rough table in his sitting-room of a quantity of theological literature by the Reverend James MacBain, of Aberdeen. Still he was not proud, and would lend any of his books or pamphlets to any white man who visited the island.

He was a fairly prosperous man, worked hard at his trading business, and, despite his assertions about the fearful future that awaited every one who had not read the Reverend Mr. MacBain's religious works, was well-liked. But few white men spent an evening in his house if they could help it. One reason of this was that whenever a ship touched at Mâdurô, the Hawaiian native teacher, Lilo, always haunted Mac-pherson's house, and every trader and trading skipper detested this teacher above all others. Macpherson liked him and said he was "earnest," the other white men called him and believed him to be, a smug-faced and sponging hypocrite.

Well, as I said, Macpherson came on board, and Packenham and Denison, the supercargo, at once noticed that he looked more than usually solemn. Instead of, as on former occasions, coming into the brig's trade-room and picking out his trade goods, he sat down facing the captain and answered his questions as to the state of business, etc., on the island, in an awkward, restrained manner.

"What's the matter, Macpherson?" said the captain. "Have you married a native girl and found out that she is related to any one on the island, and you haven't house-room enough for 'em all, or what?"

The trader stroked his bushy sandy beard, with a rough brown hand, and his clear grey eyes looked steadily into those of the captain.

"I'm no the man to marry any native girl, Captain Packenham. When I do marry any one it will be the girl who promised hersel' to me five years ago in Aberdeen. But there, I'm no quick to tak' offence at a bit of fun. And I want ye two tae help me to do a guid deed. I want ye tae come ashore wi' me at once and try and put some sense into the head of this obstinate native teacher."

"Why, what has he been doing?"

"Just pairsecuting an auld man of seventy and a wee bit of a child. And if we canna mak' him tak' a sensible view of things, ye'll do a guid action by taking the puir things awa' wi' ye to some ither pairt of the South Seas, where the creatures can at least live."

Then he told his story. Six months before, a German trading vessel had called at Mâdurô, and landed an old man of seventy and his grand-daughter—a little girl of ten years of age. To the astonishment of the people the old man proved to be a native of the island. His name was Rimé. He had left Mâdurô forty years before for Tahiti as a seaman. At Tahiti he married, and then for many years worked with other Marshall Islanders on Antimanao Plantation, where two children were born to him. The elder of these, when she was fifteen years of age, married a Frenchman trading in the Paumotu Islands.

The other child, a boy, was drowned at sea. For eight or nine years Rimé and his Tahitian wife, Tiaro, lived alone on the great plantation; then Tiaro sickened and died, and Rimé was left by himself. Then one day came news to him from the distant Paumotus—his daughter and her white husband had fallen victims to the small-pox, leaving behind them a little girl. A month later Rimé worked his way in a pearling schooner to the island where his granddaughter lived, and claimed her. His heart was empty he said. They would go to Mâdurô, though so many long, long years had passed since he, then a strong man of thirty, had seen its low line of palm-clad beach sink beneath the sea-rim; for he longed to hear the sound of his mother tongue once more. And so the one French priest on Marutea blessed him and the child—for Rimé had become a Catholic during his stay in the big plantation—and said that God would be good to them both in their long journey across the wide Pacific to far-off Mâdurô.

But changes had come to Mâdurô in forty years. When Rimé had sailed away to seek his fortune in Tahiti he and his people were heathens; when he returned he found them rigid Protestants of the Boston New England Cotton-Mather type, to whom the name of "Papist" was an abomination and a horror. And when Rimé said that he too was a Christian—a Katoliko—they promptly told him to clear out. He was not an American Christian anyway, they said, and had no business to come back to Mâdurô.

"And," said Macpherson, "I'll no suffer this—the poor creature an' the wee lit child canna git a bit to eat but what I gie them. And because I *do* gie them something to eat Lilo has turned against me, an' says I'm no a Christian. So I want ye to come ashore and reason wi' the man. He's but a bigot, I fear; though his wife is no so hard on the poor man and the child as he is; but a woman aye has a tender heart for a child. And yet, ye see, this foolish Rimé will no give in, and says he will die before he changes his faith at Lilo's bidding. They took awa' his silly brass cruceefix, and slung it into the lagoon. Then the auld ass made anither out of a broken canoe paddle, and stickit the thing up in my cook-shed! And I have no the heart to tell him to put it in the fire and warm his naked shin bones wi' it. But I think if we all tackle the native teacher together we may knock some sense into his conceited head, and make him treat the poor man better. 'Tis verra hard, too, on the poor auld fellow that these people will not give him back even a bit of his own land."

Then he went on to say that ever since Rimé had landed he and the child had been sleeping every night in his (Macpherson's) cooking-shed. The trader had given him a bundle of mats and free access to a pile of Fiji yams and a bag of rice, and sometime Louisa, Lilo's Hawaiian wife, would visit them at night, ostensibly to convert Rimé from the errors of Rome, but really to leave him a cooked fish or a piece of pork. Most of the day, however, Rimé was absent, wandering about the beaches with his grand-daughter. They were afraid to even pass near the village, for the children threw stones at them, and the men and women cursed them as Katolikos. Matters had gone on like this till two weeks before the *Palestine* arrived, when Lilo and some of his deacons had formed themselves into a deputation, and visited the trader. It was very wrong of him, they said, to encourage this wicked old man and his child. And they wanted him to cease giving them food or shelter—then when the "Katolikos" found themselves starving they would be glad to give up the "evil" religion which they had learnt in Tahiti. Then would they be baptized and food given them by the people of Mâdurô.

Macpherson tried to reason with Lilo. But neither he nor the white-shirted, but trouserless, deacons would listen to him. And furthermore, they gave him a warning—if Rimé continued obstinate, they would hold him (Macpherson) responsible and *tapu* his store. Rimé did continue obstinate, and next morning the trader found himself *tabooed*, which is a mere euphemism for boycotted.

"That's pretty rough on you, Mac," said Packenham.

"'Twill just ruin me, I fear. Ye see there's four other traders on this island besides me, and all my business has gone to them. But what can I do? The silly auld fule of a Rimé won't give in, and I canna see him starve—the damned auld Papist."

At noon, as Packenham, with his supercargo and Macpherson, stepped out of the trader's dwelling, and walked together to the Mission House, a native went through the village blowing a conch. Lilo had agreed to meet the white men and discuss matters with them. Already the big room in the teacher's house was filled with people, who sat around the walls three or four deep, talking in whispered tones, and wondering why the white men troubled so much over a miserable old man and a wretched child, who were both accursed "Katolikos."

As the captain and his friends entered, Lilo, the teacher, advanced to meet them. He was a small, slenderly built man, with a skin scarcely darker than that of an Italian, and very handsome features. After a few words of effusive welcome, and a particularly sweet smile to Macpherson, he escorted the white men to their seats—three chairs placed together at the head of the room.

Presently there was a shuffling of naked feet outside, and five or six young men entered the house, pushing before them an old man and a girl—Rimé and his grand-child. In the centre of the room was a small square mat of coconut leaf—the Marshall Island prisoners' dock. With limbs trembling with age, Rimé seated himself cross-legged; the child, kneeling at his back, placed her bony arms around his wrinkled body, and clasped him tightly; her eyes, big, black, and mournful, filled with the indifference born of despair. Then, as she saw Macpherson, a faint semblance of a smile flitted across her sallow face.

Lilo struck his hand upon a little table before which he sat, and at once the assembly was silent. Then he turned to Packenham and, in perfect English, pointing to the two figures in the centre of the room, said—

"That is Rimé and his child. They have given us much trouble, and I and the deacons of this island do not want trouble. We are Christians, and will not have any 'Katolikos' here. Mr. Macpherson says we are cruel. He is wrong. We are just, and this man and this child must give up their false faith. But because you and Mr. Denison have written me a letter about this matter I have called the people together so that we may talk. So, if you please, captain, will you speak, and I will interpret whatever you say to the people."

"Will he, the damned little sweep?" muttered the supercargo to Packenham; "tell him that we can talk Mâdurô as well as he can—and better."

So, much to the teacher's disgust, Packenham answered in the Mâdurô dialect. "'Twas better," he said, "that they should all talk Mâdurô." Lilo smiled unpleasantly, and said, "Very well."

Then Packenham, turning to the people, spoke to the point.

"Look into my face, people of Mâdurô, and listen to my words. Long before the missionaries came to this island I lived among ye for three years with my wife Nerida. And is there here one man or one woman who can say that I ever lied to him or her? So this do I say to ye all; and to thee, Lilo, the teacher of the Word of God, that ye do wrong to persecute this old man and this child. For is it not true that he hath land, which ye have denied to him? Is it not true that he is old and feeble, and his limbs tremble as he walks? Yet ye neither give him food nor drink, nor yet a mat whereon to lie his head. He is a 'Katoliko,' ye say? Are there not many thousands of 'Katolikos' in Hawaii, the land from whence comes Lilo? And I ask of thee, Lilo, do they suffer wrong from the King and the chiefs of Hawaii because of their faith? So to thee, Lilo, do I say 'beware.' Thou art but a young and ignorant man, and were I to tell the white missionaries in Honolulu (who are thy masters) that this old man and this little child would have died of hunger but that the heart of one man alone was tender to them, then wouldst thou hang thy head in shame when the mission ship comes here next year. For hath not Christ said, 'Blessed are the merciful, for they shall obtain mercy?' And so I say to ye all, let this old man dwell among ye in peace, for death is near to him, and shame will be thine if ye deny to him his right to die on his own land, of which ye have robbed him."

The teacher sprang to his feet, his dark eyes blazing with passion.

"There shall be no mercy shown to Katolikos; for they are of hell and the devil and his works!" and from the people there came a deep growl of approval, which changed into a savage hissing as Macpherson rose and stretched out his hand.

"Let me speak," he said.

"No," shouted the teacher. "Who are *you?* You are a bad man, you are——"

Packenham made two strides over to Lilo and placed his heavy hand on his shoulder—"Sit down, you damned little psalm-singing kanaka hog, or I'll knock your eye out. He *shall* speak."

"Get thee hence, thou shielder of the devil's children," said a young, fat deacon, walking up to the trader and spitting contemptuously at his feet. "We want no such white men as thee among us here in Mâdurô." In an instant Macpherson struck him between the eyes and sent him flying backwards among his fellow-deacons. Then came an angry roar from the people.

The trader turned to Packenham with a groan, "I'm a ruined man now, Captain Packenham, and all through this auld fule of a Papist." Then he again tried to speak amidst the uproar.

"Sit down, damn you," said Denison, the supercargo, "and don't excite them any more. They're ready for any mischief now. Oh, you she-devil," and he darted into the middle of the room towards Rimé and his grand-daughter. A stout muscular girl had torn the child's arms from the old man's waist, and was beating her savagely in the face with clenched fists. Denison gave her an under-clip on the jaw and sent her down, and in a few seconds the old man and child were the centre of a struggling group—the white men hitting out right and left to save them from being murdered. The teacher's wife, a tall, graceful young woman—with whom Denison had been exchanging surreptitious glances a few minutes before—weeping copiously the while, aided them by belabouring the backs of the women who were endeavouring to get at the prostrate figure of the little girl. But Packenham, Macpherson, and the supercargo were too much for the natives, and soon cleared a space around them.

"Take them to the ship, Captain Packenham," said the teacher's wife pantingly, in English. "These people are mad now. Go—go at once."

Picking up the frail figure of the old man, the captain, followed by Macpherson and the supercargo, soon gained the boat through a shower of stones and other missiles. Ten minutes later they were on board the Palestine.

"What a devil of a row!" said Packenham, as he clinked his glass against that of Macpherson, who, after the exciting events of the past hour, had been induced to take a nip to steady his nerves; "you ought to be d———d well ashamed of yourself, Mac, to be mixed up in a fight over a Papist. What would Mr. MacBain say, eh?"

"It's a verra bad business for me," said Macpherson ruefully. "Ye'll have to come back for me next month and tak' me awa' from Mâdurô. I'll do no more business here, I can see."

"Right you are, Mac," and Packenham grasped his hand. "I *will* come back for you, if it takes me a month of Sundays to beat against the trades. And you're a white man, Mac; and I'll never laugh at MacBain nor Aberdeen theology any more."

That night, as the captain of the *Palestine* slept upon the skylight, old Rimé, who, with the child, lay upon the deck just beneath Packenham, rose softly to his knees and peered into the white man's face. He was sleeping soundly. Rimé touched his grandchild with his foot. She awoke, and together they pressed their lips to the skipper's hand. Then, without a sound, they stole along the deck, clambered over the brig's low side, dropped into the water and swam ashore.

When daylight came the *Palestine* was rolling heavily to a sweeping westerly swell, with the wind piping hard through her cordage as she strained at her cable. The absence of old Rimé and the child was not discovered till coffee time; the mate thought they had gone to sleep in the hold.

"They've swum ashore in the night, Pack," said the supercargo to Packenham. "I believe the old fellow will be content to die of starvation— hallo, here's Mac coming off in his boat!"

In less than ten minutes the trader's boat was close to the ship, and Macpherson, bringing her up to the wind close under the brig's stern, hailed Packenham.

"Hae ye seen anything of the old man Rimé?"

"No," answered the captain; "the old fool cleared out last night. Isn't he on shore?"

"No. And there's a canoe missing from the beach, and I believe the auld Papist fule has taken the wee bit lassie wi' him, and thinks he can get to Ponape, whaur there's 'Katolikos' in plenty. And Ponape is sax hundred miles awa'."

"Well, come aboard and get some breakfast."

"Man, I'm going after the old fule! He's got no sail and canna be twenty mile awa'. I'll pick him up before he gets to Milli Lagoon, which is only saxty miles from here."

Packenham swore. "You infernal ass! Are you going to sea in a breeze like this by yourself? Where's your crew?"

"The deevils wadna' come wi' me to look for a Papist. And I'm not going to let the auld fule perish."

"Then come alongside and take a couple of our Savage Island boys. I can spare them."

"No, no, captain. I'm not going tae delay ye when ye're bound to the eastward and I'm going the ither way. Ye'll find me here safe enough when ye come back in anither month. And I'll pick up the auld deevil and the wee bit lassie before mid-day."

And then, with his red beard spreading out across his shoulders, Macpherson let his boat pay off before the wind. In an hour he was out of sight.

Three weeks afterwards the *Sadie Perkins* sperm whaler of New Bedford, came across a boat, five hundred miles west of Mâdurô. In the stern sheets lay that which had once been Macpherson, the "auld fule Papist, and the wee bit lassie."

A MAN OF IMPULSE

Blackett, the new trader at Guadalcanar in the Solomons, was entertaining a visitor, an old fellow from a station fifty miles distant, who had sailed over in his cutter to "have a pitch" with his nearest white neighbour. And the new man—new to this particular island—made much of his grizzled visitor and listened politely to the veteran's advice on many subjects, ranging from "doctoring" of perished tobacco with molasses to the barter of a Tower musket for a "werry nice gal."

The new trader's house looked "snugger'n anything he'd ever seed," so the old trader had told him; and Blackett was pleased and very liberal with the liquor. He had been but a few months on the island, and already his house was furnished, in a rude fashion, better than that of any other trader in the region. He was a good host; and the captains of the Fiji, Queensland, and Samoan "blackbirders" liked to visit him and loll about the spacious sitting-room and drink his grog and play cards—and tell him that his wife was "the smartest and prettiest woman in the group."

Blackett was especially vain of the young Bonin Island half-caste wife who had followed his varying fortunes from her home in the far north-west Pacific to the solitary, ghostly outlier of Polynesia—lonely Easter Island, and thence to and fro amongst a hundred other islands. He was vain of her beauty—the beauty that had led him to almost abandon any intention of returning to civilisation; he was vain of the dark, passionate eyes, the soft, wavy hair, and the proud little mouth inherited from her Lusitanian father. Of this latter person, however, neither Blackett nor Cerita, his wife, were over-proud—he was a notorious old scamp and ex-pirate, even for that part of the Pacific, and Cerita knew that Blackett had simply bought her from him as he would buy a boat, or a bolt of canvas.

Blackett, finding it impossible to make old Hutton drunk or get him to turn in, resigned himself entirely to the old pirate, who, glancing to the far end of the room, to where Cerita and his own wife, a tall, lithe-limbed Aoba woman, were lying together on a mat smoking cigarettes, proceeded to pour out the story of his countless murders and minor villainies.

Blackett himself was a negatively-moral man. He could shoot a native if necessity demanded, but would not do so hastily; and the old trader's brutal delight in recounting his pot-shots only excited a disgust which soon became visible in his face.

"*That's* all right, Mr. Blackett," said Hutton, with a hideous grin distorting his monkeyish visage; "I'm only a-tellin' you of these here things for your own good,... an' I ain't afeered of no man-o'-war a-collarin' *me*. This here island is a place where you've got to sleep with one eye open, an' the moment you sees a nigger lookin' crooked at you put a lead pill in him—that is, if he's a stranger from somewheres. An' the more you shoots the better you'll get on with your own nigs; they likes you more and treats you better."

With a weary gesture, Blackett rose from his seat. "Thank you, Hutton, for your advice. If I thought a nigger meant to send an arrow or a spear through me I'd try to get the drop on him first. But I couldn't kill any one in cold blood on mere suspicion. I could no more do that than—than you could kill that Aoba wife of yours over there."

Old Hutton rose, too, and put a detaining hand on Blackett. "Look here, now, an' I suppose you think I'm lyin'. If I thought that that there Aoba wench was foolin' me in any way—sech as givin' away my tobacco to a nigger buck, I'd have to wentilate her yaller hide or get laid out myself."

Blackett shuddered. "I'm going to turn in. Let us have another drink, Hutton. If the Dutch firm's schooner shows up this month I'll clear out of this accursed hole. I hate the place, and so does my woman." He used the term "woman" instead of wife purely out of deference to Island custom; but Hutton noticed it.

"Ain't she really your wife?" he asked inquisitively.

"No—yes—what the devil does it matter to you?" And Blackett, whose patience had quite worn out, filled the glasses, and passed one to his visitor, who uncouthly apologised. Then the two shook hands and laughed.

The night was close and sultry, and Cerita was lying on the cane-framed bed, fanning herself languidly. The man was leaning, with his face turned from her, against the open window, and looking out into the jungle blackness that encompassed the house. He was thinking of Hutton's query, "Ain't she really your wife?" His wife! No; but she would be yet. He would leave this infernal island, where one never knew when he might get a poisoned arrow or spear into him. He was making money here, yes; but money wasn't worth dying for. And 'Rita was more than money to him. She had been the best little woman in the world to him—for all her furious temper.

"Yes, he would leave these blackguardly Solomons, with their hordes of savage cannibals,... and go back to the eastward again,... and Sydney, too.

He could easily stow her away in some quiet house while he went and saw his people." And so Blackett thought and smoked away till 'Rita's voice startled him.

"Give me a match, Harry: I want to smoke. I can't sleep, it's so hot, and my arm is tired fanning, and the screen is full of mosquitoes. That devil of a girl—where is she?"

"There!" said Blackett, pointing to beneath the bed, where Europuai, his wife's attendant, lay rolled up in a mat.

"The black beast!"—and the half-blood rose from the bed, throwing the mosquito-net angrily aside—"and I thought she was sleeping near the Aoba woman, the wife of that drunken old Hutton," and, stooping down so that her black hair fell like a mantle over her bare shoulders, she seized the short, woolly head of the sleeper and dragged her out.

Blackett laughed. "Easy, 'Rita, easy! You'll frighten her so that she'll clear out from us. Let her take her mat over there in the corner. Give the poor devil a chance. She's terrified of old Hutton, so sneaked in here to hide. She's only a wild bushy"—and he looked compassionately at the almost nude figure of the girl that his wife had bought from a bush town for a musket—because she wanted "something to worry," he used jokingly to say.

The savage creature took the mat sullenly, went to the far end of the room, and covered herself up again.

"You're too soft with women," said Rita, scornfully.

"I know I am—with you," he answered, good-naturedly. And then the angry gleam in the black eyes died away, and she laughed merrily.

Two days had passed. Old Hutton had returned to his station, and Blackett was returning with a boatload of copra from a village across the bay. Heavy rain-squalls tore down upon the boat at short intervals, and Blackett, drenched to the skin, began to feel the first deadly chills and pains of an attack of island fever. Usually light-hearted, he now felt angry, and savagely cursed at his crew when the heavily-laden boat touched and ground against the coral knobs that lay scattered about her course. It was long past midnight when he reached his station, and, stepping wearily out of the boat, dragged his aching limbs along the beach. 'Rita had heard the boat, and Blackett could see that a bright fire was burning in the thatched, open-sided cook-house, and that 'Rita herself was there, with a number of native children making coffee.

The quickening agonies of fever were fast seizing him, and, entering the house and throwing himself on a seat, he felt his brain whirling, and scarcely noticed that Tubariga, the local chief, was bending over him anxiously. Then 'Rita came with the steaming coffee, and one quick glance at Blackett's crouched-up figure told her that the dreaded fever had seized him at last.

'Rita proved herself what Blackett always called her, "one of the smartest little women going." With Tubariga's help, she carried him to the bed, and sent out for some women to come and rub and thump his aching joints while she dosed him with hot rum and coffee. And then Blackett asked her what she was doing out in the cook-house. Hadn't she a cook? Then the suppressed rage of the hot-blooded girl broke out in a flood of tears. Europuai, the wild bush-girl, had been sulky all the time he was away, and she had given her a little beating with a bamboo. And then the black devil had run away, and—here the angry beauty wept again—she ('Rita) had to go out into a filthy cook-shed to boil water before a lot of man-eating savages! No one would help her, because they were all such fools that she always lost her temper with them.

Blackett—under the combined influences of rum, strong coffee, fever, and woman's tears—went into a rage, and glared angrily at the chief, Tubariga.

"You're a d— — — -d nice fellow," he said in English; "you get my wife to pay a good musket for a girl, and then as soon as I am away you let that girl run back into the bush. You're a bad friend."

Tubariga felt hurt. He prided himself on two things—his knowledge of English and his friendship for white men. He rose to his feet, grasped his rifle, and made for the door.

"Here, come back, Tubariga. Perhaps it isn't your fault. Let her stay away. She's no good, anyway."

Tubariga came back. "Tell me, white man, do you want your servant to come back?"

"Yes, d— — you!" answered Blackett, who now again was seized with that hideous brain-whirl that in fever is simple delirium, "bring her back, alive or dead."

The chief nodded and went out.

Next morning the first fierce violence of the fever had temporarily left him, and Blackett was lying covered up with rugs, when the grim figure of Tubariga entered noiselessly, and stole to his side. Motioning the trader's wife away, Tubariga's savage features relaxed with a pleased smile.

"Well, Tubariga, how are you?" said Blackett. "'Rita tell me I damn you too much last night, eh? Never mind, old chap, I was mad about that girl running away. You can tell her people to keep her—and the musket too. Rita don't want her any more. Ship come soon, then we go away.'"

Again the pleased smile spread over the chiefs face. Bending over Blackett he placed his hideous lips, blood-red with the stains of betel-juice, close to his face, and said with the simple pride of a child, *"Me pinish him."*

"What?" said Blackett, with a strange feeling at his heart—"What did you do to that girl, Tubariga?"

Sitting down with his rifle across his knees, the chief told the conscience-stricken trader that he had followed the girl to a bush village, where he, Tubariga, as their chief, had demanded her from her parents. They insisted on her going back, but she whimpered and said that the white man's wife would beat her. She sprang for the jungle, and, ere she reached it, a bullet from the chiefs rifle struck her in the side. And then, with a feeling of horror, Blackett listened to the rest of the tale—the poor wretch, with her life-blood ebbing fast, was followed up and a spear thrust through her heart.

He was sitting at the table with his face clasped in his hands when 'Rita came in. She was smoking her inevitable cigarette, and the thin wreaths of blue smoke curled upwards from her lips as she leant one arm on the table and caressed Blackett's ice-cold forehead with her shapely hand. Suddenly she stooped and sought gently to remove his hands from his face.

"Harry, are you very ill, old fellow? What can I do for you?"

"Do for me?" and the sudden misery that had smitten his heart looked out from his pallid face,... "give me back the peace of mind that was mine ten minutes ago. Leave me to die here of fever—for you I have become a murderer—a man no better than Hutton. The blood of that poor girl will for ever be between us." And then she saw that tears were falling through his trembling fingers.

"Harry," she said, "I thought you were more of a man"—and here her voice softened—"don't grieve over it. It wasn't your fault,... and I have been a good little girl to you. Don't be miserable because of such a little thing as that. If Tubariga hadn't killed her, I daresay I should have done so myself. She was a sulky little wretch."

I know Blackett well. The horror of that day has never entirely left him. But for that one dark memory he would have married 'Rita—who would have most probably run a knife into his ribs later on, when the influence of her beauty had somewhat waned and he began to look at other women. The fateful impulse of that moment when he told the chief to bring back the girl dead or alive wrecked and tortured his mind beyond description. And he can never forget.

His 'Rita and he left the island soon afterwards to wander away back to Eastern Polynesia, but his continued fits of melancholy annoyed the girl so much that she one day quarrelled with and left him, and made a fresh matrimonial engagement with a man less given to mawkish sentiment.

THE TRADER

I

The evening fires were lighting up the darkness of the coming night, when Prout, the only white man on the island, left his house on the edge of the lagoon, and, with his little daughter running by his side, walked slowly through the village.

As they passed through the now deserted pathways that intersected the straggling collection of grey, thatched-roofed houses, and Prout's heavy step crunched into the broken coral, the natives, gathered together for their evening meal, looked forth, and the brown women called out a word or two of greeting to the child, and smiled and beckoned her to leave her father for an instant and take the fruit or piece of cooked breadfruit that they held out to her with their brown hands. But only a solemn shake of the little head, and then she and the taciturn, bronzed-faced man went by, the child's tiny fingers grasping his tanned and roughened hand as they walked across the narrow island towards the sound of the muffled thunder of the surf on the outer ocean beach.

Here, with the little one perched beside him and looking wonderingly into his grave, impassive face, the white man would sit for long hours staring moodily out upon the tumbling breakers as they reared and fell upon the black, grim shelves of the reef.

Sometimes, as he sat with his chin resting on his hand, and the red glow of his pipe sending now and again a fitful gleam of light across the rugged lines of his face, the girl would get quietly down from the moss-grown coral boulder on which she rested by his side, and stepping down to the short, steep beach, play with childish solemnity with such pebbles and light shells as lay within the reach of her little hands. Perhaps, if the tide was heavy and at its flood, and a breaker heavier than the rest breached shorewards in a white wall of seething foam, and crashed and rattled together the loose coral slabs that marked the line of high-water mark, the silent, dreaming man would spring to his feet with a loud warning call. And the little one, answering his deep tones with her soft, sweet treble, would spring back to her father's side, and nestling her tender form against his gaunt frame, lay her cheek against his, and say, in the soft Tokelau tongue, "'Twas a great wave, my father!"

"Aye," he would answer, as he placed an arm round the child and gazed at her for a moment, "'twas a great wave truly, *taka taina*,{*} and thou art so small, that if it but touched thy feet thou wouldst be swept away like as a leaf in a strong wind. So stay thee here beside me, sweet one," and again his face would turn seaward, and the silence of the night, save for the soughing of the wind and the cry of the surf, fall upon them again.

* *"Little one of my heart."*

Thus the first hours of the island night would pass, till a glare of light flashed upon the blackness of the sea beyond the snow-line of surf, as the canoes from Matakatea would round the point, each one with a flaming torch of dried palm-leaves held high by a brown, tattooed hand, to dazzle the flying fish that, with wings outspread, floated motionless upon the surface of the water.

Then, because the child had no playmates, and her little life was almost as joyless and as solitary as his own, he would wait with her till the long line of canoes passed by, so that she could see the bronzed, half-naked figures of the paddlers, and the bright gleam and shimmer of the fish as they were swept up by the deadly net, and hear the warning cry from the torch-bearers, as in the depths beneath they saw the black shadow of a prowling shark rushing to seize the net, or perchance the outrigger of the canoe, in his cruel, murderous jaws.

Slowly the canoes paddled by, and as they passed, the hum of voices and laughter and the cheery lilt of island melody died away, and the paddlers looked shoreward to the motionless figure of Prout, who, with the child by his side, seemed to heed naught but the wide sweep of ocean that lay before him.

But though the voices and laughter and snatches of song ceased, many of the kindly-hearted people would, ere they passed, call out a word or two of greeting to the white man and his child, and the latter would wave her hand and smile back, while her father, as if awakened from a dream, called out, in the island tongue, the customary "May your fishing to-night be lucky." And then, as the last canoe vanished, and the glare and the smoke of the torches with it, he, with the little Mercedes by his side, walked back to his house on the lagoon.

And so, night after night, save in the stormy season of the year, when the white rain-squalls gathered together on the windward sea-line, and swept quickly down upon the island and drenched the loose, sandy soil with pouring showers, the white man had sat with his face turned seaward to the cloudless horizon of the starlit ocean and his mind dwelling upon the ever-present memories of the past.

Such, for three years past, ever since he had first landed among the people of Nukutavau, had been the existence of Prout, the silent, solitary trader.

II

Nine years before, Prout, then one of the "smartest" Englishmen in the Hawaiian Islands, had been manager of the Kalahua sugar plantation on Maui. Out of his very loneliness in the world—for except his mother, in a far-away Devonshire village, there was no one in the outside world that cared aught for him—there grew upon him that quiet, reserved temperament that led the other white men on the plantation to call him in kindly jest, "Prout, the Hermit."

But although he never mixed with the men on the Kalahua Estate in the wild revelries with which they too often sought to break the monotony of their existence and celebrate a good season, he was by no means a morose or unsociable man; and Chard, the merry-hearted Belgian sugar-boiler, often declared that it was Prout alone who kept the estate going and the native labourers from turning on the white men and cutting their throats, out of sheer revenge for the brutal treatment they received from Sherard, the savage, drunken owner of Kalahua.

Between Roden Sherard and Prout there had been always, from the first day almost of the latter entering upon his duties, a silent, bitter antagonism. And the reason of it was known only to the two men themselves.

In those times the native labour for the Hawaiian sugar plantations was recruited from the islands of the Mid-Pacific, and from the chains of sandy atolls lying between the Bonins and the Radack Archipelago of the Marshall Group. On Kalahua there were some three hundred natives, and within a month of Prout taking charge, he had changed their condition so much for the better, that not one of the wild-eyed, half-naked beings who toiled from sunrise to dark but would give him a grateful glance as he rode through the cane fields. And Sherard, who rode with him, would see this, and scowl and tell Prout that as soon as his engagement terminated, he, Sherard, would bring back Fletcher, the former manager, "a man who would thump a kanaka into a pulp if he dared to look sideways at him."

"If you are not satisfied with me you can bring him here to-morrow if you like," Prout had said coldly to him one day. "I've managed bigger places than this in Demerara, and on no one of them have I ever seen a nigger struck. But then, you see, in Demerara the planters are Englishmen, and Englishmen as a rule don't shine at nigger walloping."

Sherard, a black-visaged Marylander, snapped his teeth together and, smothering his rage, tried to laugh the matter off.

"Well, I suppose you're right, Prout. I know I have got a good man in you; but at the same time, God never intended these damned saucy niggers to be coddled and petted."

Prout laughed ironically as he repeated Sherard's words "coddled and petted!" And then long-suppressed wrath boiled out, and, swinging his horse's head round, he faced the owner of Kalahua.

"Look here, Sherard, give me the control of these three hundred natives for the next two seasons and I'll stake my life that they'll do more work for you than you have ever had done by that brute Fletcher when he had five hundred here. Do you think that these people *knew* what was in store for them when they came here?—that in place of an encouraging word they would get a threat or a blow? That those of them who have wives and daughters can forget what has befallen *them?* Do you think that I don't know that you speak of me to your friends with contempt as 'a nigger-loving Britisher'? And yet, Sherard, you know well that, were I to leave Kalahua tomorrow, every native on the estate would leave too—not for love of me, but to get away from *you*."

Sherard laughed coarsely.

"You've got more in you than I thought, Prout. What you say is true enough. Let us quit quarrelling. I know you can do more with them than Abe Fletcher could; and I guess I'm not going to interfere with you."

But, for all that, Prout did not trust Sherard, and he made up his mind to leave the estate when his two years' engagement came to an end.

"The *Mana* is in Honolulu with a cargo of Line Island boys, Prout," said Sherard to him about a month or two after this; "I wish you would get away down there, and try to obtain some more hands. You talk the language like a Line Islander, and will have no trouble in getting all the men we want."

But when Prout boarded the labour schooner *Mana* there was not a native left. The other planters on Oahu had been there before him, and the master—Captain Courtayne—called him down to have a drink in the cabin.

"You are the new manager on Kalahua, hey? Well, I'm sorry you've had your trip for nothing; but, at the same time, I'm real glad to see Sherard left out in the cold. He's a bad man, sir, and although you might think that because I'm in this trade I'm not particularly soft, I can tell you that I'd be thundering sorry to see any of the crowd I've brought up go to him."

"Your feelings do you honour, Captain; but I can assure you that the Kalahua boys are well treated now," said Prout, as he took the cigar the seaman handed him.

The quiet manner and truthful look in Prout's face made the master of the schooner regard him intently for a few moments, then he said abruptly:

"Do you know Honolulu well?"

Prout did not; his visits there had been few and far between.

"Do you know any decent people here who could take care of my daughter for me till I come back from my next trip?"

"No, Captain, I do not."

"Take another whisky, sir, and I'll tell you the fix I'm in. You see I'm new to this business. I had a trading station down on one of the Ellice Islands where I've lived for the last twenty years. This schooner came there about six months ago, and the captain died in my house. As the mate couldn't navigate, and I am an old shell-back, I sold out my trading station, took charge of her, brought my daughter aboard and filled the schooner with Line Island labourers."

"Her mother is dead, I suppose?"

Captain Courtayne coloured and shifted about in his seat. "Well, no, not as far as I know; but, you see, down there in the south-east a man has to change his wives occasionally. For instance, if you marry a Samoa girl you must live in Samoa; she won't leave there to go and live on Nanomea or Vaitupu, where the people have different ideas and customs. And, as we poor traders have to shift about from one island to another sometimes, we can't afford to study a woman's whims."

Prout grasped the situation at once. "I see; your daughter, then, is your child by a former wife?"

"Just so. Her mother was a Hervey Island half-caste whom I married when I was trading on Manhiki. We drifted apart somehow—perhaps it was my fault. I was a careless, hard-drinking man in those days. But, here I am telling you a lot of things that don't interest you, when I ought to tell you at once what it is I thought you might help me with. You see, Mr. Prout, my little Marie has lived with me all her life. Since she was five years old she has never left me for a day, and I've done my best to educate her. She's as good and true as gold, and this is what troubles me—I don't want to take her away again in the schooner if I can help it. Do you think—do you know—of any English or American family here that would take her to live with them till I return from this voyage? I'm willing to pay well for her keep."

Prout shook his head. "I should advise you to take her back with you, Captain. How old is she?"

The captain went to the companion-way and called out:

"Marie."

"Yes, father," answered a girl's soft voice.

"Come below a minute."

Prout heard some one getting out of a hammock that was slung over the skylight, and presently a small slippered foot touched the first step of the companion-way; and then a girl, about fifteen or sixteen, came into the cabin, and bowing to him, seated herself by the captain of the schooner. Then, as if ashamed of the formal manner of her greeting, she rose again, and a smile lit up her beautiful face, as she offered her hand to him.

Prout, one of those men whose inborn respect for women often makes them appear nervous, constrained, and awkward in their presence, flushed to the roots of his hair as she let her soft hand touch his.

"That is Marie, sir," and the skipper glanced somewhat proudly at the graceful, muslin-clad figure of his daughter. "Marie, this gentleman says he does not know any English or American ladies here."

The sweet red mouth smiled and the dark eyes danced.

"I'm very glad, father; I would rather go away with you to sea in the *Mana* than stay in a strange place."

But Marie Courtayne did not go away; for next morning her father, through Prout, learned that the French Sisters were willing to take her as a boarder till the schooner returned, and so to them she went, with her tender mouth twitching, and her eyes striving to keep back the tears that would come as she bade her father goodbye.

"You'll go and see my little Marie sometimes, I hope, Mr. Prout?" said Courtayne, as he bade farewell to the manager of Kalahua.

Prout murmured something in reply, and then the captain of the *Mana* and he parted.

Three months later the American cruiser *Saranac* brought the news that she had spoken the labour schooner *Mana*, Captain Courtayne, off the island of Marakei, in the Gilbert Group, "all well, and wished to be reported at Honolulu." After that she, her captain and crew, and the two hundred Kanaka labourers she had on board, were never heard of again.

For nearly a year Prout and Marie Courtayne waited and hoped for some tidings of the missing ship, but none came. And every now and then, when business took him to Honolulu, Prout would call at the Mission School and try to speak hopefully to her.

"He is dead," she would say apathetically, "and I wish I were dead, too. I think I shall die soon, if I have to live here."

Then Prout, who had grown to love her, one day plucked up courage to tell her so, and asked her to be his wife.

"Yes," she said simply, "I will be your wife. You are always kind to me," and for the first time she put her face up to his. He kissed her gravely, and then, being a straightforward, honourable man, he went to the Sisters and told them. A week afterward they were married.

When he returned to Kalahua with his wife, Sherard met them on the verandah of his house, and Prout wondered at the remarkable change in his manner, for even to women Sherard was coarse and tyrannical.

From the moment he first saw Marie's fresh young beauty Sherard determined to have a deadly revenge upon her husband. But he went about his plans cautiously. Only a few days previously he had made a fresh agreement with Prout to remain for another two years. Before those two years had expired he meant to put his plan into effect. There was on the plantation a ruffianly Chileno who, he knew, would dispose of Prout satisfactorily when asked to do so.

When Marie's child was born, Sherard acted the part of the imperatively good-natured employer, and told Prout that as soon as his wife was strong enough, he was to leave the house he then occupied and take up his quarters permanently in the big house.

"This place of yours will do me, Prout," he said, when his manager protested; "and your wife's only a delicate little thing. There's all kinds of fixings and comforts there that she'll appreciate, which you haven't got here. D———n my thick skull, I might have done this before."

"Thank you, Sherard," said Prout, with a genuine feeling of pleasure. "You are very good to us both. But I won't turn you out altogether; you must remain there too."

Sherard laughed. "Not I. You'll be far happier up there together by yourselves, like a pair of turtledoves. But I'll always be on hand in the smoking-room when you want me for a game of cards."

The change was soon made, and Moreno, the Chilian overseer, grinned when he saw the white-robed figure of the manager's wife lying on one of the verandah lounges, playing with her child.

"Bueno," he said to Sherard that night, as they drank together, "the plan works. Make the bird learn to love its pretty nest. *Dios*, when am I to feel my knife tickling Senor Prout's ribs?"

"At the end of the crushing season, I think," answered Sherard coolly; "the brat will be old enough to be taken from her by then."

It is a bad thing for a man to "thump" either a Chilian, or a Peruvian, or a Mexican. And Prout had "thumped" the evil-faced Chileno very badly one day for beating a native nearly to death. Had he been wiser he would have taken the little man's knife out of his belt and plunged it home between his ribs, for a Chileno never forgives a blow with a fist.

III

"Are you going over to Halaliko to-night, Prout?" asked Sherard, walking up to where his manager and Marie sat enjoying the cool of the evening. He threw himself in a cane chair beside them and puffed away at his cheroot, playing the while with the little Mercedes.

"Yes, I might as well go to-night and see how the Burtons have got on," and Prout arose and went to the stables.

Sherard remained chatting with Marie till Prout returned, and then, raising his hat to her, bade them good-night."

"Don't let Burton entice you to Halaliko, Prout," he said with a laugh; "he knows that your time here is nearly up."

Prout laughed too. "I don't think that Marie would like me to give up Kalahua for Halaliko—would you, old girl?"

She shook her head and smiled. "No, indeed, Mr. Sherard. I am too happy here to ever wish to leave."

Whistling softly to himself, Prout rode along the palm-bordered winding track. It was not often he was away from Marie, but he meant to take his time this evening. It was nearly five miles to Burton's plantation at Halaliko, and half an hour would finish his business there. He knew that, as soon as he left, Marie would tell the native servant to go to her bed in the coolie lines, and then she would herself retire; and when he returned he would find her lying asleep with her baby beside her.

To the right the road wound round a great jagged shoulder of rocky cliff, and clung to it closely; for on the left there yawned a black space, the valley of Maunahoehoe, and, as he rode, Prout could see the glimmer of the natives' fires below—fires that, although they were but distant a few hundred feet, seemed miles and miles away.

A slight sound that seemed to come from the face of the cliff above him caused him to look upwards, and the next instant a heavy stone struck him slantingly on the side of his head. Without a sound he fell to the ground, staggered to his feet, and then, failing to recover himself, vanished over the sloping side of the cliff into the valley beneath.

A shadowy, supple figure clambered down from the inky blackness of cliff that overhung the road, and peered over the valley of Maunahoehoe. It was Moreno, the Chilian.

"Better than a knife after all; Holy Virgin, he's gone now, and I forgive him for all the blows he struck me."

Long before daylight, Prout, with his face and shoulders covered with gory stains, staggered into the native village at Maunahoehoe and asked the people to lend him a horse to take him back to Kalahua.

When within half a mile of Kalahua, almost fainting from loss of blood and exhaustion, he pulled up his horse at a hut on the borders of the estate and got off. There were some five or six natives inside, and they started up with quick expressions of sympathy when they saw his condition.

"Give me a weapon, O friends," he said. "Some man hath tried to kill me."

A short squat native smiled grimly, reached to the rafters of the dwelling, and took down a heavy carbine, which he loaded and then handed to the white man.

"'Tis Moreno who hath hurt thee," said the native; "at midnight he rode by here in hot haste."

With the native supporting him, Prout rode along the road to the Estate gates.

As he reeled through he heard a faint cry.

In another minute he was on the verandah and looking through the French lights into Marie's dimly-lighted bedroom. An inarticulate cry of anguish burst from him. Sherard and his wife were together.

Steadying himself against a post he took aim at the trembling figure of his wife, and fired. She threw up her arms and fell upon her face, and then Sherard, pistol in hand, dashed out and met him.

Ere he could draw the trigger, Prout swung the heavy weapon round, and the stock crashed into the traitor's brain.

"It is the death of a dog," said the native, spurning the body with his naked foot.

She was dying fast when Prout, with love and hate struggling for mastery in his frenzied brain, stood over her.

"He took my child away from me," she said.... "He said he would kill her before me,... and it was to save her. Only for that I would have died first. Oh, Ned, Ned——"

Then with a look of unutterable love from her fast-dimming eyes, she closed them in death.

That was why Prout, after two years of madness in a prison, had stepped on board Hetherington's schooner and asked the captain to take him away somewhere—he cared not where—so that he could be away from the ken of civilised and cruel mankind and try and forget the dreadful past.

IV

They are a merry-hearted, laughter-loving race, the people of white-beached Nukutavau, with whom the trader lived. To them the grave-faced, taciturn man, who cared not to listen to their songs or to watch their wild dances on the moonlit beach—as had been the custom of those white men who had dwelt on the island before him—was but as one afflicted with some mental disease, and therefore to be both pitied and feared. At first, indeed, when he had landed, carrying his child in his arms, to bargain with Patiaro, the chief, that the people should build him a house, the women of the island had clustered around him as he stepped out of the boat, and with smiles upon their faces, extended their arms to him for the child. But no answering smile lit up the man's rugged features, though, to avoid the appearance of discourtesy (to which all island races are so keenly sensitive) he gave the infant into the keeping of old Malineta, the mother of the chief.

Patiaro, the chief, holding the stranger's right hand in both his own, looked searchingly into his calm, deep-set eyes with that dignified curiosity which, while forbidding a native to put a direct question to an utter stranger, yet asks it by the expression of his face. But Prout, whose anxious glance followed the movements of the grey-haired mother of the chief, as she pressed his child to her withered bosom, seemed to notice not his questioning look.

Following the stranger's gaze, the chief broke the silence: ·

"'Tis my mother, *ariki papalagi*.{*} who carries thy child—Malineta, the mother of Patiaro, the chief of Nukutavau, he who now speaks to thee. And I pray thee have no fear for the little one."

* *White gentleman.*

The quiet, dignified courtesy with which the chief addressed him recalled the white man to himself, and a pleasant smile lit up the native's features when the stranger answered him in Tokelau—the *lingua franca* of the equatorial isles of the Pacific—north and south.

"Nay, I fear not for the child, Patiaro, chief of Nukutavau, but yet it may not be well for her to be taken to the village awhile; for with thee and thy people doth it rest whether the child and I remain here, or return to the ship and seek some other island whereon I may build my house and live in peace. And I will pay thee that which is fair and just for house and land."

But in those days, before too much civilisation had brought these simple people deadly disease, Christianity, and the knowledge of the great Pit of Fire, the brown men thought much of a white man; and so Patiaro, the chief, made haste to answer:

"Let the child go with my mother, and tell thou the men in the boat that everything thou desirest of me and my people to do shall be done. Five rainy seasons have come and gone since a white man has lived here; so I pray thee, stay."

The white man inclined his head; then he turned and walked to the boat, and spoke to the captain of the little vessel which, to bring him to the island, had dropped her anchor just outside the current-swept passage of the lagoon.

"I am remaining here, Captain Hetherington. Will you let your men put my gear out on the beach?"

Hetherington, the skipper, looked at his passenger curiously, and then answered:

"Cert'nly. But I'm real sorry you are leaving us, I don't want to pry inter any man's business, and you know these islands as well as I do; but I guess I wouldn't stay here if I war you. Why, it won't pay a man to stay and trade on a bit of a place like this," and he cast a deprecatory look around him.

The trader made him no answer, and the skipper of the schooner, ordering his crew to take out his passenger's goods and carry them to the village, stepped ashore, and held out his hand to the chief, whose fine, expressive features showed some signs of fear that the captain's remarks were intended to dissuade the stranger from remaining on the island.

Motioning to the white men to follow him, the stalwart young chief led the way to the *fale kaupale*, or council-house of the village, where food and young coconuts for drinking were brought in and placed before them by the young women.

Sitting directly in front of his guests, the chief served them with food with his own hands, in token of his desire for friendship and to do them honour, and then quietly withdrew to direct the natives who were carrying the trader's goods up from the boat to his own house, further back in the village.

"I would wish ter remark, mister," said the American skipper as he pulled out his pipe and commenced to fill it, "thet, ez a rule, I don't run any risk ev bustin' myself with enthoosiastic admiration fer Britishers in general—principally because they air the supporters of er low-down, degradin' system ev Government, which hez produced some bloody wars and sunk my schooner the *Mattie Casey*, with a cargo of phosphates valued et four thousand dollars."

"It was a heavy loss to you, Captain Hetherington, but you surely do not dislike all Englishmen because the *Alabama* sunk your vessel?" said the trader, with a melancholy smile, whilst his restless eye sought the village houses to discern the movements of the chief's mother with his child.

The American pulled his long, straggling beard meditatively. "Wal, I don't know, they're a darned mean crowd anyway." And then, with a sudden change of manner, "Say, look here, mister; hev yew finally made up your mind ter remain on this island among a lot ev outrageous, unclothed, ondelikit females, whar every prospeck pleases an' on'y man is vile; or air yew game ter come in pardners with me in the schooner an' run her in the sugar trade between 'Frisco and Honolulu?"

Prout grasped the old man's hand, but shook his head.

"You are a generous man, Captain Hetherington, but I cannot do it. I am no seaman, and, what is more to the point, I have no money to put into the venture."

"Thet's jest it," the American answered quickly, "but yew hev a long head—fer a Britisher, a darned long head—an' I reckon yew an' me will pull together bully; so jes' tell the chief here to get the traps back inter the boat again, an' yew an' me an' little Mercedy will get aboard agin——"

"No, no, no," and the trader rose to his feet and walked quickly to and fro—"no, Hetherington; I cannot do as you wish. Here, among these islands, it is my wish to live; and here, or on such another island as this, and among such wild, uncivilised beings, must I die."

"So?" and the hard-featured American raised his shaggy eyebrows interrogatively. "Waal, I reckon yew regulates your own affairs ter your own fancy; but look here, mister," and the kindly ring in the old skipper's voice appealed to the man before him—"what about little Mercedy? Yew ain't agoin' to let thet pore child grow up among naked, red-skinned savages, hey?"

A deep flush overspread the trader's face, and then it paled again, and he ceased his hurried, agitated walk.

"Hetherington!... do not, I implore you, say another word to me on the subject. It is better for me to remain here with my little Mercedes.... So, here, give me that honest hand of yours and leave me.... But, stop, I forgot," and he thrust his hand into a large canvas pouch that hung suspended from his shoulder, "I did indeed forget this, Captain; but forget the kindness that you have shown to me and my child during the four months I have been with you, I never can."

The Yankee skipper's face was visibly perturbed as he heard the jingle of money in the canvas pouch, and he worked his jaws violently, while his heavy, bushy brows met together as if he were in deep study, and uneasy mutterings escaped from his lips. Suddenly he rose and left his companion.

As he shambled away to the far end of the council-house, he caught sight of a number of native women and children advancing towards himself and his passenger. Foremost among them was the old woman Malineta, her lean and wrinkled face wreathed in smiles, for the white man's child, whom she still carried, had placed one arm around her neck. As she drew near the American, the little one smiled and made as if she wished to go to him, or to her father who stood near by.

Holding out his arms to the child, the skipper took her from the old woman, and then he turned to Prout.

"Say, I've jest been reckonin' up an' I make out yew hev been jest four months aboard o' my hooker thar, an' I reckon thet twenty dollars a month ain't more'n a fair an' square deal."

Again the red flush mantled to the trader's brow. "No, no, Hetherington. I am poor, but not so poor that I should insult you by such an insignificant sum as that. Two hundred and fifty dollars I can give you easily, and freely and willingly," and advancing to the captain he offered him a number of twenty-dollar gold pieces.

An angry "Pshaw!" burst from the captain. He thrust the proffered money aside, and then, with his leathern visage working in strange contortions, he walked quickly outside, and sitting down upon an old unused canoe, bent his grizzled head, and strained the child to his bosom. And presently Prout and the natives heard something very like the sound of a sob.

Then, as if ashamed of his emotion, he suddenly rose, and kissing the child tenderly, gave her back to the woman Malineta. Then he turned to Prout.

"Waal, I guess I'll be goin'.... Naow, jest yew put them air cursed dollars back again. It's jest like yew darned Britishers, ter want ter shove money inter a man's hand, jest like ez if he war a nigger, an' hadn't a red cent ter buy a slice of watermelon with," and then all his assumed roughness failed him, and his eyes grew misty as he grasped the Englishman's hand for the last time.

"Thet thar Mercedy.... Why, I hed sich a little mite once...." and he chewed fiercely at the fresh plug he had thrust into his cheek.

"Dead?" queried Prout, softly.

"Yes; diphthery. Yew see it came about th' way. When I got back ter Cohoes—thet's whar I belong—after that cussed pirut Semmes sunk my hooker, an' 'Riar sees me standin' in front ev her without givin' her any warnin' I was comin', she gets that skeered that she drops kerwallop on the floor, an' when she come to, an' heerd that the *Mattie Casey* was gone, waal, thet jest sorter finished her. Waal, she hung on ter life fur a year or so, kep' getting more powerful weak in the intelleck every day; an' when she died, my little Hope was on'y four years old. An' Hope died when I was away servin' in the *Iroquois* lookin' fur Semmes,... an' I ain't got no one else to keer fur me naow.... Waal, goodbye, Prout; I guess I'll beat up ter windward of this grewp, and then make a bee-line fur Honolulu."

In another minute he had shambled down to the boat, and as the sun sank below the line of coconuts on the lee side of Nukutavau, the schooner swept away into the darkness. Then Prout, taking the little girl in his arms, followed old Malineta to the house of Patiaro the chief, and again took up the thread of his lonely existence.

Four years had come and gone. In his quiet house, under the shadow of the ever-rustling palms, Prout lay upon his rough couch of coarse mats, and little Mercedes stood beside him with her tiny hand upon his death-dewed forehead.

The missionary ship had just anchored in the lagoon, and Patiaro and his men had paddled off to her, so that, save for the low murmur of voices of women and children in the houses near by, the village lay silent.

Weeping softly, the child placed her tender cheek against the rugged face of the dying man, and whispered:

"What is it, my father, that aileth thee?"

He drew her slender figure to him with his failing hands and kissed her with pallid lips, and then Prout the trader gave up the battle of life.

MRS. CLINTON

I

As the sun set blood red, a thick white fog crept westward, and the miserable fever-stricken wretches that lay gasping and dying on the decks of the transport *Breckenbridge* knew that another day of calm—and horror—waited them with the coming of the dawn on the morrow.

Twenty miles away the dark outline of the Australian shore shone out green and purple with the dying sunshafts, and then quickly dulled again to the sombre shades of the coming night and the white mantle of fog.

On the starboard side of the high quarterdeck of the transport the master stood gazing seaward with a worn and troubled face, and as he viewed the gathering fog a heavy sigh broke from him.

"God help us!" he muttered, "ninety-six dead already, and as many more likely to die in another week if this calm keeos up."

A hand was laid on his shoulder, and turning he met the pale face of the surviving surgeon of the fever-stricken ship.

"Seven more cases, Belton—five prisoners and two marines."

The master of the *Breckenbridge* buried his face in his hands and groaned aloud.

"Can nothing be done, doctor? My God! it is terrible to see people perishing like this before our eyes when help is so near. Look! over there, only twenty miles away, is Twofold Bay, where there is a settlement, but I dare not send a boat ashore. There are not ten sound men in the ship, and if an easterly wind springs up I could not keep my ship from going ashore."

The young surgeon made no answer for awhile. Ever since the *Breckenbridge* had left Rio, one or more of the convicts, seamen, or military guard had died day after day; and he had striven hard since the outbreak of the fever to stay its deadly progress. The cause he knew well: the foul, overcrowded 'tween decks, where four hundred human beings were confined in a space not fit to hold a hundred, the vile drinking-water and viler provisions, the want of even a simple disinfectant to clear the horrible, vitiated atmosphere, and the passage, protracted long beyond even the usual time in those days, had been the main causes of their present awful condition.

Presently the surgeon spoke—

"Nothing can be done, Belton."

"How is Lieutenant Clinton, sir?" asked the master, as the surgeon turned to leave him.

"Dying fast. Another hour or so will see the end."

"And his wife and baby?"

"She bears up well, but her infant cannot possibly live another day in such weather as this. God help her, poor little woman! Better for her if she follows husband and child."

"Who is with Mr. Clinton, doctor?" asked the master presently.

"Adair—No. 267. I brought him into the cabin. Indeed, Clinton asked me to do so. He thinks much of the young fellow, and his conduct ever since the outbreak occurred deserves recognition. He has rendered me invaluable assistance with Clinton and the other sick in the main cabin."

"He's a fine young fellow," said Belton, "and his good example has done much to keep the others quiet. Do you know, doctor, that at any time during the last three weeks the ship could have been captured by a dozen even unarmed men."

"I do know it; but the poor wretches seem never to have thought of rising."

"What was Adair sent out for?" asked Belton.

"Lunacy; otherwise, patriotism. He's one of a batch of five—the five best conducted men on the ship—sentenced to end their days in Botany Bay for participating in an attack on a party of yeomanry at Bally-somewhere or other in Ireland. There was a band of about fifty, but these five were the only ones captured—the other forty-five were most likely informers and led them into the mess."

A hurried footstep sounded near them, and a big man, in a semi-military costume, presented himself abruptly before them. His dark, coarse race was flushed with anger, and his manner insolent and aggressive. Not deigning to notice the presence of the surgeon, he addressed himself to the master of the transport.

"Mr. Belton, I protest against the presence in the main cabin of a ruffianly convict. The scoundrel refuses to let me have access to Lieutenant Clinton. Both on my own account and on that of Mr. Clinton, who needs my services, I desire that this man be removed immediately."

"What right, sir, have you, a passenger, to protest?" answered Belton surlily. "Mr. Clinton is dying and Prisoner Adair is nursing him."

"That does not matter to me, I— —"

The surgeon stepped in front of the newcomer.

"But it *shall* matter to you, Mr. Jacob Bolger, Government storekeeper, jailer, overseer, or commissary's runner, or whatever your position is. And I shall see that No. 267 suffers no molestation from you."

"Who are you, sir, to threaten me? The Governor shall hear of this when we arrive at the settlement. A pretty thing that I should be talked to like this by the ship's doctor!"

"By God, sir, I'll give you something to talk about," and the surgeon's Welsh blood leapt to his face. Advancing to the break of the poop, he called—

"Sergeant Matthews!"

The one remaining non-commissioned officer of the diminished convict-guard at once appeared and saluted.

He was a solemn-faced, taciturn man, devoted to Clinton.

"Mr. Belton," said the doctor, "in the serious illness of Lieutenant Clinton I now assume charge of the military guard and convicts on this ship, and as a first step to maintain proper discipline at such a critical time, I shall confine Mr. Bolger to his cabin. Sergeant, take him below and lock him in."

Bolger collapsed at once. "I beg your pardon, doctor, for my hastiness. I did not know.... I was— —"

The surgeon cut his apologies short. "Go to your cabin, sir. I shall not have you locked in, but, by heavens! if you attempt to go into Mr. Clinton's cabin I'll put you in irons, Government official though you are. I am well aware that your presence is particularly objectionable to Mrs. Clinton."

With an evil look Bolger left them, and the surgeon, turning to Belton, said: "That settles *him*, anyway, for a time. He's a thorough scoundrel, I believe. Mrs. Clinton has a positive horror of the man; yet the brute is continually pestering her with offers of his services. Now I must go below again to poor Clinton."

In the dimly lighted cabin the young officer lay breathing heavily, and as the doctor softly entered he saw that the time was now very near. By her husband's side sat Marion Clinton, her loosened wavy brown hair hiding from view her own face and the dying hand which she held pressed to her quivering lips. At her feet, on a soft cushion on the floor, lay her infant, with one thin waxen hand showing out from the light shawl that covered it; at the further end of the cabin stood a young, broad-shouldered man in grey convict garb. As the doctor entered he stood up and saluted.

The sound of the opening door made Clinton turn his face. "Is that you, Williams?" he said, in slow, laboured tones. "Marion, my girl, bear up. I know I am going, old fellow. Do what you can for her, Williams. The Governor will see to her returning to England, but it may be long before a ship leaves.... Marion!"

"Yes," she answered brokenly.

"Is baby no better?"

"No," she answered with a sob, as she raised her tear-stained face to Surgeon Williams, who shook his head. "There is no hope for her, Harry."

His hand pressed hers gently. "God help you, dear! Only for that it would not be so hard to die now; and now I leave you quite alone."

She stooped down and lifted the fragile infant, and Williams and No. 267 turned their faces away for awhile. Presently Clinton called the surgeon.

"Williams," and his eyes looked wistfully into the doctor's, "do what you can for her. There is something like a hundred guineas among my effects—that will help. Thank God, though, she will be a rich woman when my poor old father dies. I am the only son."

The surgeon bent down and took his hand. "She shall never want a friend while I live, Clinton, never."

A light of thankfulness flickered in Clinton's eyes, and the pallid lips moved; and then as wife and friend, each holding a hand, waited for him to speak, there came the sound of a heavy sob. Convict 267 was kneeling and praying for the departing soul.

Slowly the minutes passed, the silence broken but by the creaking and straining of the ship as she rose and fell to the sea, and now and again the strange, mournful cry of some night-fishing penguin.

"Marion," Clinton said at last, "I would like to speak to Adair before I die. He has been good to you and to me."

Walking softly in his stockinged feet, Adair advanced close to the bed.

"Give me your hand, Adair. God bless you," he whispered.

"And God bless you, sir, and all here," answered the young Irishman in a husky, broken voice.

"Hush," said the surgeon warningly, and his eyes sought those of the watching wife, with a meaning in them that needed no words. Quickly she passed her arm around Clinton, and let his head lie upon her shoulder. He sighed heavily and then lay still.

The surgeon touched the kneeling figure of Convict Adair on the arm, and together they walked softly out of the cabin.

"Come again in an hour, Adair," said Dr. Williams; "you can help me best. We must bury him by daylight. Meanwhile you can get a little sleep."

No. 267 clasped his hands tightly together as he looked at the doctor, and his lips worked and twitched convulsively. Then a wild beseeching look overspread his face. "For God's sake don't ask me!" he burst out. "I implore you as man to man to have pity on me. I *cannot* be here at daylight!"

"As you please," answered Williams, with a surprised expression; and then as he went on deck he said to himself, "Some cursed, degrading Irish superstition, I suppose, about a death at sea."

Slowly the hours crept on. No noise disturbed the watcher by her dead save the low voices of the watch on deck and the unknown sounds that one hears at night alone. Prisoner Adair was sitting in the main cabin within near call of Mrs. Clinton, and, with head upon his knees, seemed to slumber. Suddenly the loud clamour of five bells as the hour was struck made him start to his feet and look quickly about him with nervous apprehension. From the dead officer's state-room a narrow line of light from beneath the door sent an oblique ray aslant the cabin floor and crossed the convict's stockinged feet.

For a moment he hesitated; then tapped softly at the door. It opened, and the pale face of Marion Clinton met his as he stood before her cap in hand.

"Have you come to take"—the words died away in her throat with a sob.

"No," he answered, "I have but come to ask you to let me say goodbye, and God keep and prosper you, madam. My time here is short, and you and your husband have made my bitter lot endurable."

She gave him her hand. He clasped it reverently in his for a moment, and his face flushed a dusky red. Then he knelt and kissed her child's little hand.

"Are you leaving the ship? Are we then in port or near it?" she asked.

He looked steadfastly at her for a moment, and then, pushing the door to behind him, lowered his voice to a whisper.

"Mrs. Clinton, your husband one day told me that he would aid me to regain my freedom. Will you do as much?"

"Yes," she answered, trembling; "I will. I shall tell the Governor how you——"

He shook his head. "Not in that way, but now, now."

"How *can* I help you now?" she asked wonder-ingly.

"Give me Mr. Clinton's pistols. Before daylight four others and myself mean to escape from the ship. The guard are all too sick to prevent us even if we are discovered. There is a boat towing astern, lowered with the intention of sending it ashore to seek assistance. Water and provisions are in it. But we have no firearms, and if we land on the coast may meet with savages."

Without a word she put her husband's pistols in his hands, and then gave him all the ammunition she could find.

"Do not shed blood," she began, when the convict clutched her arm. A sound as of some one moving came from the next cabin—the one occupied by Jacob Bolger—and a savage light came into Adair's eyes as he stood and listened.

"He would give the alarm in a moment if he knew," he muttered.

"Yes," she answered; "he hates you, and I am terrified even to meet his glance."

But Mr. Jacob Bolger made no further noise; he had heard quite enough, and at that moment was lying back in his bunk with an exultant smile, waiting for Adair to leave the cabin.

Then the convict, still crouching on the floor, held out his hand.

"Will you touch my hand once more, Mrs. Clinton?" he said huskily.

She gave it to him unhesitatingly.

"Goodbye, Adair. I pray God all will go well with you."

He bent his face over it and whispered "Goodbye," and then went up on deck.

As No. 267 stumbled along the main deck he saw that all discipline was abandoned, and even the for'ard sentry, that for the past week had been stationed to guard the prisoners when on deck, had left his post.

At the fore-hatch four shadowy forms approached him, and then the five men whispered together.

"Good," said Adair at last. Then they quickly separated.

Six bells had struck when Jacob Bolger opened his cabin door, peered cautiously about, and then, stepping quickly to Mrs. Clinton's door, turned the handle without knocking, and entered.

"Why do you come here, Mr. Bolger?" said Marion Clinton, with a terrified look in her dark eyes. "Do you not know that my husband is dead and my child dying?" And, holding the infant in her arms, she barred a nearer approach.

"I am sorry to disturb you, Mrs. Clinton; but I come as a friend, first to offer you my poor services in your great affliction, and secondly—but as a friend still—to warn you of the dangerous step you have taken in assisting a party of convicts to escape from the ship."

"For Heaven's sake, Mr. Bolger, have some pity on me! My dear husband is dead, my child has but a few hours—perhaps minutes—to live. Do not add to my misery."

"I shall not betray *you!*" and he advanced a step nearer to her; "but it is my duty," and his cunning eyes watched her shrinking figure keenly, "to prevent these men from escaping." And then he turned as if to go.

Her courage came back. "Mr. Bolger"—and she placed her hand on his cuff, shuddering as she did so—"you are not a rich man. Will you—can I—will a hundred guineas buy your silence? It is all I have. Forget that which you know. Let these wretched men escape. What harm can it do you?"

His savage, brutal nature came out, and he laughed coarsely.

"None, but—but you would like to see them get away, would you not?"

"Yes," she answered, looking at him with dulled eyes, "Adair has been very good to us."

"Well, look here; money cannot buy my silence, but *you* can. Now do you know what I mean?"

"No," she answered despairingly. "How should I? What is it you wish me to do?"

"This"—and he bent his evil-eyed face close to hers—"promise to marry me three months from now."

She gave a gasping cry, and sank back upon her seat. He followed and stood over her, and then spoke quickly—

"Ever since I first saw you I have loved you. You are a free woman now, and I shall have a good position at the settlement."

She made a gesture of horror, and his voice grew savage and threatening. "And unless you make me that promise I'll give the alarm now, and Adair and his confederates shall hang together. Come, think, and decide quickly—their life or death rests in your hands."

For some moments she bent her gaze upon the pinched and sunken features of her dying child; then she raised her head, and a swift gleam of fire came into her eyes.

"I will do as you wish. Now go."

Without a word Bolger turned and left the cabin.

As he walked quickly through the main cabin he did not see the tall figure of Sergeant Matthews standing a few feet aft from Mrs. Clinton's cabin-door. The moment Bolger disappeared the sergeant tapped and called—

"Mrs. Clinton!"

A new terror beset her as she recognised the sergeant's voice; but she bravely stifled it and bade him come in.

The solemn, wooden-faced soldier looked at her steadily for a second or so, and then, being a man of few words, got through with them as quickly as possible.

"Beg pardon, madam, doctor sent me with a message to Mr. Bolger, telling him he was at liberty to leave his cabin; found he was gone; heard his voice in here; waited to see if could be of any assistance to you, madam."

There was a kindly ring in his voice which encouraged her.

"Matthews, did you hear what Mr. Bolger was saying?"

The sergeant looked stolidly before him. "I did, madam—part of it."

"Part?" she repeated agitatedly.

"Yes, madam—about Adair and some other men."

She pressed her hand to her throat. Matthews was an old, tried servant of her husband's in former years. "Close the door!" she said suddenly.

Opening a locker, she took out a leathern-bound writing-desk, unlocked it, and in a moment or two more turned to the sergeant with a small but heavy purse in her hand.

"Sergeant," she said quietly; "this money, nearly a hundred guineas, is for you. I may not live to reach the settlement at Port Jackson. And I would like to reward you for—for——" The rest died away.

Matthews understood. He took the money, saluted, and with softened tread left the cabin. He was not a hard man, and had meant to do his duty when he heard Bolger speak of Adair's intended escape; but a hundred guineas was a large sum to him.

As the door closed after the sergeant, Marion Clinton, holding the infant close to her bosom, saw the grey shadow deepen on the pallid race, as with a gentle tremor of the frail body the child's head fell back upon her arm.

No one on board heard a soft splashing of the Water as Adair swam to the boat towing astern and cut the painter where it touched the water-line; the dense fog hid everything from view. Holding the line in his left hand he swam silently along, drawing the boat after him, till he reached the fore-chains. Then four figures clambered noiselessly over the bulwarks and got into the boat, which was at once pushed off.

Wrapped in the white mantle of fog, they drifted slowly away, watching with bated breath the misty outlines of the towering spars grow feinter and fainter, and then vanish altogether, till, although they were but forty yards away, the position of the *Brekenbridge* was discernible only by a dull blur of sickly light that came from her stern ports. Then suddenly there came the sound of a splash, followed by tramping of feet and Captain Belton's hoarse voice.

"Hands to the boat, here! Mrs. Clinton and her baby have fallen overboard."

Lights appeared on the deck, and then a voice called out, "The boat is gone, sir!"

"Clear away the starboard-quarter boat, then!" roared Belton; "quick!"

But before the quarter-boat could be lowered, the sound of oars was heard, a boat dashed up, and a man, leaning over the side, grasped the drowning woman and lifted her in, her dead baby still clasped tightly in her arms.

"Have you got her?" called out Williams and Belton together.

"No," came the answer, and those in the boat began rowing again, but instead of approaching the ship, she seemed to be swallowed up in the fog, and the *click clack* of the oars momentarily sounded feinter.

"By heavens, the scoundrels are pulling away!" shouted Belton. "After them, you fellows in the quarter-boat!"

But the dense, impenetrable mantle of fog made pursuit useless, and the quarter-boat returned an hour later with an exhausted crew.

At ten o'clock next morning a keen, cold air came from the southeast, and two days later the *Breckenbridge* brought her load of misery into Sydney Cove, and her master reported the escape of Edward Adair, Michael Terry, William O'Day, Patrick O'Day, and Daniel McCoy, and the death by drowning of Mrs. Clinton, who, with her baby in her arms, had jumped overboard on the same night.

II

Till dawn the convicts urged the boat along through the fog, then they ceased rowing and ate ravenously of the food in the boat's locker.

Lying upon the sail in the bottom, of the boat, Mrs. Clinton slept. The night was warm, her wet clothing did her no harm, and her sleep was the sleep of physical and mental exhaustion. As the rising sun sent its rays through the now lifting fog, Adair touched the sleeping woman on her shoulder.

She opened her eyes and looked wildly about her, then at the outline of a little figure that lay beside her covered with a convict's coarse jacket, and seizing it in her arms, looked at the five men with eyes of such maddened terror, they thought her reason was gone.

But rough, unkempt and wild-looking as were Adair's four companions, they treated her with the tenderest pity, and watched in silent sympathy the bitter tide of grief that so quickly possessed her. As the sun rose higher, the glassy water rippled here and there in dark patches, and the men looked longingly at the sail on which she sat, holding the infant, but hesitated to disturb her. Away to the westward the dim summits of a range of mountains showed faintly blue, but of the *Breckenbridge* there was no sign, and a grey albatross sailing slowly overhead was their only companion. Already Adair and the others had cast away their hated convict garb, and clothed themselves in tattered garments given them by some of the transport's crew.

Another hour passed, and then helping Mrs. Clinton to a seat in the stern, they hoisted the mainsail and jib, and headed the boat for the land, for the breeze was now blowing freshly.

What Adair's intentions were regarding Mrs. Clinton the others did not ask. Theirs was unquestioning loyalty, and they were ready to follow him now with the same blind and fateful devotion that had brought them with him on board the *Breckenbridge* in manacles.

As the boat sped over the sunlit sea Adair spoke—

"Mrs. Clinton, I shall try to reach a settlement near here. There we may be able to put you ashore."

She only smiled vacantly, and with a feeling of intense pity Adair saw her again bend her head and heard her talking and crooning to the dead child.

"Sure 'tis God's great pity has desthroyed her raison, poor darlin'," muttered a grey-headed old prisoner named Terry; "lave her alone. We'll take the babe from her by an' by."

Between the boat and the faint blue outline of the distant land lay the rounded wooded slopes of Montagu Island, showing a deep depression in the centre. As the boat sailed round its northern point a small bay opened out, and here in smooth water they landed without difficulty. Carrying Mrs. Clinton to a grassy nook under the shade of the cliffs, she unresistingly allowed old Terry to take the infant from her arms, and her dulled eyes took no heed of what followed.

Forcing their way through the thick, coarse grass that clothed the western side of the island, and disturbing countless thousands of breeding gulls and penguins, Adair and Terry dug a tiny grave on the summit under a grove of low, wide-branched mimosa trees, and there the child was buried.

As they were about to descend, the old man gave a shout and pointed seaward—there, not a mile away, was a large ship, whose many boats showed her to be a whaler, and quite near the shore a boat was pulling swiftly in towards the landing-place.

Rushing down to their companions they gave the alarm, and then a hurried consultation was held.

"We must meet them," said Adair, "we can't hide the boat. If they mean mischief we can take to the woods."

In another five minutes the newcomers saw the little group and gave a loud, friendly hail. Stepping out from his companions, who followed him closely, Adair advanced to meet the strangers.

A young, swarthy-faced man, who steered, jumped out of the boat and at once addressed him. He listened with interest to Adair's story that they had escaped from a ship that had gone ashore on the coast some weeks before, and then said quietly—

"Just so. Well, I'm glad that I can assist you. I've just come from Port Jackson, and am bound to the East Indies, sperm-whaling. Come aboard, all of you, and I'll land you at one of the Dutch ports there."

Adair's face paled. Something told him that his story was not believed. What should he do?

The captain of the whaler beckoned him aside. "Don't be alarmed. I can guess where you come from. But that doesn't concern me. Now look here. My ship—the *Manhattan*, of Salem—is a safer place for you than an open boat, and I'm short-handed and want men. You can all lend a hand till I land you at Amboyna or Ternate. Is that your wife?"

"Yes."

"Well, what are you going to do—stay here or come aboard?"

"We accept your offer gladly," answered Adair, now convinced of the American's good intentions.

"Very well; carry your wife down to the boat while my men get some gulls' eggs."

For two weeks after Mrs. Clinton was carried up the whale-ship's side she hovered between life and death. Then, very, very slowly, she began to mend. A month more and then the *Manhattan* hove-to off the verdant hills and shining beaches of Rotumah Island.

"You cannot do better than go ashore here," the captain had said to Adair a few hours before. "I know the natives well. They are a kind, amiable race of people, and many of the men, having sailed in whale-ships, can speak English. The women will take good care of Mrs. Clinton" (Adair had long since told him hers and his own true story); "have no fear of that. In five months I ought to be back here on my way to Port Jackson, and I'll give her a passage there. If she remains on board she will most likely die; the weather is getting hotter every day as we go north, and she is as weak as an infant still. As for yourself and old Michael, you will both be safe here on Rotumah. No King's ship has ever touched here yet; and if one should come the natives will hide you."

That evening, as the warm-hearted, pitying native women attended to Mrs. Clinton in the chiefs house, Adair and Terry watched the *Manhattan's* sails disappear below the horizon.

There for six months they lived, and with returning health and strength Marion Clinton learned to partly forget her grief, and to take interest in her strange surroundings. Ever since they had landed Adair and old Michael Terry had devoted themselves to her, and as the months went by she grew, if not happy, at least resigned. To the natives, who had never before had a white woman living among them, she was as a being from another world, and they were her veriest slaves, happy to obey her slightest wish. At first she had counted the days as they passed; then, as the sense of her utter loneliness in the world beyond would come to her, the thought of Adair and his unswerving care for and devotion to her would fill her heart with quiet thankfulness. She knew that it was for her sake alone he had remained on the island, and when the six months had passed, her woman's heart told her that she cared for him, and that "goodbye" would be hard to say.

But how much she really did care for him she did not know, till one day she saw him being carried into the village with a white face and blood-stained garments. He had been out turtle-fishing, the canoe had capsized on the reef, and Adair had been picked up insensible by his native companions, with a broken arm and a deep jagged cut at the back of his head.

Day by day she watched by his couch of mats, and felt a thrill of joy when she knew that all danger was past.

One afternoon while Adair, still too weak to walk, lay outside his house thinking of the soft touch and gentle voice of his nurse, there came a roar of voices from the village, and a pang shot through his heart— the *Manhattan* was back again.

But it was not the *Manhattan*, and ten minutes afterwards four or five natives, headed by old Terry, white-faced and trembling, came rushing along the path.

"'Tis a King's ship!" the old man gasped, and then in another minute Adair was placed on a rude litter and carried into the mountains.

It was indeed a King's ship, bound to Batavia to buy stores for the starving settlers at Port Jackson, and in want of provisions even for the ship's company. Almost as soon as she anchored, the natives flocked off to her with fruit, vegetables, and such poultry as they had to barter. Among those who landed from the ship was a tall, grave-raced Sergeant of Marines, who, after buying some pigs and fowls from the natives on the beach, had set out, stick in hand, for a walk along the palm-lined shore. At the request of the leading chief, all those who came ashore carried no weapons, and, indeed, the gentle, timid manner of the natives soon convinced the white men that there was no need to arm themselves. A quarter of a mile walk hid the ship from view, and then Sergeant Matthews, if he did not show it, at least felt surprised, for suddenly he came face to face with a young, handsome white woman dressed in a loose jacket and short skirt. Her feet were bare, and in one hand she carried a rough basket, in the other a heavy three-pronged wooden crab-spear. He recognised her in a moment, and drawing himself up, saluted, as if he had seen her but for the first time.

"What do you want?" she asked trembling; "why have you come here— to look for me?"—and as she drew back a quick anger gave place to fear.

"No, Madam," and the sergeant looked, not at her, but away past her, as if addressing the trees around him, "I am in charge of the Marine guard on board the *Scarborough*. Put in here for supplies. Ship bound to Batavia for stores, under orders of Deputy-Commissary Bolger, who is on board."

"Ah!" and she shuddered. "Matthews, do not tell him I am here. See, I am in your power. I implore you to return to the ship and say nothing of my being here. Go, go, Matthews, and if you have pity in your heart for me do all you can to prevent any of the ship's company from lingering about the village! I beg, I pray of you, to ask me no questions, but go, go, and Heaven reward you!"

The sergeant again saluted, and without another word turned on his heel and walked leisurely back to the boat.

An hour before sunset, Adair, from his hiding-place in the mountains, saw the great ship fill her sails and stand away round the northern point. Terry had left him to watch the movements of the landing party, and Adair but waited his return. Soon through the growing stillness of the mountain forest he heard a footfall, and then the woman he loved stood before him.

"Thank God!" she cried, as she clasped her hands together; "they have gone."

"Yes," he answered huskily, "but... why have you not gone with them? It is a King's ship,... and I hoped—oh! why did you stay?"

She raised her dark eyes to his, and answered him with a sob that told him why.

Sitting beside him with her head on his shoulder, she told him how that morning she had accompanied a party of native women to a village some miles distant on a fishing excursion, and knew nothing of the ship till she was returning and met Sergeant Matthews.

"And now," she said, with a soft laugh, "neither King's ship nor whale-ship shall ever part us."

Another month went by all too swiftly now for their new-found happiness, and then the lumbering old *Manhattan* came at last, and that night her captain and Adair sat smoking in the latter's thatched hut.

"That," said the American, pointing to a heavy box being borne past the open door by two natives, "that box is for Mrs. Clinton. I just ransacked the Dutchmen's stores at Amboyna, and bought all the woman's gear I could get. How is she? Old Terry says she's doing 'foine.'"

"She is well, thank you," said Adair, with a happy smile, and then rising he placed his hand on the seaman's shoulder, while his face reddened and glowed like a boy's.

"Oh, that's it, is it?" said the American with a good-natured laugh. "Well, I'm right pleased to hear it. Now look here. The *Manhattan* is a full ship, and I'm not going to Port Jackson to sell my oil this time. I'm just going right straight home to Salem. And you and she are coming with me; and old Parson Barrow is going to marry you in my house; and in my house you and your wife are going to stay until you settle down and become a citizen of the best country on the earth."

And the merry chorus of the sailors, as they raised the anchor from its coral bed, was borne across the bay to old Terry, who sat watching the ship from the beach. No arguments that Adair and the captain used could make him change his mind about remaining on the island. He was too old, he said, to care about going to America, and Rotumah was a "foine place to die in—'twas so far away from the bloody redcoats."

As he looked at the two figures who stood on the poop waving their hands to him, his old eyes dimmed and blurred.

"May the howly Saints bless an' kape thim for iver! Sure, he's a thrue man, an' she's a good woman!"

Quickly the ship sailed round the point, and Marion Clinton, with a last look at the white beach, saw the old man rise, take off his ragged hat, and wave it in farewell.

THE CUTTING-OFF OF THE
"QUEEN CHARLOTTE"

One day, early in the year 1814, the look-out man at the South Head of Port Jackson saw a very strange-looking craft approaching the land from the eastward. She was a brigantine, and appeared to be in ballast; and as she drew nearer it was noticed from the shore that she seemed short-handed, for when within half a mile of the Heads the wind died away, the vessel fell broadside on to the sea and rolled about terribly; and in this situation her decks were clearly visible to the lightkeeper and his men, who could see but three persons on board. In an hour after the north-easter had died away, a fresh southerly breeze came up, and then those who were watching the stranger saw that her sails, instead of being made of canvas, were composed of mats stitched together, similar to those used by South Sea Island sailing canoes. Awkward and clumsy as these looked, they yet held the wind well, and soon the brigantine came sweeping in through the Heads at a great rate of speed.

Running close in under the lee of the land on the southern shore of the harbour the stranger dropped anchor, and shortly after was boarded by a boat from the shore, and to the surprise of those who manned her the vessel was at once recognised as the *Queen Charlotte*, which had sailed out of Port Jackson in the May of the preceding year.

The naval officer in charge of the boat at once jumped on board, and, greeting the master, a tall, bronzed-faced man of thirty, whose name was Shelley, asked him what was wrong, and where the rest of his crew were.

"Dead! Lieutenant Carlisle," answered the master of the brigantine sadly. "We three—myself, one white seaman, and a native chief—are all that are left."

Even as far back as 1810 the port of Sydney sent out a great number of vessels all over the South Seas. The majority of these were engaged in the whale fishery, and, as a rule, were highly successful; others, principally smaller craft, made long but very remunerative cruises among the islands of Polynesia, Melanesia, and Micronesia, trading for coconut oil, sandal-wood, and pearl shell. A year or two before, an adventurous trading captain had made a discovery that a vast group of islands named by Cook the Dangerous Archipelago, and lying to the eastward of Tahiti, was rich in pearl shell. The inhabitants were a race of brave and determined savages, extremely suspicious of, and averse to, the presence of strangers; but yet, once this feeling was overcome by just treatment, they were safe enough to venture among, provided a good look-out was kept, and the vessel well armed to resist an attempt at cutting-off.

The news of the wealth that lay hidden in the unknown lagoons of the Dangerous Archipelago (now called the Paumotu Group) was soon spread from one end of the Pacific to the other, and before two years had passed no less than seven vessels had appeared among the islands, and secured very valuable cargoes for a very trifling outlay. Among those who were tempted to hazard their lives in making a fortune quickly was Herbert Shelley, the master and owner of the *Queen Charlotte*.

Leaving Sydney on May 14, with a crew of nine men all told, the brigantine arrived, thirty-one days later, at Matavai Bay in Tahiti. Here she remained some days, while the master negotiated with the chiefs of the district for the services of some of their men as divers. Six were secured at Tahiti; and then, after wooding and watering, and taking on board a number of hogs, fowls, and turtle, presented to Captain Shelley and his officers by the chief Pomare, the vessel stood away north-west to the island of Raiatea, with a similar purpose in view. Here the master succeeded in obtaining three fine, stalwart men, who were noted not only for their skill in diving but for their courage and fidelity as well.

Among those natives secured at Tahiti was a chief named Upaparu, a relative of Pomare, and hereditary ruler of the district of Taiarapu. He was a man of herculean proportions, and during the stay of Captain Bligh, of the *Bounty*, at Tahiti, was a constant visitor to the white men, with whom he delighted to engage in friendly wrestling matches and other feats of strength and endurance. Fletcher Christian, the unfortunate leader of the mutiny that subsequently occurred, was the only one of all the ship's company who was a match for Upaparu in these athletic encounters, and until thirty years ago there remained a song that recounted how the unfortunate and wronged master's mate of the *Bounty* and the young chief of Taiarapu once wrestled for half an hour without either yielding an inch, though "the ground shook and quivered beneath the stamping and the pressing of their feet." And although twenty-three years had passed since Upaparu had seen the barque sail away from Tahiti for the last time, when Christian and his fated comrades bade the people farewell for ever, the native chief was still, despite his fifty years, a man of amazing strength, iron resolution, and dauntless courage.

The voyage from the fertile and beautiful Society Islands to the low, sandy atolls of the Dangerous Archipelago was a pleasant one; for not only was the weather delightfully fine, but there prevailed on board a spirit of harmony and comradeship among Captain Shelley, his officers, and crew, that was not often seen. A brave and humane man himself, the master of the *Queen Charlotte* was particularly fortunate in having for his first and second officers two young men of similar dispositions. This was their second voyage among the islands of the Society and Dangerous Archipelago Islands; and their kindness to the natives with whom they had come into contact, their freedom from the degrading licentiousness that, as a rule, marked the conduct of seamen associating with the natives, and the almost brotherly regard that they evinced for each other made them not only respected, but loved and admired by whites and natives alike. Both were men of fine stature and great strength; and, indeed, Upaparu one day jestingly remarked that he and Captain Shelley's two officers were a match for three times their number.

For some eight or nine days the *Queen Charlotte* beat steadily to the eastward against the gentle southeast trades, which, at that time of the year, blew so softly as to raise scarce more than tiny ripples upon the bosom of the ocean. Then, one day, there appeared against the horizon the faint outline of a line of coco-trees springing from the ocean, and by and by a white gleam of beach showed at their base as the vessel lifted to the long ocean swell, and then sank again from view; but up aloft on the brigantine's foreyard, the native pearl-divers, with their big, luminous eyes shining with excitement, gazed over and beyond the tops of the palm-trees, and saw the light-green waters of a noble lagoon that stretched northwest and south-east for fifty miles, and twenty from east to west.

Aft, on the skylight, Captain Shelley and his mate, with Upaparu, the chief, leaning over their shoulders, peered over a rough chart of the Dangerous Archipelago which showed a fairly correct outline of the island before them. Twelve months before, the master of the brigantine had heard from the captain of a South Seaman—as whaleships were called in these days—that this island of Fakarava abounded in pearl shell, and had determined to ascertain the truth of the statement. As he carefully studied the chart given him by the captain of the whaler, and read aloud the names of the villages that appeared here and there, the Tahitian chief nodded assent and confirmation.

"That is true," he said to the white man, "I have heard these names before; for long before Tuti the Wise{*} came to Tahiti, we had heard of these people of Fakarava and their great lagoon, so wide that even if one climbs the tallest coconut-tree on one side he cannot see across to the other. And once, when I was a boy, I saw bonito hooks of thick pearl shell, that were brought to Taiarapu from this place by the Paniola.{**}

* *Captain Cook.*

* *The Spaniards—two Spanish ships fitted out by the Viceroy of Peru had visited these islands before Cook.*

"But then," he went on to say, "O friends of my heart, we must be careful, for these men of Fakarava are all *aitos* (fighting men), and no ship hath ever yet been inside the great lagoon, for the people swarm off in their canoes, club and spear in hand, and, stripped to the loins, are ready to fight to the death the stranger that sets foot on their land."

Somewhat disquieted at this intelligence, the master of the *Queen Charlotte* was at first in doubt whether to venture inside or not; but, looking round him and noting the eager, excited faces of his white crew and their native messmates, he decided at least to attempt to see for himself whether there was or was not pearl shell in the lagoon.

By this time the brigantine was within a mile or so of the entrance, which, on a nearer inspection, presented no difficulties whatever. As the vessel passed between the roaring lines of surf that thundered and crashed with astounding violence on the coral barriers enclosing the placid lagoon, a canoe shot out from the beach a quarter of a mile away, and approached the ship. But four natives were in the tiny craft, and when within a cable-length of the brigantine they ceased paddling, and conversed volubly with one another, as if debating whether they should venture on board the strange ship or not. Paddles in hand, they regarded her with the most intense curiosity as a being from another world; and when, the ship bringing up to the wind, the anchor was let go, a loud cry of astonishment burst forth from them, and with a swift backward sweep of their paddles the canoe shot shorewards like an arrow from a bow full fifty feet astern.

Clambering out on the end of the jib-boom, Upaparu seized hold of a stay and hailed them in a semi-Tahitian dialect, the *lingua franca* of Eastern Polynesia—

"*Ia ora na kotore teie nei aho!*" ("May you have peace this day!"), and then, bidding them await him, he sprang overboard and swam to them. In a few minutes he was alongside the canoe, holding on the gunwale and holding an animated conversation with its crew, one of whom, evidently the leader, at last bent down and rubbed noses with the Tahitian in token of amity. Then they paddled alongside, and after some hesitation clambered up on deck.

Tall and finely made, with light copper-coloured skins deeply tattooed from their necks to their heels, and holding in their hands wooden daggers set on both edges with huge sharks'-teeth as keen as razors, they surveyed the vessel and her crew with looks of astonishment. Except for a narrow girdle of curiously-stained pandanus leaves, each man was nude, and their stiff, scanty, and wiry-looking beards seemed to quiver with excitement as they looked with lightning-like rapidity from one object to another.

Advancing to them with his hand outstretched, the master of the brigantine took the leader's hand in his, and pointed to the poop, and Upaparu told them that the white chief desired them to sit and talk with him. Still grasping their daggers they acceded, and followed Shelley and the Tahitian chief to the poop, seated themselves on the deck, while the crew of the brigantine, in order not to embarrass or alarm them, went about their work as if no strangers were present.

In a very short time Upaparu had so far gained their confidence that they began to talk volubly, and answered all the questions he put to them. "Pearl shell? Yes, there be plenty of it. Even here, beneath the ship. Let us show thee!" and one of them, springing over the side, in another minute or two reappeared with a large pearl shell in his hand, which he placed in the hands of the master of the brigantine.

Convinced that he had done well in venturing inside, Captain Shelley strove his utmost to establish friendly relations with his visitors, and so far succeeded, through the instrumentality of the Tahitian chief, that the leader of the natives, who was a leading chief of the island named Hamanamana, promised to show them where the thickest patches of pearl shell lay in the lagoon. Then, after making them each presents of a sheath-knife and some other articles, the master and his officers watched them descend into their canoe again, and paddle swiftly back to their village, which lay within full view of the ship, a quarter of a mile away.

At a very early hour on the following day, the ship was surrounded by some fifty or sixty canoes, all filled with natives of both sexes, who proffered their services as divers, and seemed animated by the kindliest feelings towards the white men. Lowering the largest boat, the master, accompanied by Upaparu and the other Tahitians, was soon on his way to a place in the lagoon, where his guides assured him there was plenty of pearl shell. For some hours the first and second officers watched their captain's movements with the liveliest anxiety; for, despite the apparent friendliness of the natives, they were by no means confident.

But when, four hours later, the master returned with nearly a ton of pearl shell in the boat, and excitedly told them that their fortunes were made, the young men could not but feel highly elated, and sought by every means in their power to increase the good impression that they and the rest of the ship's company seem to have made upon the islanders.

That night, when the natives had returned to the shore, and the bright blaze of the fires shot out across the sleeping lagoon, and their voices were borne across the water to those in the ship, the two young officers sat and talked together on the poop. A month or two in such a place as this and they would be made men, for it was evident that no other vessel had yet been inside the lagoon, which undoubtedly teemed with pearl shell. And up for'ard the white sailors and their dark-skinned shipmates grew merry, and talked and sang, for they, too, would share in the general good luck. Then, as the lights from the houses on shore died out, and the murmur of voices ceased, the crew of the *Queen Charlotte*, officers and men, lay down on deck and went to sleep.

One for'ard and one aft, the two sentries paced to and fro, and only the slight sound of their naked feet broke the silence of the tropic night. Now and then a fish would leap out of the water and fall back again with a splash, and the sentries watched the swell and bubble of the phosphorescent water for a minute or so, and then again resumed their walk.

But though so silent, the darkness of the night was full of danger to the unsuspecting ship's company of the *Queen Charlotte*. A hundred yards away, swimming together in a semicircle, were some two hundred savages, each with a dagger in his mouth and short ebony club held in the left hand. Silently, but quickly, they swam towards the dark shadow of the brigantine, whose lofty spars stood silhouetted against the white line of beach that lay astern.

Suddenly fifty naked, dripping savages sprang upon the deck, and ere the sentries could do more than fire their muskets the work of slaughter had begun. Nearly all the white seamen, and many of the Tahitians, were lying upon the main hatch, and these were slain almost ere they had time to awake and realise their dreadful fate. As the loud reports of the sentries' muskets reverberated across the motionless waters of the lagoon, the master of the brigantine and his two officers awoke, and, cutlasses in hand, tried bravely to defend those terrified and unarmed members of the crew who had not yet been slaughtered. For some ten minutes or so these three men, with Upaparu beside them, defended the approaches to the poop, and succeeded in killing no less than fifteen of their assailants. Swinging a short, heavy axe in his right hand, the Tahitian chief fought like a hero, till a club was hurled at him with such force that it broke two of his ribs. As he sank down he saw the wild rush of naked bodies pass over him, and heard the death-cries of the first and second officers, who, borne down by numbers, were ruthlessly butchered. After that he remembered no more, for he was dealt another blow on the head, which left him stunned.

When he came to his senses in the cold grey of the morning he found the ship in possession of the people of Fakarava, and of all his shipmates but two remained alive—Captain Shelley and a seaman named Ray; all the rest had been slain and thrown overboard.

Apparently satisfied with the dreadful slaughter they had committed, the natives now began plundering the ship, and Captain Shelley, who seems to have been spared merely for the same reason that Upaparu was not killed—because he was a chief, and therefore sacred—had to sit by and watch them.

After stripping the vessel of everything movable, and even taking all her canvas except the spanker and topsails, the natives went ashore, and their leader, addressing Upaparu, told him that the ship was at liberty to go away.

With the aid of the seaman Ray and the gallant chieftain, Captain Shelley managed to get under weigh, and sailed for Tahiti, which he reached safely. Here he stayed for some months, and then, having made a new suit of sails from native mats, he returned to Port Jackson to relate the story of his fateful voyage.

THE PERUVIAN SLAVERS

About north-west from turbulent and distracted Samoa lie a group of eight low-lying coral atolls, called the Ellice Islands. Fifty years ago, when the white cotton canvas of the ships of the American whaling fleet dotted the blue of the Pacific from the west coast of South America to the bleak and snow-clad shores of the Siberian coast, these lonely islands were perhaps better known than they are now, for then, when the smoky flames of the whaleships' try works lit up the night-darkened expanse of the ocean, and the crackling of the furnace fires and the bubble of the boiling oil made the hardy whalemen's hearts grow merry, many a white man, lured by the gentle nature and amiable character of the Ellice Islanders, had built his house of thatch under the shadow of the rustling palms, and dwelt there in peace and happiness and overflowing plenty. Some of them were traders—men who bartered their simple wares, such as red Turkey twill, axes, knives, beads, tobacco, pipes, and muskets, for coconut oil and turtle shell. Others were wild, good-for-nothing runaways from whaleships, who then were generally known as "beach-combers"—that is, combing the beach for a living—though that, indeed, was a misnomer, for in those days, except one of these men was either a murderer or a tyrant, he did not "comb" for his living, but simply lived a life of luxurious, sensuous ease among the copper-coloured people with whom he dwelt. He had, indeed, to be of a hard and base nature to incur the ill-will or hostility of the denizens of the eight islands.

Twenty years had passed, and, save for a few wandering sperm whalers, the great fleet of the olden days had vanished; for the Civil War in America had borne its fruit even put upon the placid Pacific, and Waddell, in the Confederate cruiser *Shenandoah*, had swept northwards from Australia, bent on burning every ship that flew the hated Stars and Stripes. So, with fear in their hearts, the Yankee whaling skippers hurried into neutral ports for shelter; and not a day too soon, for the rebel war-vessel caught four of them at Ponapé Island, burnt them and went up to the Arctic to destroy the rest.

Then followed years of quiet, for only a very few of the whaleships returned, and, one by one, most of the white men wandered away to the far distant isles of the north-west, taking their wives and families with them, till there were but five or six remaining in the whole Ellice Group.

Among those who sailed away one day in a whale-ship was a trader named Harry. His surname was never known. To his fellow white men and the natives of the island of Nukufetau on which he lived he was simply "Harry"; to those of the other islands of the group he was *Hari Tino Kéhé*, Big Harry.

It was not that he was wearied of the monotony of his existence on Nukufetau that had led Harry to bid his wife and two children farewell, but because that he had heard rumours of the richness in pearl-shell and turtle-shell of the far distant isles of the Pelew Group, and desired to go there and satisfy himself as to the truth of these sailors' tales; for he was a steady, honest man, although he had run away from his ship, a Sydney sandal-wooding vessel; and during his fifteen years' residence on Nukufetau he had made many thousands of dollars by selling coconut oil to the Sydney trading ships, and provisions to the American whalers. A year after his arrival on the island he had married a native woman named Te Ava Malu (Calm Waters). She was the daughter of the chief's brother, and brought her husband as her dowry a long, narrow strip of land richly covered with countless thousands of coco-palms, and it was from these groves of coconuts that Harry had earned most of the bright silver dollars, which, in default of a strong box, he had headed up in a small beef keg and buried under the gravelled floor of his thatched dwelling-house.

Children had been born to him—two fair-skinned, dark-eyed, and gentle-voiced girls, named Fetu and Vailele. The elder, Fetu (The Star), was a quiet, reserved child, and had her father's slow, grave manner and thoughtful face. The younger, Vailele (Leaping Water), was in manner and her ever merry mood like her name, for she was a restless, laughing little maid, full of jest and song the whole day long.

When the time came for Big Harry to say farewell, he called to him his wife and the two girls—Fetu was fourteen, and Vailele twelve—and, bidding them lower down the door of plaited thatch so that they might not be observed, he unearthed the keg of dollars, and, knocking off the two topmost hoops, took out the head. Then he took out nine hundred of the bright, shining coins, and, placing them in the lap of Te Ava Malu, quickly headed up the keg again, and put it back in its hiding-place.

"Listen now to me, O wife and children," said he in the native tongue. "See this money now before us. Of the nine hundred dollars I shall take seven hundred; for it is to my mind that if these tales I hear of these far-off islands be true, then shall I buy from the chiefs there a piece of land, and get men to build a house for me; and if all goeth well with me, I shall return here to Nukufetau within a year. Then shall we sail thither and dwell there. And these other two hundred dollars shalt thou keep, for maybe a ship may come here, and then thou, Te Ava Malu, shalt go to thy father and place them in his hand, and ask him to go to the ship and buy for me a whaleboat, which, when we leave this land together, we shall take with us."

Then, giving his wife the two hundred dollars, he placed the rest in a canvas pouch slung round his waist, and, embracing them all tenderly, bade them farewell, and walked down to the shining beach to where the boat from the whaleship awaited his coming.

Drawing her children to her side, Te Ava Malu stood out upon the sand and watched the whaler loosen her canvas and heave up anchor. Only when the quick *click, click* of the windlass pauls reached their listening ears, as the anchor came up to the song of the sailors and the ship's head swung round, did the girls begin to weep. But the mother, pressing them to her side, chid them, and said that a year was but a little time, and then she sank down and wept with them.

So, with the tears blinding their eyes, they saw the whaler sail slowly out through the passage, and then, as she braced her yards up and stood along the weather shore of the island, they saw Big Harry mount halfway up the mizzen lower rigging. He waved his broad leaf hat to them three times, and then soon, although they could see the upper canvas of the ship showing now and then above the palms, they saw him no more.

Seven months had come and gone, and every day, when the great red sun sank behind the thick line of palms that studded the western shore of Nukufetau, Fetu and Vailele would run to a tall and slender *fau* tree that grew on their mother's land, and cut on its dark brown bark a broad notch.

"See," said Vailele to her sister on this day, "there are now twenty and one marks" (they were in tens) "and that maketh of days two hundred and ten."

"Aue!" said the quiet Fetu. "Cut thou a fresh one above. One hundred and fifty and five more notches must there be cut in the tree before Hari, our father, cometh back; for in the white men's year there are, so he hath told me, three hundred and sixty and five days."

"O-la!" and Vailele laughed. "Then soon must we get something to stand on to reach high up. But yet, it may be that our father will come before the year is dead."

Fetu nodded her dark head, and then, hand in hand, the two girls walked back to their mother's house through the deepening gloom that had fallen upon the palm grove.

Ten miles away, creeping up to the land under shortened canvas, were a barque and a brig. No lights showed upon their decks, for theirs was an evil and cruel mission, and the black-bearded, olive-skinned men who crowded her decks spoke in whispers, lest the sound of their voices might perhaps fall upon the ears of natives out catching flying fish in their canoes.

Closer and closer the ships edged in to the land, and then, as they opened out the long white stretch of beach that fringed the lee of the island, they hove-to till daylight.

But if there were no lights on deck there were plenty below, and in the barque's roomy cabin a number of men were sitting and talking together over liquor and cigars. They were a fierce, truculent-looking lot, and talked in Spanish, and every man carried a brace of revolvers in his belt. All round the cabin were numbers of rifles and carbines and cutlasses; and, indeed, the dark faces of the men, and the profusion of arms that was everywhere shown, made them look like a band of pirates, bent upon some present enterprise. Pirates they were not; but they were perhaps as bad, for both the brig and the barque were Peruvian slavers, sent out to capture and enslave the natives of the South Sea Islands to work the guano deposits of the Chincha Islands.

At one end of the cabin table sat the captain of the barque—a small-made, youthful-looking man, of not more than twenty-five years of age. Before him was spread a sheet-chart of the Ellice Group, and another of the Island of Nukufetau, which he was studying intently.

Standing at the back of the captain's chair was a short, stout, broad-shouldered man, with a heavy black moustache and hawk-like features, who followed with interest the movements of the captain's slender brown hand over the chart. This was Senor Arguello, the owner of the two vessels, and the leading spirit in the villainous enterprise.

"There is the passage into the lagoon, Senor Arguello," said the young captain, pointing to the place on the chart; "and here, on this islet, the last one of the three that form the western chain of the atoll, is the native village. Therefore, if we can succeed in landing our boats' crews between the islet and the one next to it, we can cut off all chances of the natives escaping in that direction."

"Good, Captain Martinas. But what if they escape into the forest?"

"As you see, Senor," said the captain politely, "the islet is but narrow, and offers no chance of concealment unless there are mangrove scrubs in the wider portions. We can secure every one of them in a few hours. There is no possible way of escape but by the sea, and that we have provided against—the brig's boats will watch both sides of the islet, three on the lagoon side, and two on the ocean side."

"Excellent, Captain," said the fat ruffian Arguello. "I must compliment you upon your exactitude of your arrangements. I trust that we shall be as successful here as we were at Nukulaelae.{*} Captain Hennessy," and here he bowed to a man who sat at the other end of the table, "will, I am sure, see that none of these people are drowned in their silly efforts to escape, as occurred at other places."

* *Nukulaelae was almost entirely depopulated by these*
slavers.

Captain Peter Hennessy, once a dashing officer of the Peruvian navy, now a dissipated, broken-down master of a slaving brig, for answer struck his hand heavily on the table, and swore an oath.

"That was not my fault. But, by the God above me, I am sick of this business! I undertook to sail the brig and fill her with natives, but I did not undertake to have a hand in the bloody deeds that have happened. And now that I am on board, I may as well tell you all that the moment I see a shot fired at any of these poor devils I back out of the concern altogether."

"The brave Captain Pedro is tender-hearted," sneered the young captain of the barque, showing his even white teeth under his jet-black moustache.

"No words from you, Captain Martinas," retorted the Irishman. "I am prepared to go on now; but mind you—and you know me—the first man that I see lift a rifle to his shoulder, that man will I send a bullet through, be he black or white."

Then, with a curt nod to his fellow-associates in crime, the captain of the brig *Chacahuco* strode out of the cabin, and calling his boat, which was towing astern of the barque, he got into her and pulled off to shore.

Just as the first flushes of the rising sun tinged the sea to windward with streaks of reddish gold, the decks of the slavers bustled with activity. Boats were lowered, and the crews of cut-throat Chilenos and Peruvians swarmed eagerly into them, and then waited for the signal to cast off.

Suddenly the look-out on the barque, who was stationed on the foreyard, hailed the deck and reported that three canoes had pushed off from the beach and were paddling towards the ship.

A savage curse broke from Porfiro Arguello. He and Martinas had hoped to get part of the landing party posted between the two islets before the natives could see the ships. Now it was too late.{*}

> * Three vessels were engaged in this nefarious business, a
> barque and two brigs. The most dreadful atrocities were
> committed. At Easter Island they seized nearly the whole
> population; at Nukulaelae, in the Ellice Group, they left
> but thirty people out of one hundred and fifty.

"Let all the boats go round to the port side," said Martinas. "The canoes will board us on the starboard side, Senor Arguello, and once we get these people safely on board we shall still be in time to block the passage between the islets."

The boats were quickly passed astern, and then hauled up alongside on the port side; and Martinas, having signalled to the brig to do the same with her boats, lest the natives, seeing armed men in them, should make back for the shore, quietly lit a cigar and waited.

On came the three canoes, the half-naked, stalwart rowers sending them quickly over the ocean swell. In the first canoe were four men and two young girls; in the others men only. Unconscious of the treacherous intentions that filled the hearts of the white men, the unfortunate people brought their canoes alongside, and, with smiling faces, called out in English—

"Heave a rope, please."

"Aye, aye," responded a voice in English; and the natives, as the rope was thrown to them, made fast the canoes and clambered up the sides, the two girls alone remaining in the first canoe, and looking with lustrous, wondering eyes at the crowd of strange faces that looked down at them from the barque's decks.

Ten minutes before Martinas had ordered two sentries who stood guard, one at the break of the poop and the other on top of the for'ard deckhouse, to disappear; and so, when the natives gained the deck there was nothing to alarm them. But at the heavy wooden gratings that ran across the decks, just for'ard of the poop and abaft the for'ard deckhouse, they gazed with eyes full of curiosity. As for the main hatch, that was covered with a sail.

"Good morning, cap'en," said the leader of the natives, a tall, handsome old man about fifty. "Where you come from?"

"From California," answered Martinas, making a sign to one of his officers, who slipped away down to the main deck.

"What you come here for, sir?" resumed the native amiably; "you want fowl, pig, turtle, eh?" And then, unfastening a small bag tied round his naked waist, he advanced and emptied out a number of silver dollars.

"What is that for?" said Martinas, who spoke a little English.

The native laughed pleasantly.

"Money, sir." And then he looked round the ship's decks as if seeking something. "Me want buy boat. Where all your boat, cap'en? Why boat no here?" pointing to the davits and the pendant boat-falls.

"Sea break all boat," said the Peruvian quickly. And then, seeing the look of disappointment on the man's face, he added, "But never mind. You come below. I have handsome present for you."

"All right, cap'en," answered the old man with a pleased smile, as he turned and beckoned to the other natives to follow him.

An exultant smile showed on the grim features of Senor Arguello as he saw the captain's ruse. But just then the second mate came up.

"The girls won't come up on deck," he muttered in Spanish to the captain. "They laugh, and shake their heads."

"Let them stay, Juan, until I get these fellows below quietly. Then let one of the boats slip round and seize them."

Great results sometimes attend upon the merest trifles, and so it fell about now, for by a simple accident were some hundreds of these innocent, unsuspecting people of Nukufetau saved from a dreadful fate; for just as Mana, who was the chiefs brother and the uncle of the two poor half-caste children in the canoe, was about to go below, followed by his people, one of the boat's crew on the starboard side dropped the butt of his musket heavily on the naked foot of a young Chileno boy, who uttered an exclamation of pain.

Wondering where the cry came from, the old native, before he could be stayed, ran to the port side and looked over. There, lying beneath him, were four boats filled with armed men.

Suspicion of evil intent at once flashed through his mind, and, springing back, he gave voice to a loud cry of alarm.

"Back, back, my children!" he cried. "There be many boats here, and in them are men with guns and swords." And then he and those with him rushed for the break of the poop, only to meet the black muzzles of carbines and the glint of twenty cutlasses.

Alas! poor creatures, what hope was there for them, unarmed and almost naked, against their despoilers? One by one they were thrown down, seized, and bound; all but the old man, who, with his naked hands, fought valiantly, till Martinas, seizing a cutlass from a seaman, passed it through his naked body.

With one despairing cry, the old man threw up his arms and fell upon his face, and Martinas, drawing out his bloody weapon, ran to the side and looked over. The canoes were there, but the two girls were gone.

"Curses on you, Juan!" he shouted. "Why did you not seize them?"

But Senor Arguello, with a grim smile, took him by the arm and pointed to where Juan, the second mate, was chasing the two girls in his boat. At the sound of the struggle on deck they had jumped overboard, and, fearless of the sharks, were swimming swiftly for the reef, not a quarter of a mile away.

Standing on the poop-deck of the barque, the captain and Arguello watched the chase with savage interest. Halfway to the shore they saw Juan stand up and level his carbine and fire. The ball struck the water just ahead of the two girls, who were swimming close together. Then, in another two or three minutes, Juan was on top of them, and they saw the oars peaked.

"Saints be praised! He's got one," said Arguello. "They are lifting her into the boat."

"And the other little devil has dived, and they will lose her. Perdition take their souls! A bullet would have settled her," said Martinas. "She will easily get ashore now and alarm the whole village."

Then, with a volley of oaths and curses, he ordered the rest of the boats away to the little strait separating the two islets.

But ere they had sped more than halfway to the shore, the girl who had dived had swum in between the jagged, isolated clumps of coral that stood out from the reef, and rising high upon a swelling wave, they saw her lifted bodily upon its ledge, and then, exhausted as she was, stagger to her feet and run shorewards along its surface.

On, on, she ran, the sharp coral rock tearing her feet, till she gained the white sand of the inner beach, and then she fell prone, and lay gasping for her breath. But not for long, for in a few minutes she was up again, and with wearied limbs and dizzy brain she struggled bravely on till the houses of the village came in sight, and the wondering people ran out to save her from falling again.

"Flee! flee!" she gasped. "My uncle, and Fetu, and all with them are killed.... The white men on the ships have killed them all."

Like bees from their hives, the terrified natives ran out of their houses, and in ten minutes every soul in the village had fled to the beach, and launching canoes, were paddling madly across the lagoon to the main island of Nukufetau lagoon. Here, in the dense puka and mangrove scrub, there was hope of safety.

And, with rage in their villains' hearts, the slavers pursued them in vain; for before the boats could be brought round to the passage the canoes were nearly across the lagoon. But two of the canoes, being overloaded, were swamped, and all in them were captured and bound. Among those who escaped were the wife of Big Harry and her daughter Vailele.

That afternoon, when the boats returned to the ships, Captain Peter Hennessy and his worthy colleague, Captain Martinas, of the barque *Cid Campeador* quarrelled, and the young Peruvian, drawing a pistol from his belt, shot the Irish gentleman through the left arm, and the next moment was cut down upon his own deck by a sweeping blow from Hennessy's cutlass. Then, followed by Arguello's curses, the Irish captain went back to his brig and set sail for Callao, leaving Martinas to get the better of his wound and swoop down upon the natives of Easter Island six weeks later.

And down below in the stifling, sweating hold, with two hundred miserable captives like herself, torn from various islands and speaking a language akin to her own, lay the heart-broken and despairing daughter of Big Harry of Nukufetau.

And now comes the strange part of this true story. Two years had passed, when one cold, sleety evening in Liverpool, a merchant living at Birkenhead returned home somewhat later than his usual hour in a hired vehicle. Hastily jumping out, he pulled the door-bell, and the moment it was opened told the domestic to call her mistress.

"And you, Mary," he added, "get ready hot flannels, or blankets, and a bed. I found an unfortunate young foreign girl nearly dead from cold and exhaustion lying at the corner of a side street. I am afraid she is dying."

In another minute the merchant and his wife had carried her inside, and the lady, taking off her drenched and freezing garments, set about to revive her by rubbing her stiffened limbs. A doctor meanwhile had been sent for, and soon after his arrival the girl, who appeared to be about sixteen years of age, regained consciousness, and was able to drink a glass of wine held to her lips. For nearly an hour the kindly hearted merchant and his wife watched by the girl's bedside, and with a feeling of satisfaction saw her sink into a deep slumber.

The story she told them the next day, in her pretty broken English, filled them with the deepest interest and pity. She had, she said, been captured by the crew of one of two slave ships and taken to a place called Callao. On the voyage many of her ill-fated companions had died, and the survivors, upon their arrival at Callao, had been placed upon a vessel bound to the Chincha Islands. She, however, had, the night before the vessel sailed, managed to elude the sentries, and, letting herself drop overboard, swam to an English ship lying nearly a quarter of a mile away, and clambered up her side into the main-chains. There she remained till daylight, when she was seen by one of the crew. The captain of the ship, at once surmising she had escaped from the slave barque, concealed her on board and, the ship being all ready for sea, sailed next day for Japan. For nearly ten months the poor girl remained on board the English ship, where she was kindly treated by the captain and his wife and officers. At last, after visiting several Eastern ports, the ship sailed for Liverpool, and the girl was taken by the captain's wife to her own lodgings. Here for some weeks she remained with this lady, whose husband meantime had reported the girl's story to the proper authorities, and much red-tape correspondence was instituted with regard to having her sent back to her island home again. It so happened, however, that the girl, who was deeply attached to the captain's wife, was one day left alone, and wearied and perhaps terrified at her mistress not returning at dark, set out to look for her amid the countless streets of a great city. In a very short time she was hopelessly lost, and became so frightened at the strangeness of her surroundings that she sank exhausted and half-frozen upon the pavement of a deserted street. And here she was found as related.

For some months the girl remained with her friends, the merchant and his wife, for the captain of the ship by which she had reached Liverpool had, with his wife, consented to her remaining with them.

One evening, some few months after the girl had been thus rescued, a tall, sunburnt man, dressed like a seaman, presented himself at the merchant's house and asked to see him.

"Send him in," said Mr.——

As the stranger entered the room, Mr. —— saw that he carried in his hand a copy of a Liverpool newspaper.

"I've come, sir," he began, "to ask you if you are the gentleman that I've been reading about——"

Just then the door opened, and the merchant's wife, followed by a girl, entered the room. At the sound of their footsteps the man turned, and the next moment exclaimed—

"My God! It's my little girl!"

And it was his little girl—the little Fetu from whom he had parted at Nukufetau two years before.

Sitting with his great arms clasped lovingly around his daughter, Big Harry told his tale. Briefly, it was this:—After reaching the Pelew Islands and remaining there a few weeks, he had taken passage in a vessel bound to Manila, in the hope that from that port he could get a passage back to Nukufetau in another whaler. But the vessel was cast away, and the survivors were rescued by a ship bound for Liverpool. Landed at that port, and waiting for an opportunity to get a passage to New Bedford, from where he could return to his island home in a whaler, he had one day picked up a paper and read the account of the slavers' onslaught upon the Ellice Islands, and the story of the escape of a young half-caste girl. Never dreaming that this girl was his own daughter—for there are many half-castes in the eight islands of the group—he had sought her out, in the hope that she would be pleased to hear the sound of her native tongue again, and perhaps return with him to her native land.

Nearly a year passed before Big Harry, with his daughter Fetu, sailed into the placid waters of Nukufetau Lagoon, and of the glad meeting of those four happy souls there is no need to tell.

A QUESTION OF PRECEDENCE

Denison, the supercargo of the *Indiana* was always reproaching Packenham, the skipper, for getting the ship into trouble by his inconsiderate and effusive good-nature—"blind stupidity," Denison called it. And whenever Packenham did bring trouble upon himself or the ship's company by some fresh act of glaring idiotcy, he would excuse himself by saying that it wouldn't have happened if Nerida had been with him that trip. Nerida was Packenham's half-caste Portuguese wife. She was a very small woman, but kept her six-foot husband in a state of placid subjection and also out of much mischief whenever she made a cruise in the *Indiana*. Therefore Denison loved her as a sister, and forgave her many things because of this. Certainly she was a bit of a trial sometimes to every living soul on board the brig, but then all skippers' wives are that, even when pure white. And Nerida's doings would make a book worth reading—especially by married women with gadabout husbands like Packenham. But on this occasion Nerida was not aboard, and Denison looked for trouble.

For four days and nights the little *Indiana* had leapt and spun along, before a steady southerly gale, rolling like a drunken thing a-down the for'ard slopes of mountain seas, and struggling gamely up again with flattened canvas from out the windless trough; a bright, hot sun had shone upon her swashing decks from its slow rosy dawn to its quick setting of fiery crimson and blazing gold; and at night a big white moon lit up an opal sky, and silvered the hissing froth and smoky spume that curled in foaming ridges from beneath her clean-cut bows.

The brig was bound from Auckland to Samoa and the islands of the north-west, and carried a cargo of trade goods for the white traders who hoisted the *Indiana's* house-flag in front of their thatched dwellings. Packenham thought a good deal of this flag—it bore the letters R. P. in red in a yellow square on a blue ground—until one day Hammerfeld, the German supercargo of the *Iserbrook*, said it stood for Remorseless Plunderer. Some one told this to Packenham, and although he gave the big Dutchman a bad beating for it, the thing travelled all over the South Seas and made him very wroth. So then he got Nerida to sew another half turn in red to the loop of the P, and thereby made it into a B.

"That'll do fine," he said to Denison. "'Bob Packenham' instead of 'Robert Packenham,' eh?"

"Ye-s," answered, Denison thoughtfully, "I daresay it will be all right." And a month later, when Captain Bully Hayes came on board the *Indiana* in Funafuti Lagoon, he gravely told Packenham that a lot of people were saying the letters stood for "Bloody Pirate."

But all this has nothing to do with this story.

As I have said, the brig was running before a stiff southerly gale. Packenham came on deck, and flinging his six feet of muscular manhood upon the up-ended flaps of the skylight, had just lit his cigar when Alan the bos'un came aft and said that the peak of Tutuila was looming high right ahead, thirty miles away.

"Bully old ship!" said the skipper, "give the *Indiana* a good breeze that catches her fair and square in the stern and she'll run like a scared dog with a tin-pot tied to his tail. Denison, you sleepy beast, come up on deck and look at Samoa the Beautiful, where every prospect pleases and only the German trader is vile."

And so as he and Denison sat aft on the skylight drinking their afternoon coffee and smoking their Manilas, and the brown-skinned native crew sat below in the dark and stuffy foc's'le and gambled for tobacco, the *Indiana* foamed and splashed and rolled before the gale till she ran under the lee of the land into a sea of transparent green, whose gentle rollers scarce broke in foam as they poured over the weed-clad ledges of the barrier-reef into the placid waters or the islet-studded lagoon encompassing the mainland about the village of Sa Lotopa.

Then as some of the merry-hearted kanaka crew ranged the cable, and others ran aloft to clew-up the sails, Packenham steered the brig between a narrow reef-bound passage till she brought up abreast a sweeping curve of sandy beach, shining white under the wooded spurs of a mountain peak two thousand feet above. Back from the beach and showing golden-brown among the sunlit green lay the thatched houses of a native village, and as the brig came head to wind, and the cable clattered through the hawse-pipes, the brown-skinned people ran joyously down to their canoes and swarmed off to the ship. For they all knew Pakenami the *kapeni*, and Tenisoni the supercargo, and Alan the half-caste bos'un, and the two mates, and the Chinaman cook, and every one else on board, and for years past had laughed and joked and sang and hunted the wild boar with them all; and sometimes lied to and robbed and fought with them, only to be better friends than ever when the white men came back again, and the skipper and Denison made the young men presents of meerschaum pipes and condemned Snider rifles; and Alan the Stalwart "asked" every fourth girl in the village when he got drunk at a dance and denied it when sober, yet paid damages like an honourable man (2 dols, in trade goods for each girl) to the relatives.

In a few minutes the first batch of canoes reached the ship, and the occupants, men, women, and children, clambered up the brig's side, and then rushed aft to the poop to rub noses with Packenham and Denison, after the custom of the country, and then for a time a wild babble of voices reigned.

"Hallo, Iakopo, how are you!" said the skipper, shaking hands with a fat-faced, smiling native, who was clad in a white duck suit, and was accompanied by a pretty, dark-eyed girl; "how's the new church getting on? Nearly finished, is it. Well, I didn't forget you. I've brought you down the doors and windows from Auckland."

Iakopo (*Anglicè* Jacob), who was the local teacher and rather a favourite with the *Indiana's* company, said he was very glad. He was anxious to get the church finished before the next visit of the missionary ship, he said. That vain fellow Pita, the teacher at Leone Bay, had been boasting terribly about *his* church, and he (Iakopo) meant to crush him utterly with these European-made doors and windows, which his good friend Pakenami had brought him from Nui Silani.

"You bet," said the skipper; "and what's more, I'll help you to take the shine out of Pita. I'll fix the doors and windows for you myself," and he winked slily at the teacher's daughter, who returned it as promptly as any Christian maiden, knowing that Nerida wasn't on board, and that she had nothing to fear.

"I wish to goodness that fellow hadn't come aboard," grumbled Denison to Packenham, after the missionary and his daughter had gone ashore. "Peter Deasy and the Dutchman don't like it, I can see, or they would have been aboard before now. No white man likes boarding a ship *after* a native teacher, and both these fellows are d— —d touchy. The chances are that they won't come aboard at all to-day."

"That's true," said the captain thoughtfully; "I didn't think of that." (He never did think.) "Shall I go ashore first, and smooth down their ruffled plumage?"

Denison said he thought it would be a good thing to do. Deasy and the Dutchman (*i.e.*, the German) were both independent traders, who had always bought their trade goods from and sold their produce to the *Indiana* for years past, and were worth humouring. So Packenham went ashore, leaving Denison to open out his wares in the brig's trade room in readiness for the two white men.

Now both Peter Deasy and Hans Schweicker were feeling very sulky—as Denison imagined—and at that moment were talking to each other across the road from their respective doorways, for their houses were not far apart. They had intended boarding the ship the moment she anchored, but abandoned the idea as soon as they saw the teacher going off. Not that they disliked Iakopo personally, but then he was only a low-class native, and had no business thrusting himself before his betters. So they sat down and waited till Denison or the captain came ashore.

Peter wore a pair of clean white moleskins and a bright pink print shirt covered with blue dogs; and as the lower portion of this latter garment was hanging outside instead of being tucked inside his moleskins, quite a large number of dogs were visible. Hans, dressed in pyjamas of a green and yellow check, carefully starched, smoked a very bad German cigar; Deasy puffed a very dirty clay dhudeen.

Presently one of Hans's wife's numerous relatives ran up to him, and told him that the captain was coming ashore, and the atmosphere at once cleared a little. Deasy was the elder trader, and by right of custom expected the skipper would come to his house first. Hans, however, was the "warmest" man of the two, and thought *he* should be the honoured man, especially as he had the larger quantity of copra and other island produce to sell Packenham. Both men were very good friends at that moment, and had been so for years past. They had frequently lied manfully on each other's behalf when summoned before the Deputy-Commissioner for selling arms and ammunition to the natives. But while in social matters—such as getting drunk, circumventing the missionaries, and making fools of her Majesty's representatives—the two were in perfect and truly happy accord, they were often devoured with the bitterest business jealousies, and their wives and relatives generally shared this feeling with them. And as Mrs. Deasy and Mrs. Schweicker each had a large native following who all considered *their* white man was the better of the two, the question of commercial supremacy between Peter Deasy and Hans Schweicker was one of much local importance.

As the word was passed along that the captain was coming, the female inmates of the two houses each surrounded their respective head, and looked anxiously over his shoulders at the approaching visitor. Deasy's wife had put on her best dress; so had Schweicker's. Pati-lima—otherwise Mrs. Peter Deasy—who was a huge eighteen stone creature, with a round good-humoured face and a piping childish voice, had arrayed her vast proportions in a flowing gown of Turkey-red twill, and the radiant glory thereof had a pleasing and effective background in the garments of her three daughters, who were dressed in 'green, yellow, and blue respectively. Manogi—Mrs. Schweicker—who had no children, and was accounted the prettiest woman in Samoa, was clothed, like her husband, in spotless white, and her shining black tresses fell in a wavy mantle down to her waist. Unlike Pati-lima's daughters, whose heads were encircled by wreaths of orange blossoms, Manogi wore neither ornament nor decoration. She knew that her wavy hair drooped gracefully down her clear-cut, olive-hued face like the frame of a picture, and set off her bright eyes and white teeth to perfection; and that no amount of orange blossoms could make her appear more beautiful. So in the supreme and blessed consciousness of being the best-dressed and best-looking woman in the whole village, she sat behind her husband fanning herself languidly, and scarce deigning to answer the Deasy girls when they spoke to her.

Presently the boat touched the beach. The captain jumped out, shook hands with a number of natives who thronged around him, and stepped along the path. Half-way between the white men's houses was the unfinished church, and near to that the teacher's house, embowered in a grove of orange and lemon trees. As Packenham walked along he looked up the road, smiled and nodded at the Deasy and Schweicker crowd, then deliberately turned to the left and walked into the teacher's dwelling! And Manogi and all the Deasy women saw Miriamu, the teacher's daughter, come to the open window and make a face at them in derision. Peter and Schweicker looked at each other in speechless indignation.

"The swape av the wurruld!" and Deasy dashed his pipe down at his feet and smashed it in small pieces, "to go to a native's house first an' white min sthandin' awaitin' his pleasure. By the sowl av' me mother, Hans, devil a foot does he put inside my door till he explains phwat he manes by it."

"Shoost vat you mide expeg from a new chum!" replied Hans, who had lived in Australia. Then they both went back to their respective houses to await events.

Now Packenham meant no harm, and had not the faintest idea he was giving offence. But then, as Denison said, he never would think. Yet on this occasion he had been thinking. Iakopo had told him that he had collected enough money to pay for the doors and windows right away, and then Packenham, who knew that this would surprise and please Denison, told the teacher that he would call for the money when he came ashore.

"Come to my father's house first—before you go to the white men's," said Iakopo's daughter, with a side look at the captain. She hated all the

Deasy girls and Manogi in particular, who had "said things" about her to Denison, and knew that they would feel furiously jealous of her if Packenham called at her father's house first. And Packenham said he would do so.

Half an hour passed, and then the skipper having been paid the money by the teacher, and having smoked a couple of cigarettes rolled for him by Miriamu, said he must go. And Miriamu, who wanted to triumph over the Deasy girls and Manogi, said she would come too. On the Scriptural principle of casting bread upon the waters she had given Packenham some presents—a fan, a bottle of scented coconut-oil, and two baked fowls. These she put into a basket and told her little brother to bring along—it would annoy the other girls.

During this time Deasy and Hans had been talking over the matter, and now felt in a better temper. Manogi had said that Denison was a more important man than Packenham. *He* wouldn't have gone into the teacher's house first; and then most likely Miriamu, who was no better than she ought to be, had called the captain in.

"Why let this vex thee?" she said, "this captain for ever forgetteth *faà Samoa* (Samoan custom), and hath been beguiled by Miriamu into her father's house."

After awhile Deasy and Hans agreed with her, and so when Packenham came up to them with outstretched hand, they greeted him as usual; but their women-folk glared savagely at Miriamu, who now felt frightened and stuck close to the captain.

"Bedad, it's hot talking here in the sun," said Deasy, after Packenham had shaken hands with Mrs. Deasy and Mrs. Hans and the girls, "come inside, captain, and sit down while I start my people to fill the copra bags and get ready for weighing."

"Veil, I don't call dot very shentlemanly gonduck," grunted Hans, who, naturally enough, wanted *his* copra weighed first so that he could get away on board the brig and have first pick of Denison's trade room.

Deasy fired up. "An' I tell ye, Hans, the captain's going to plase himself intoirely. Sure he wouldn't turn his back on my door to plase a new man like you——"

Manogi pushed herself between them: "You're a *toga fiti* man (schemer), Paddy Deasy," she said in English, with a contemptuous sniff.

"Yes," added Hans, "you was no good, Deasy; you was alvays tarn shellous——"

"An' you're a dirty low swape av a Dutchman to let that woman av yours use a native wor-rud in the captain's hearin'," and Deasy banged his fellow-trader between the eyes, as at the same moment Manogi and Pati-lima sprang at each other like fiends, and twined their hands in each other's hair. Then, ere Manogi's triumphant squeal as she dragged out a handful of the Deasy hair had died away, half a dozen young lady friends had leapt to her aid, to be met with cries of savage fury by the three Misses Deasy, and in ten seconds more the whole lot were fighting wildly together in an undistinguishable heap, with Deasy and the Dutchman grasping each other's throats underneath.

Packenham jumped in on top of the struggling mass, and picking up three women, one after another, tossed them like corks into the arms of a number of native men who had now appeared on the scene, and were encouraging the combatants; but further movement on his part was rendered impossible by Miriamu, who had clasped him round the waist and was imploring him to come away. For a minute or so the combat continued, and then the tangle of arms, legs, and dishevelled hair was heaved up in the centre, and Deasy and Hans staggered to their feet, glaring murder and sudden death at each other.

Freeing himself from the grasp of the minister's daughter, who at once leapt at Manogi, Packenham seized Schweicker by the collar, and was dragging him away from Deasy when he got a crack on the side of his head from Manogi's mother, who thought he meant to kill her son-in-law, and had dashed to the rescue with a heavy tappa mallet. And then, as Packenham went down like a pithed bullock, there arose a wild cry from some one that the white captain was being murdered. Denison heard it, and with five of the *Indiana's* crew, armed with Winchester rifles, he jumped into the boat and hurried ashore.

By this time some thirty or forty stalwart Samoans, under the direction of the teacher, had flung themselves upon the women who were still rending each other in deadly silence, and in some way separated them. Packenham was lying apart from the rest, his head supported by a white-haired old native who was threatening every one present with the bloody vengeance of a man-of-war. Deasy and Hans were seated on the sward, still panting and furious. Deasy had one black eye; Hans had two.

"Are yez satisfied, Dutchy?" inquired Deasy.

"Shoost as mooch as you vas!" answered the German.

Now here the matter would have ended, but just at that time Pati-lima, who was being fanned by a couple of her friends, caught sight of the slight figure of Manogi, her white muslin gown torn to ribbons and her bosom heaving with excitement. Her beautiful face, though white with rage, was un-marred by the slightest scratch, while Pati-lima's was deeply scored by her enemy's nails. This was hard to bear.

Raising herself on one elbow, Mrs. Deasy pointed contemptuously to Manogi's husband and called out—

"Ah, you conceited Manogi! Take home thy German *pala-ai* (coward). My man hath beaten him badly."

"Thou liest, thou great blubbering whale," was the beauty's scornful reply; "he could beat such a drunkard as thy husband any day."

The two women sprang to their feet, and were about to engage again when Denison ran in between them, and succeeded in keeping them apart. Deasy and Hans looked on unconcernedly.

"What is all this?" said Denison to Packenham.

Packenham groaned, "I don't know. An old woman hit me with a club."

"Serve you right. Now then, Deasy, and you, Hans, send all these women away. I thought you had more sense than to encourage such things," and then Denison, who excelled in vituperative Samoan, addressed the assemblage, and told the people to go home.

Still glaring defiance, the two factions slowly turned to leave the field, and again all would have been well but for Manogi, who was burning to see the thing out to its bitter end. So she had her try.

Pati-lima came from Manono, the people of which island eat much shell-fish, and suffer much in consequence from the sarcastic allusions of the rest of the Samoan people. And they don't like it, any more than a Scotsman likes his sacred haggis being made the subject of idiotic derision. So as the two parties moved off, Manogi faced round to Pati-lima.

"Pah! *Manono ai foli*" (Manono feeds on shellfish).

"*Siamani vao tapiti elo*" (Germans gorge on stinking cabbage) was the quick retort of Mrs. Deasy, who pointed scornfully at Manogi's husband, and instantaneously the whole assemblage, male and female, were engaged in hideous conflict again, while Denison and his boat's crew, "Wond'ring, stepped aside," and let them fight it out.

What the result would have been had not the encounter been stopped is hard to say; but in the midst of this second struggle the young yellow-haired local chief bounded into the fray, and smote right and left with a heavy club, ably seconded by Denison and his men and Iakopo. The appearance of the chief was, however, enough—the opposing factions drew off from each other and retired, carrying their wounded with them.

"What a brace of detestable ruffians!" said Captain De Groen, of her Majesty's ship *Dawdler*, to Denison a day or two afterwards. The doctor of the man-of-war had gone ashore to patch up the wounded, and Denison had been telling the commander how the affair occurred.

Now Captain De Groen was wrong. Both Deasy and Schweicker were as decent a pair of men as could be found in the Pacific—that is to say, they did no harm to a living soul except themselves when under the influence of liquor, which was not infrequent. But it was all Packenham's fault. Had he kept clear of the teacher's house, Deasy and Hans would not have felt affronted, Manogi and Pati-lima would not have said nasty things to each other, and Denison would not have been reported upon officially by her Majesty's High Commissioner for the Western Pacific as a person who, "with a Mr. Packenham, master of the brig *Indiana*, incited the native factions of Sa Lotopa to attack each other with murderous fury."

A TOUCH OF THE TAR-BRUSH

Dr. Te Henare Rauparaha, the youngest member of the New Zealand House of Representatives, had made his mark, to a certain extent, upon the political life of the colony. Representing no party, and having no interests but those of the Maori race, he seldom rose to speak except on questions of native land-grants, or when similar matters affecting the Maori population were under discussion. Then his close, masterly reasoning and his natural eloquence gained him the most profound attention. Twice had he succeeded in inducing the House to throw out measures that would have perpetrated the grossest injustice upon certain Maori tribes; and ere long, without effort on his part, he became the tacit leader of a small but growing party that followed his arguments and resisted tooth and nail the tendency of certain Ministers to smooth the path of the land-grabber and company-promoter. Later on in the session his powers of debate, undeviating resolution, and determined opposition to Governmental measures that he regarded as injurious to the natives began to make Ministers uneasy; and although they cursed him in secret for a meddling fool and mad-brained enthusiast, they no longer attempted to ride rough-shod over him in the House, especially as the Labour members, who held the balance of power, entertained very friendly feelings towards the young man, and gave him considerable support. Therefore he was to be conciliated, and accordingly the curt nods of recognition, which were all that were once given him, were exchanged for friendly smiles and warm hand-grasps. But Rauparaha was not deceived. He knew that in a few evenings a certain Bill to absolutely dispossess the native holders of a vast area of land in the North Island would be read, and that its mover, who was a Government member, was merely the agent of a huge land-buying concern, which intended to re-sell the stolen property to the working people on magnanimous terms for village settlements; and although sorely afraid at heart that he would have to bear the brunt of the battle in opposing the Bill, the young doctor was hopeful that the Labour members would eventually come to his support when he exposed the secret motives that really had brought it into existence. But he did not know that the Labour members had already been "approached," and had given promises not to support him and not to vote against the measure; otherwise some concessions regarding railway contracts, which the Government were prepared to make to the great Labour party, would be "matters for future consideration" only. And, therefore, rather than offend the Government, the honest men agreed to let Rauparaha "fight it out himself against the Government," and "ratted" to a man. Every one of their number also expected to be appointed a Director of a Village Settlement, and were not disposed to fly in the face of a Providence that would give them each a permanent and comfortable billet, especially as their parliamentary career was doomed—not one of them had the faintest hope of re-election.

And so Dr. Rauparaha made the effort of his life, and the House listened to him in cold and stony silence. From the first he knew that he was doomed to failure, when he saw two or three of his once ardent admirers get up and sneak out of the Chamber; but, with a glance of contemptuous scorn at their retreating figures, he went on speaking. And then, at the close of an impassioned address, he held up in his right hand a copy of the Treaty of Waitangi.

"And this, honourable members, is the solemn bond and testimony of a great nation, the written promise of our Queen and her Ministers to these people that their lands and their right to live in their country should be kept inviolate! How has that promise been kept? Think of it, I pray you, and let your cheeks redden with shame, for the pages of this Treaty are blotted with the blackest treachery and stained a bloody red. And the Bill now before the House to rob and despoil some hundreds of native families of land that has been theirs before a white man ever placed his foot in the country is the most shameful and heartless act of all. I say 'act' because I recognise how futile is my single voice raised on behalf of my race to stay this bitter injustice. Rob us, then, but offer us no longer the ghastly mockery of parliamentary representation. Better for us all to die as our forefathers have done, rifle in hand, than perish of poverty and starvation on the soil that is our only inheritance."

"Rot!" called out a short, fat man wearing a huge diamond ring and an excessively dirty white waistcoat. This was the Minister for Dredges and Artesian Bores, a gentleman who hoped to receive a C.M.G. ship for his clamorous persistency in advocating the claim of the colony to "'ave a Royel dook as its next Governor."

"Shut up!" said an honourable member beside him. "Rauparaha doesn't talk rot. You do—always."

The Minister muttered that he "didn't approve of no one a-usin' of inflammetery langwidge in the 'Ouse," but made no further remark.

Rauparaha resumed his seat, the proposer of the Bill made his reply, and the House voted solidly for the measure.

That evening, as the young man sat in his chambers gazing moodily into the glowing embers of the fire, and thinking bitterly of the utter hopelessness of the cause that lay so near his heart, his door opened, and Captain Lionel Brewster, a member of the House and a favoured *protégé* of the Government, walked in and held out his hand.

"How are you, doctor?" and he showed his white teeth in a smile of set friendliness. "I hear you are leaving Wellington at the close of the session for the North Island. I really am sorry, you know—deuced sorry—that your splendid speech was so quietly taken this afternoon. As a matter of fact, both — — — and — — — have the most friendly feeling towards you, and, although your political opponents in this matter, value and esteem you highly."

"Thanks, Captain Brewster," answered Rau-paraha coldly. He knew that this polished gentleman had been sent to him merely to smooth him down. Other land-grants had yet to come before the House, and Dr. Rauparaha, although he stood alone, was not an enemy to be despised or treated with nonchalance. One reason was his great wealth, the second his influence with a section of the Press that attacked the Government native policy with an unsparing pen. But, as a matter of fact, his visitor had a second and more personal motive.

However, he asked Brewster to be seated; and that gentleman, twirling his carefully-trimmed moustache, smiled genially, and said he should be delighted to stay and chat a while.

"By the way, though, doctor," he said cordially, "my people—my aunt and cousin, you know—have heard so much of you that I have promised to take you down to our place for a few days if I can induce you to come. They were both in the gallery yesterday, and took the deepest interest in your speech. Now, my dear fellow, the House doesn't meet again till Tuesday. Come down with me to-morrow."

"Thanks," and the doctor's olive features flushed a deep red; "I will come. I think I have fired my last shot in Parliament, and intend to resign, and so do not care much whether I ever enter the House again. And I shall have much pleasure in meeting your aunt and cousin again; I was introduced to them some weeks ago."

"So they told me," and Brewster smiled sweetly again. "Then you won't come as a stranger. Now I must be off. I shall call for you after lunch tomorrow."

As Lionel Brewster threw himself back in his cab and smoked his cigar he cursed vigorously. "Damn the cursed half-breed of a fellow! He's clever enough, and all that; but what the devil Helen can see in him to make me invite him down to Te Ariri I don't know. Curse her infernal twaddle about the rights of humanity and such fustian. Once you are my wife, my sweet, romantic cousin, I'll knock all that idiotic bosh on the head. It's bad enough to sit in the House and listen to this fellow frothing, without having to bring a quarter-bred savage into one's own family. However, he's really not a man to be ashamed of, so far as appearances go.... And I must humour her. Five thousand a year must be humoured."

"Well, Helen, and what do you think of your savage?" said Mrs. Torringley to her niece, late the following evening, as she came to the door of Helen's room before she said good-night.

The girl was lying on a couch at the further end of the room, looking through the opened window out into the shadows of the night. The pale, clear-cut face flushed. "I like him very much, auntie. And I have been thinking."

"Thinking of what, dear?"

"Wondering if my father ever thought, when he was leading his men against the Maoris, of the cruel, dreadful wrong he was helping to perpetrate."

"'Cruel'! 'dreadful'! My dear child, what nonsense you talk! They were bloodthirsty savages."

"Savages! True. But savages fighting for all that was dear to them—for their lands, their lives, their liberties as a people. Oh, auntie, when I read of the awful deeds of bloodshed that are even now being done in Africa by English soldiers, it makes me sicken. Oh, if I were only a man, I would go out into the world and——"

"My dear child," said the older lady, with a smile, "you must not read so much of—of Tolstoy and other horrible writers like him. What would Lionel say if he thought you were going to be a Woman with a Mission? Good-night, dear, and don't worry about the Maoris. Many of them are real Christians nowadays, and nearly all the women can sew quite nicely."

Outside on the broad gravelled walk the young doctor talked to himself as he paced quickly to and fro. "Folly, folly, folly. What interest can she have in me, except that I have native blood in my veins, and that her father fought our people in the Waikato thirty years ago?"

Brewster had gone back to town for a day or two; but as he bade his aunt and cousin goodbye, he warmly seconded their request to the doctor to remain at Te Ariri till he returned, although inwardly he swore at them both for a pair of "blithering idiots." And as he drove away to the station he congratulated himself on the fact that while his fiancée had a "touch of the tar-brush," as he expressed it, in her descent, her English bringing-up and society training under her worldly-minded but rather brainless aunt had led her to accept him as her future husband without difficulty.

For the next two days Dr. Rauparaha had much writing to do, and passed his mornings and afternoons in the quiet library. Sometimes, as he wrote, a shadow would flit across the wide, sunlit veranda, and Helen Torringley would flit by, nodding pleasantly to him through the windows. Only two or three times had he met her alone since he came to Te Ariri, and walked with her through the grounds, listening with a strange pleasure to her low, tender voice, and gazing into the deep, dark eyes, that shone with softest lustre from out the pale, olive face, set in a wealth of wavy jet-black hair. For Helen Torringley was, like himself, of mixed blood. Her mother, who had died in her infancy, was a South American quadroon, born in Lima, and all the burning, quick passions and hot temperament of her race were revealed in her daughter's every graceful gesture and inflexion of her clear voice.

It was late in the afternoon, and Dr. Rauparaha, pushing his papers wearily away from him, rose from his seat. His work was finished. To-morrow he would bid these new friends goodbye—this proud English lady and her beautiful, sweet-voiced niece—the girl whose dark eyes and red lips had come into his day-dreams and visions of the night. And just then she came to the library door, carrying in her hand a portfolio.

"Are you very busy, Dr. Rauparaha?" she said, as she entered and stood before him.

"Busy! No, Miss Torringley. Are these the sketches you told me Colonel Torringley made when he was in New Zealand?" and as he extended his hand for the book, the hot blood surged to his sallow forehead.

"Yes, they were all drawn by my father. I found them about a year since in the bottom of one of his trunks. He died ten years ago."

Slowly the young man turned them over one by one. Many of them were drawings of outposts, heads of native chiefs, &c. At last he came to one, somewhat larger than the others. It depicted the assault and capture of a Maori *pah*, standing on a hill that rose gradually from the margin of a reedy swamp. The troops had driven out the defenders, who were shown escaping across the swamp through the reeds, the women and children in the centre, the men surrounding them on all sides to protect them from the hail of bullets that swept down upon them from the heights above the captured fortress.

A shadow fell across the face of Dr. Rauparaha, and his hand tightened upon and almost crumpled the paper in his grasp; then he smiled, but with a red gleam in his dark eyes.

"'The assault on Maungatabu by the 18th Royal Irish,'" he read.

"The brave Irish," he said, with a mocking smile, raising his head and looking intently into the pale face of the girl; "the brave Irish! So ardent for liberty themselves, such loud-mouthed clamourers to the world for justice to their country—yet how they sell themselves for a paltry wage to butcher women and children"—then he stopped suddenly.

"Pardon me, I forgot myself. I did not remember that your father was an officer of that regiment."

She gave him her hand, and her eyes filled. "No, do not ask my pardon. I think it was horrible, horrible. How can such dreadful things be? I have heard my father say that that very victory filled him with shame.... He led the storming party, and when the *pah* was carried, and he saw the natives escaping—the men surrounding the women and children—he ordered the 'Cease firing' to be sounded, but— —" and her voice faltered.

"But— —" and the lurid gleam in Rauparaha's eyes made her face flush and then pale again.

"The men went mad, and took no notice of him and the other two officers who were both wounded—the rest were killed in the assault. They had lost heavily, and were maddened with rage when they saw the Maoris escaping, and continued firing at them till they crossed the swamp, and hid in the long fern scrub on the other side."

"And even then a shell was fired into them as they lay there in the fern, resting their exhausted bodies ere they crept through it to gain the hills beyond," added the young man slowly.

"Yes," she murmured, "I have heard my father speak of it. But it was not by his orders—he was a soldier, but not a cruel man. See, this next sketch shows the bursting of the shell."

He took it from her hand and looked. At the foot of it was written, "The Last Shot at Maungatabu."

His hand trembled for a moment; then he placed the drawing back in the portfolio, and with averted face she rose from the table and walked to the window.

For a moment or two she stood there irresolutely, and then with the colour mantling her brow she came over to him.

"I must ask *your* pardon now. I forgot that—that—that——"

"That I have Maori blood in my veins. Yes, I have, my father was a Pakeha Maori,{*} my mother a woman of one of the Waikato tribes. She died when I was very young." Then, in a curiously strained voice, he said: "Miss Torringley, may I ask a favour of you? Will you give me that sketch?"

* A white man who had adopted Maori life and customs.

She moved quickly to the table, and untied the portfolio again.

"Which, Dr. Rauparaha? The last——"

"Yes," he interrupted, with sudden fierceness, "the Last Shot at Maungatabu."

She took it out and came over to him. "Take it, if you wish it; take them all, if you care for them. No one but myself ever looks at them.... And now, after what you have told me, I shall never want to look at them again."

"Thank you," he said, in softer tones, as he took the picture from her. "I only wish for this one. It will help to keep my memory green—when I return to my mother's people."

"Ah," she said, in a pained voice, "don't say that. I wish I had never asked you to look at it. I have read the papers, and know how the Maori people must feel, and I am sorry, oh! so sorry, that I have unthinkingly aroused what must surely be painful memories to you."

"Do not think of it, Miss Torringley. Such things always will be. So long as we live, breathe, and have our being, so long will the strong oppress and slay the weak; so long will the accursed earth-hunger of a great Christian nation be synonymous for bloodshed, murder, and treachery; so long will she hold out with one hand to the children of Ham the figure of Christ crucified, and preach of the benefits of civilisation; while with the other she sweeps them away with the Maxim gun; so long will such things as the 'Last Shot at Maungatabu'—the murder of women and children, always be."

With bated breath she listened to the end, and then murmured—

"It is terrible to think of, an unjust warfare. Were any women and children killed at Maungatabu?"

"Yes," he almost shouted back, "many were shot as they crossed the swamp. And when they gained the fern two more were killed by that last shell—a woman and child—my mother and my sister!"

He turned away again to the window, but not so quickly but that he could see she was crying softly to herself, as she bent her face over the table.

Three days after, Mrs. Torringley showed her nephew a note that she had found on her niece's dressing-table:—

> "Do not blame me. I cannot help it. I love him, and am going
> away with him to another country. Perhaps it is my mother's
> blood. Wipe me out of your memory for ever."

THE TRADER S WIFE

Years ago, in the days when the "highly irregular proceedings," as naval officers termed them in their official reports, of the brig *Carl* and other British ships engaged in the trade which some large-minded people have vouched for as being "absolutely above reproach," attracted some attention from the British Government towards the doings of the gentlemanly scoundrels engaged therein, the people of Sydney used to talk proudly of the fleet of gunboats which, constructed by the New South Wales Government for the Admiralty, were built to "patrol the various recruiting grounds of the Fijian and Queensland planters and place the labour-traffic under the most rigid supervision." The remark quoted above was then, as it is now, quite a hackneyed one, much used by the gallant officers who commanded the one-gun-one-rocket-tube craft aforementioned. Likewise, the "highly irregular proceedings" were a naval synonym for some of the bloodiest slaving outrages ever perpetrated, but which, however, never came to light beyond being alluded to as "unreliable and un-authenticated statements by discharged and drunken seamen who had no proper documentary evidence to support their assertions."

The Australian slave-suppressing vessels were not a success. In the first place, they could not sail much faster than a mud-dredge. Poor Bob Randolph, the trader, of the Gilbert and Kingsmill Groups, employed as pilot and interpreter on board, once remarked to the officer commanding one of these wonderful tubs which for four days had been thrashing her way against the south-east trades in a heroic endeavour to get inside Tarawa Lagoon, distant ten miles (and could not do it), that "these here schooners ought to be rigged as fore-and-afters and called 'four-and-halfters; for I'll be hanged if this thing can do more than four and a half knots, even in half a gale of wind, all sail set and a smooth sea." But if the "four-and-halfters," as they were thenceforth designated in the Western Pacific, were useless in regard to suppressing the villainies and slaughter that then attended the labour trade, there was one instance in which one of the schooners and her captain did some good by avenging as cruel a murder as was ever perpetrated in equatorial Oceania.

One Jack Keyes was a trader on the island of Apiang, one of the Gilbert Group, recently annexed by Great Britain. He was very old, very quiet in his manner, and about the last kind of man one would expect to see earning his living as a trader among the excitable, intractable native race which inhabit the Line Islands. His fellow-trader, Bob Randolph, a man of tremendous nerve and resolution, only maintained his prestige among the Apiang natives by the wonderful control he had learnt to exercise over a naturally fiery temper and by taking care, when knocking down any especially insulting native "buck," never to draw blood, and always to laugh. And the people of Apiang thought much of Te Matân Bob, as much as the inhabitants of the whole group—from Arorai in the south to Makin in the north—do to this day of quiet, spectacled Bob Corrie, of wild Maiana, who can twist them round his little finger without an angry word. Perhaps poor Keyes, being a notoriously inoffensive man, might have died a natural death in due time, but for one fatal mistake he made; and that was in bringing a young wife to the island.

A white woman was a rarity in the Line Islands. Certainly the Boston mission ship, *Morning Star*, in trying to establish the "Gospel according to Bosting—no ile or dollars, no missn'ry," as Jim Garstang, of Drummond's Island, used to observe, had once brought a lady soul-saver of somewhat matured charms to the island, but her advent into the Apiang *moniap* or town hall, carrying an abnormally large white umbrella and wearing a white solar topee with a green turban, and blue goggles, had had the effect of scaring the assembled councillors away across to the weather-side of the narrow island, whence none returned until the terrifying apparition had gone back to the ship. But this white woman who poor old Keyes married and brought with him was different, and the Apiang native, like all the rest of the world, is susceptible to female charms; and *her* appearance at the doorway of the old trader's house was ever hailed with an excited and admiring chorus of "*Te boom te matân! Te boom te matân!*" (The white man's wife.) But none were rude or offensive to her, although the young men especially were by no means chary of insulting the old man, who never carried a pistol in his belt.

One of these young men was unnecessarily intrusive. He would enter the trader's house on any available pretext, and the old man noticed that he would let his savage eyes rest upon his wife's figure in a way there was no mistaking. Not daring to tackle the brawny savage, whose chest, arms, and back were one mass of corrugations resulting from wounds inflicted by sharks' teeth spears and swords in many encounters, old Jack one day quietly intimated to his visitor that he was not welcome and told him to "get." The savage, with sullen hate gleaming from cruel eyes that looked out from the mat of coarse, black hair, which, cut away in a fringe over his forehead, fell upon his shoulders, rose slowly and went out.

Early next morning old Keyes was going over to Randolph's house, probably to speak of the occurrence of the previous day, when his wife called him and said that some one was at the door waiting to buy tobacco.

"What have you to sell?" called out the old man.

"*Te moe motu*" (young drinking-coconuts), was the answer, and the old man, not recognising the voice as that of his visitor of the day before, went unsuspectingly to take them from the native's hand, when the latter, placing a horse-pistol to the trader's heart, shot him dead, with the savage exclamation—

"Now your wife is mine!"

The poor woman fled to Bob Randolph for safety, and, dreading to remain on the island, went away in a schooner to her home in New Zealand. Nearly a year passed, and then a man-of-war came and endeavoured to capture the murderer; but in vain, for the captain would not use force; and "talk" and vague threats the natives only laughed at. So the ship steamed away; and then the natives began to threaten Randolph, and talk meaningly to each other about his store being full of *te pakea* and *te rom* (tobacco and gin). A long, uneasy six months passed, and then the little "four-and-halfter" Renard, Commander ——— sailed into Apiang lagoon, and the naval officer told Randolph he had come to get the man and try him for the murder.

The commander first warped his vessel in as near as possible to the crowded village, and moored her with due regard to the effectiveness of his one big gun. Then, with Randolph as interpreter, negotiations commenced.

The old men of the village were saucy; the young men wanted a fight and demanded one. Randolph did his part well. He pointed out to the old men that unless they gave the man up, the long gun on the ship would destroy every house and canoe on the island, even if no one were killed. That meant much to them, whereas one man's life was but little. But, first, the natives tried cunning. One and then another wretched slave was caught and bound and taken off to the naval officer as the murderer, only to be scornfully rejected by Randolph and the captain. Then the officer's patience was exhausted. If the man who murdered Keyes was not surrendered in an hour he would open fire, and also hang some of the chiefs then detained on board as hostages.

Randolph's gloomy face quickened their fears. This captain could neither be frightened nor fooled. In half an hour the slayer of the trader was brought on board. The old men admitted their attempt at deception, but pleaded that the murderer was a man of influence, and they would rather the two others (who were absolutely innocent) were hanged than this one; but their suggestion was not acted upon. The trial was just and fair, but short, and then Randolph urged the captain to have the man executed on shore by being shot. It would impress the people more than hanging him on board. And hanging they regarded as a silly way of killing a man.

The naval officer had no relish for work of this nature, and when Randolph told him that the natives had consented to execute the prisoner in his (Randolph's) presence (and the captain's presence also if necessary) he, no doubt, felt glad. Bob Randolph then became M.C., and gave his instructions to the old men. The whole village assembled in front of Randolph's to see the show. An old carronade lying in the corner of the copra house was dragged out, cleaned, and loaded with a heavy blank charge. Then the prisoner, sullen and defiant to the last, but wondering at the carronade, was lashed with his back to the muzzle, and, at a signal from one of the old men, a firestick was applied to the gun. A roar, a rush of fragments through the air, and all was finished. Bob Randolph's fox-terrier was the only creature that seemed to trouble about making any search for the remnants of the body. Half an hour afterwards, as Bob was at supper, he came in and deposited a gory lump of horror at his master's feet.

NINA

When Captain Henry Charlton—generally known as "Bully Charlton"—stepped on shore at Townsville in North Queensland with his newly-wedded wife, his acquaintances stared at them both in profound astonishment. They had heard that he had married in Sydney, and from their past knowledge of his character expected to see a loudly-attired Melbourne or Sydney barmaid with peroxided hair, and person profusely adorned with obtrusive jewelry. Instead of this they beheld a tall, ladylike girl with a cold, refined face, and an equally cold and distant manner.

"Well, I *have* seen some curious things in my time," said Fryer, the American master of a Torres Straits pearling schooner, to the other men, as they watched Charlton and his wife drive away from the hotel, "but to think that *that* fellow should marry a lady! I wonder if she has the faintest idea of what an anointed scoundrel he is?"

"He's been mighty smart over it, anyway," said a storekeeper named Lee. "Why, it isn't six months since Nina drowned herself. I suppose it's true, Fryer, that she did bolt with Jack Lester?"

The American struck his hand upon the table in hot anger. "That's a lie! I know Lester well, and Nina Charlton was as good a woman as ever breathed."

"Well, you see, Fryer, we don't know as much as you do about the matter. But when Nina cleared out from her husband and Lester disappeared a day or two later and went no one knows where, it did look pretty queer."

"And I tell you that Lester never saw Mrs. Charlton after the day he took it out of Charlton. He's a gentleman. And if you want to know where he is now I'll tell you. He's pearling at Thursday Island in Torres Straits. And Nina Charlton, thank God, is at rest. After the fight between Lester and her husband she ran away, and reached Port Denison almost dead from exposure in the bush. Shannon, of the *Lynndale*, who had known her in her childhood, gave her a passage to Sydney. Two days before the steamer reached there she disappeared—jumped overboard in the night, I suppose."

"Well, I'm sorry I repeated what is common gossip; but Charlton himself put the story about. And the papers said a lot about the elopement of the wife of a well-known plantation manager.'"

Fryer laughed contemptuously. "Just the thing Charlton would do. He's an infernal scoundrel. He told Lester that he'd make it warm for him—the beast. But I'm sorry for that sad-faced girl we saw just now. Fancy the existence she will lead with an unprincipled and drunken brute like Charlton! Good-bye; I'm off aboard. And look here, if ever any of you hear any more talk about Lester and Nina Charlton and repeats it in my hearing I'll do my best to make him sorry."

Lester was the manager of a mine and quartz-crushing battery near Charlton's plantation on the Lower Burdekin River when he "took it out" of its owner. He was a quiet, self-possessed man of about thirty, and occasionally visited Charlton and his wife and played a game of billiards—if Charlton was sober enough to stand. Sometimes in his rides along the lonely bush tracks he would meet Mrs. Charlton and go as far as the plantation gates with her. She was a small, slenderly built woman, or rather girl, with dark, passionate eyes, in whose liquid depths Lester could read the sorrows of her life with such a man as Henry Charlton. Once as he rode beside her through the grey monotone of the lofty, smooth-barked gum-trees she told him that her father was an Englishman and her mother a Portuguese.

"I married Captain Charlton in Macao. He was in the navy, you know; and although it is only four years since I left my father's house I feel so old; and sometimes when I awake in the night I think I can hear the sound of the beating surf and the rustle of the nipa-palms in the trade wind. And, oh! I so long to see— —" Her eyes filled with tears, and she turned her face away.

Perhaps Lester's unconsciously pitying manner to her whenever they met, and the utter loneliness of her existence on the Belle Grace Plantation made Nina Charlton think too much of the young mine manager, and, without knowing it, to eagerly look forward to their chance meetings.

One day as Lester was walking through Charlton's estate, gun in hand, looking for wild turkeys, he met her. She was seated under the widespreading branches of a Leichhardt-tree, and was watching some of her husband's labourers felling a giant gum.

"I came out to see it fall," she said. "It is the largest tree on Belle Grace. And it is so dull in the house." She turned her face away quickly.

Lester muttered a curse under his breath. He knew what she meant. Charlton had returned from Townsville the day before in a state of frenzy, and after threatening to murder his servants had flung himself upon a couch to sleep the sleep of drunkenness.

As the men hewed at the bole of the mighty tree Lester and Nina Charlton talked. She had spent the first year of her married life in Sydney, which was Lester's native town, and in a few minutes she had quite forgotten the tree, and was listening eagerly to Lester's account of his wanderings through the world, for his had been an adventurous career—sailor, South Sea trader, pearl-sheller, and gold miner in New Guinea and the Malayan Archipelago.

"And now here I am, Mrs. Charlton, over thirty years of age, and not any the richer for all my roving. Of course," he added, with boyish candour, "I know when I'm well off, and I have a good billet here and mean to save money. And I intend to be back in Sydney in another fortnight."

"But you will return to Queensland, will you not?" she said quickly.

Lester laughed. "Oh yes, I suppose I shall settle down here finally. But I'm going to Sydney to be married. Would you care to see my future wife's photograph? You see, Mrs. Charlton, you're the only lady I've ever talked to about her, and I should like you to see what she is like."

She made no answer, and Lester in wondering ignorance saw that her face had paled to a deathly white and that her hands were trembling.

"You are ill, Mrs. Charlton. You must be getting a touch of fever. Let me take you home."

"No," she answered quickly; "let me stay here. I shall be better in a minute." And then she began to sob passionately.

Charlton, awakening from his drunken sleep, looked at them from the window of the sitting-room. He hated his wife because she feared him, and of late had almost shuddered when he touched her. Picking up his whip from the table, he walked out of the house to where she was sitting.

"So this is your little amusement, is it?" he said savagely to Nina; "and this fellow is the cause of all my trouble. I might have known what to expect from a woman like you. Your Portuguese nature is too much for you. Go back to the house, and leave me to settle with your lover."

The next instant Lester launched out and struck him on the mouth. He lay where he fell, breathing heavily, and when he rose to his feet he saw Lester carrying his wife, who had fainted, to the house.

Placing Mrs. Charlton in the care of a servant, Lester returned quickly to where Charlton, who was no coward, awaited him.

"You drunken scoundrel!" he burst out; "I've come back to settle up with you!"

And Lester did "settle up" to his heart's content, for he half-killed Charlton with his own whip.

A week later, however, Charlton had his first bit of revenge. Lester was dismissed, the directors of the mine being determined, as they said, to show their disapproval of his attack upon "a justice of the peace and one of their largest shareholders."

Lester sat down and wrote to the "girl of his heart," and told her that he could not see her for another year or so. "I have had to leave the mine, Nell, dear," he said. "I won't tell you why—it would anger you perhaps. But it was not all my fault. However, I have decided what to do. I am going back to my old vocation of pearler in Torres Straits. I can make more money there than I could here."

The following morning, as he was leaving Belle Grace, he heard that Mrs. Charlton had left her husband two days previously, and had made her way through the bush to Port Denison, from where she had gone to Sydney.

Soon after Lester had sailed for Torres Straits in Fryer's schooner, the owner of Belle Grâce Plantation received a telegram from Sydney telling him that his wife was dead—she had jumped overboard on the passage down. And, later on, Lester heard it also.

Lester was doing well, but wondering why Nellie March did not write. He little knew that Charlton was in Sydney working out his revenge. This he soon accomplished.

From the local postmistress at Belle Grace Charlton had learned the address of the girl Lester was to marry; and the first thing he did when he arrived in Sydney was to call upon her parents, and tell them that Lester had run away with his wife. And they—and Nellie March as well—believed his story when he produced some Queensland newspapers which contained the accounts of the "elopement." He was a good-looking man, despite his forty years of hard drinking, and could lie with consummate grace, and Nellie, after her first feelings of shame and anger had subsided, pitied him, especially when he said that his poor wife was at rest now, and he had forgiven her. Before a month was out she married him.

Then Charlton, who simply revelled in his revenge, sent the papers containing the announcement of his marriage to Lester.

Lester took it very badly at first. But his was a strong nature, and he was too proud a man to write to the woman he loved and ask for an explanation. It was Charlton's money, of course, he thought. And as the months went by he began to forget. He heard of Charlton sometimes from the captains of passing vessels. He was drinking heavily they said, and whenever he came to town boasted of having "got even" with the man who had thrashed him. Lester set his teeth but said nothing, and in time even such gossip as this failed to disturb him. But he swore to give Charlton another thrashing when the opportunity came.

A year had come and gone, and Lester found himself in Sydney. He liked the free, open life among the pearlers, and intended to go back after a month or so of idleness in the southern city. One evening he strolled into the bar of Pfahlerts Hotel and ordered a whisky-and-soda. The girl he spoke to looked into his face for a moment and then nearly fainted—it was Nina Charlton!

"Give me your address," she said quickly, as she put out her hand. "I will come and see you in an hour from now."

She came, and in a few minutes told him her history since he had seen her last. The captain of the *Lynniale* pitying her terror at the prospect of her husband following her, had concealed her when the steamer was near Sydney, and it was he who telegraphed to Charlton that his wife had disappeared on the passage and was supposed to have jumped or fallen overboard. And she told Lester that she knew of her husband's second marriage and knew who it was whom he had married.

What was she going to do? Lester asked.

Nothing, she said. She would rather die than let Charlton know she was alive. When she had saved money enough she would go back to her own people.

Lester walked home with her. At the door of the hotel she bade him good-night.

"We shall meet sometimes, shall we not?" she asked wistfully. "I have not a friend in all Sydney."

"Neither have I," he said, "and I shall only be too happy to come and see you." She was silent a moment, then as she placed her hand in his she asked softly—

"Have you forgotten *her* altogether?"

"Yes," he answered, "I have. I did cut up a bit at first. But I'm over it now."

Her fingers pressed his again, and then with an almost whispered "Good-night" she was gone.

Before a month was over Lester was honestly in love with her. And she knew it, though he was too honourable a man to tell her so. Then one day he came to her hurriedly.

"I'm going back to Torres Straits to-morrow," he said. "I may be away for two years.... You will not forget me."

"No," she answered, with a sob, "I shall never forget you; you are all the world to me. And go now, dear, quickly; for I love you—and I am only a woman."

But there is a kindly Providence in these things, for when Lester reached Thursday Island in Torres Straits he heard that Charlton was dead. He had been thrown from his horse and died shortly after. His widow, Lester also heard, had returned to Sydney.

So Lester made quick work. Within twenty-four hours he had sold his business and was on his way back to Sydney.

He dashed up in a cab to his old lodgings. In another hour he would see Nina. He had sent her a telegram from Brisbane, telling her when the steamer would arrive, and was in a fever of excitement. And he was late. As he tumbled his things about, his landlady came to the door with a letter.

"There was a lady called here, sir, a week ago, and asked for your address. I had just got your telegram saying you were coming back to-day, and she said she would write, and this letter came just now."

Lester knew the handwriting. It was from Nellie. He opened it.

> *"I know now how I have wronged you. My husband, before he died, told me that he had deceived me. My life has been a very unhappy one, and I want to see you and ask for your forgiveness. Will you send me an answer to-night?—Nellie!"*

Lester held the letter in his hand and pondered. What should he do? Answer it or not? Poor Nellie!

He sat down to think—and then Nina Charlton opened the door and flung her arms around his neck.

"I could not wait," she whispered, "and I am not afraid *now* to say I love you."

That night Lester wrote a letter to the woman he had once loved. "I am glad to know that Charlton told you the truth before he died," he said. "But let the past be forgotten."

He never told Nina of this. But one day as they were walking along the "Block" in George Street, she saw her husband raise his hat to a tall, fair-haired woman with big blue eyes.

"Is that she, Jack?" murmured Nina.

Lester nodded.

"She's very lovely. And yet I felt once that I could have killed her—when you and I sat together watching the big tree fall. But I couldn't hate *any one* now."

THE EAST INDIAN COUSIN

Nearly eighty years ago, when the news of Napoleon's downfall at Waterloo had not yet reached England's colonies in the Far East, a country ship named the *Nourmahal* sailed from Madras for the Island of Singapore. The object of her voyage was not known except, perhaps, to the leading officials of the Company's establishment at Madras; but it was generally believed that she carried certain presents from the Indian Government to the then Sultans of Malacca, Johore, and Pahang. Sir Stamford Raffles, it was known, had urged the occupation and fortification of Singapore as a matter of importance to England's supremacy in the Eastern seas. And, indeed, three years later he began the work himself.

But the presents destined for the Rajahs never reached them; for from the day that she sailed from Madras roadstead the *Nourmahal* was never heard of nor seen again; and a year later no one but the relatives of the few Europeans on board thought any more about her. She had, it was conjectured, foundered in a typhoon, or been captured by pirates on her way through the Straits of Malacca.

The master of the missing ship was an Englishman named John Channing. For twenty-five or more years he had served the East India Company well, and his brave and determined conduct in many a sea-fight had won him not only a high place in the esteem of the directors, but considerable wealth as well. In those days it was not unusual for the captains of the larger ships belonging to or chartered by the Honourable Company to accumulate fortunes as the result of half a dozen successful voyages between England and Calcutta, and Captain John Channing had fared as well—or even better—than any of his fellow-captains in the service. For many years, however, he had not visited England, as, on account of his intimate and friendly relations with both the Portuguese and Dutch in the East Indies, the Government kept him and his ship constantly employed in those parts. Jealous and suspicious as were both the Dutch and Portuguese of English influence, they yet accorded Channing privileges granted to no other Englishman that sailed their seas. The reasons for these concessions from the Dutch were simple enough. A Dutch war-vessel conveying treasure to Batavia had been attacked by pirates, and in spite of a long and gallant defence was almost at the mercy of her savage assailants when Channing's ship came to her rescue and escorted her to port in safety. With the Portuguese merchants he was on most friendly terms, for twenty years before the opening of this story he had married the daughter of one of the wealthiest of their number, who was settled at Macassar, in Celebes. They had but one child, Adela, who when the *Nourmahal* sailed from Madras was about eighteen years of age, and she, with her mother, had accompanied her father on his last and fateful voyage. In England the missing seaman had but one relative, a nephew named Francis Channing, who was a lieutenant in the Marines. Nearly a year after the departure of his uncle's ship from India, all hope of his return was abandoned, and as he had left no will an official intimation was sent to the young man by John Channing's Calcutta bankers, informing him of his uncle's supposed death, and suggesting that he should either obtain a lengthened leave or resign from the service and come out to India to personally confer with them and the proper authorities as to the disposal of the dead man's property, which, as the owner had died intestate, would, of course, be inherited by his sole remaining relative. But the ship by which this letter was sent never reached England. A week after she sailed she was captured by a French privateer, one of several which, openly disregarding the proclamation of peace between England and France, still preyed upon homeward-bound merchantmen; and all the letters and despatches found on board the captured vessel were retained by the privateer captain, and were doubtless lost or destroyed.

Meanwhile Lieutenant Channing, quite unconscious of his good fortune, had sailed in His Majesty's ship *Triton* for the Cape and East Indies. With no influence behind him, and nothing but his scanty pay to live on, he had nothing to hope for but that another year's or two years' service would gain him his captaincy. Of his uncle in India he had scarcely ever heard, for his father and John Channing had quarrelled in their early lives, and since then had not corresponded.

Although at times quiet and reflective in his manner, his genial, open-hearted disposition soon made the young officer of Marines a general favourite with every one on board the *Triton*. The captain of the frigate, one of those gallant old seamen who had distinguished themselves under Nelson and Hyde Parker, knew Channing's worth and bravery well, for they had served together in some of the bloodiest engagements that had ever upheld the honour of England's flag. Unlike many other naval captains who in those days were apt to regard somewhat slightingly the services rendered by the Marines, Captain Reay was, if not an ardent admirer of the corps, at least a warm-hearted advocate for and friend to it. Perhaps much of the feeling of friendship shown to Channing was due to the fact that before he joined the *Triton* her captain had told his officers a story of his experiences in the West Indies, in which the officer of Marines was the central figure. Captain Reay had been sent by the senior officer of the squadron to demand the surrender of a fort on the Island of Martinique, when by an act of treachery he and his boat's crew were made prisoners and confined in the fortress, where he was treated with almost savage brutality by the commandant. The frigate at once opened fire, but after four hours' bombardment had failed to silence a single gun in the fort. At midnight it was carried in an attack led by young Channing, then a mere lad, and who, although two-thirds of his small force fell ere the walls were reached, refused to draw back and abandon Reay and his men. From that day Reay became his warm and sincere friend.

The best part of a year had passed since the *Triton* had sailed from Portsmouth, and now, with only the faintest air filling her canvas, she was sailing slowly along the shores of a cluster of islands, high, densely wooded, and picturesque. They formed one of the many minor groups of the beautiful and fertile Moluccas. Ten days before, the frigate had left Banda, and, impelled upon her course by but the gentlest breezes, had crept slowly northward towards Ternate, where Captain Reay was touching for letters before reporting himself to the Admiral at Singapore. On the quarter-deck a party of officers were standing together looking over the side at the wonders of the coral world, over which the ship was passing. For many hours the *Triton* had sailed thus, through water as clear as crystal, revealing full sixty feet below the dazzling lights and ever-changing shadows of the uneven bottom. Now and again she would pass over a broad arena of sand, gleaming white amid encircling walls of living coral many-hued, and gently swaying weed and sponge of red and yellow, which, though so far below, seemed to rise and touch the frigate's keel and then with quivering motion sink again astern. And as the ship's great hull cast her darkening shadow deep down through the transparency, swarms of brightly coloured fishes, red and blue and purple and shining gold, and banded and striped in every conceivable manner, darted away on either side to hide awhile in the moving caverns of weed that formed their refuge from predatory enemies. So slowly was the frigate moving, and so clear was the water, that sometimes as she sailed over a valley of glistening sand the smallest coloured pebble or fragment of broken coral could be as clearly discerned upon the snowy floor as if it lay embedded in a sheet of flawless crystal; and then again the quivering walls of weed and sponge would seem to rise ahead as if to bar her way, then slowly sink astern in the frigate's soundless wake.

But if the strange world beneath was wondrous and fascinating to look upon, that around was even more so. Three miles away on the starboard hand a group of green and fertile islands shone like emeralds in the morning sun. Leaning over the rail, Francis Channing gazed at their verdant heights and palm-fringed beaches of yellow sand with a feeling but little short of rapture to a man with a mind so beauty-loving and poetic as was his. Familiar to the wild bloom and brilliance of the West Indian islands, the soft tropical beauty of the scene now before him surpassed all he had ever seen, and, oblivious of the presence and voices of his brother officers as they conversed near him, he became lost in reflective and pleased contemplation of the radiant panorama of land, sea, and almost cloudless sky around him. Thirty miles away, yet so distinctly defined in the clear atmosphere that it seemed but a league distant from the ship, a perfect volcanic cone stood abruptly up from out the deep blue sea, and from its sharp-pointed summit a pillar of darkly-coloured smoke had risen skywards since early morn; but now as the wind died away it slowly spread out into a wide canopy of white, and then sank lower and lower till the pinnacle of the mountain was enveloped in its fleecy mantle.

As the young officer watched the changes of the smoky pall that proclaimed the awful and mysterious forces slumbering deep down in the bosom of the earth, he was suddenly aroused from his reflective mood by the shrill whistles and hoarse cries of the boatswain's mates, and in another minute the watch began to shorten sail: a faint greenish tinge in the western sky, quickly noted by the master, who was an old sailor in Eastern seas, told of danger from that quarter.

Although the typhoon season had not yet set in, and both Captain Reay and the master knew that in that latitude (about 4 deg. south) there was not very much probability of meeting with one, every preparation was made, as violent squalls and heavy rain, at least, were certain to follow the greenish warning in the sky. In a very short time their surmise proved correct, for by four in the afternoon the *Triton* under short canvas, was battling with a mountainous sea and furious gusts of wind from the W.N. W. The presence of so much land around them, surrounded by networks of outlying reefs, the strong and erratic currents, and the approaching night, gave Captain Reay much concern, and it was with a feeling of intense relief that he acceded to the master's suggestion to bring the ship to an anchor in a harbour situated among the cluster of islands that the ship had passed early in the day.

"We can lie there as snugly as if we were in dock," said the master; "the holding ground is good, and there is room for half a dozen line-of-battle ships." Then, pointing to the chart lying before him, he added, "The place is called Tyar, and, curiously enough, was first made known to the Admiral at Calcutta by a Captain Channing, one or the Company's men. This plan of the harbour is a copy of the one he made ten years ago."

"Channing's uncle, very probably," said Captain Reay, who had been told by his Marine officer that he had an unknown uncle in the Company's service. "Very well, Mr. Dacre, let us get in there by all means. I am most anxious to see the ship out of this before darkness sets in and we get piled up on a reef."

A mighty downpour of rain, which fell upon the frigate's deck like a waterspout, cut short all further speech by its deafening tumult, and although it lasted but a few minutes, it killed the fury of the squall to such an extent that the ship, unsteadied by her canvas, rolled so violently that no one could keep his feet. Suddenly the torrent ceased, and a short, savage, and gasping puff struck and almost sent her over on her beam-ends, then swept away as quickly as it came, to be followed a minute later by another almost as fierce but of longer duration.

Without further loss of time the reefs were shaken out of the topsails, for darkness was coming on, and, wearing ship at a favourable opportunity, the Triton kept away for Mr. Dacre's harbour. The wind, now blowing with steady force, sent her through the confused and lumpy sea at such a speed that before sundown she ran through the entrance to the harbour, and, bringing to under a high, wooded bluff, dropped anchor in ten fathoms of water, quite close to a narrow strip of beach that fringed the shores of a little bay.

The place in the immediate vicinity of the ship appeared to be uninhabited, but as darkness came on, a glimmer of lights appeared along the shore some miles away, and at daylight a number of fishing prahus approached the frigate, at first with hesitation, but when they were hailed by the master in their own tongue, and told that the ship was English, they came alongside and bartered their fish. They assured the master that the stormy weather was sure to continue for some days, until the moon quartered, and Captain Reay was pleased to learn from them that a certain amount of provisions, fish, vegetables, and fruit, would be brought off daily to the ship for sale.

The wind still blew with violence, and although the ship lay in water as smooth as a mill-pond, the narrow strip of open ocean visible from her decks was whipped foaming white with its violence.

In their conversation with the master, the natives had told him that at a village some miles away from where the Triton was anchored, there was a white man and his wife living—French people, so they said. A year before, a French privateer, running before a heavy gale and a wild, sweeping sea, had struck upon the barrier reef of one of the outer low-lying islands of the group, and, carried over it by the surf, had foundered in the lagoon inside.

Only ten people were saved, and among them were the Frenchman and his wife. Two months afterwards eight of the male survivors took passage in a prahu belonging to the Sultan of Batchian, having heard that there was a French ship refitting at that island.

"Why did the two others remain?" asked Mr. Dacre.

The natives laughed. "Ah! the one man who stayed was a clever man. When the prahu from Batchian came here he said he was sick, and that his wife feared to sail so far in a small prahu. He would wait, he said, till a ship came."

"And then?" asked Dacre.

"And then, after the other Frenchmen had gone, he came to our head man and said that if they would keep faith with him he would make them rich, for he knew that which none else knew. So he and they made a bond to keep faith with one another, and that day he took them to where the ship had sunk, and pointing to where she lay beneath the water he said: 'Is there any among ye who can dive down so far?' They laughed, for the wreck was but ten single arm lengths below, and then they said: 'Is this where thy riches lie? Of what use to us is this sunken ship, save for the guns on her decks?'

"Then he said: 'In that ship is gold and silver money enough to cover as a carpet the beach that lies in front of the village, but to get it the decks must be torn up. I, who was second in command, know where the treasure lieth in the belly of the ship. Now let us talk together and make a plan whereby we can get this money. It was for this I lied to those who have gone and said I was sick.'

"Then as soon as the tides were low, the Frenchman and the head men made rafts of bamboos and timber, and floating them on the wreck they took thick ropes of rattan, and divers went down and lashed the ends thereof to the cross-beams under the decks. Then when this was done more bamboos were added to the rafts above, and as the tide flowed the rattan ropes stood up like iron bars. For two days the people worked at this, and yet the decks kept firm, but on the third day a great piece tore out, and the sunken rafts sprang to the surface. And then the divers again went down, and by and by they brought up money in bags of canvas, and wooden boxes. And half of which was gotten up the Tuan took, and half he gave to the head men, according to the bond. And much more money is yet in the ship, for it is only when the water is clear and the current is not swift can we dive. Yet every time do we get money."

"The rascal!" said Captain Reay, when Dacre translated this. "I suppose this money was from plundered English prizes. Only that we are at peace with France, I'd like to take every coin from both the piratical scoundrel himself and his Malay partners. And, indeed, if the *Triton* were not a King's ship, I'd send a boat there and take it now. But I suppose I can't interfere— confound the fellow!—now that we are at peace with France."

The wind was still blowing with great force, and as there appeared no prospect of the weather breaking for another day or two, Captain Reay and his officers made preparations for excursions into the country. The natives showed a very great friendliness towards the *Triton's* people, and at about ten in the morning two boats left the ship for the shore, and Channing, accompanied by one of his Marines, who carried a fowling-piece, set out by themselves along the winding path that encircled the narrow littoral of the island off which the frigate lay. The captain had ordered that the shore party was not to remain later than sunset; so, determined to see as much of the place as possible, Channing and Private Watts set off at a brisk pace. A three hours' walk brought them to the windward side of the island, and then emerging from the palm-shaded path, they suddenly came upon the principal village of the island. Their appearance was hailed by the natives with every manifestation of pleasure, and a number of young men escorted them to the house of the principal head man, where they offered a simple repast of fish and fruit, and small drams of arrack served in coconut shells.

Leaving Private Watts to amuse himself with the villagers, who apparently took much interest in his uniform and accoutrements, Francis Channing set out for a walk. The path led along through the sweet-smelling tropical forest at about a cable's length from the shore, and then suddenly emerged upon a little cove, the beach of which was strewn with wreckage; spars, hempen cables, and other ship's gear covering the sand at high-water mark. Several rudely constructed rafts of wreckage, timber, and bamboo, were moored a little distance off, and Channing at once surmised that the spot was used as a landing-place by the wreckers working at the sunken privateer.

As he stood looking about him, uncertain whether to go on or turn back, a man approached him from a house that stood at the furthest point of the bay, and saluted him politely in French.

"I presume, sir," he said, as he bowed and extended his hand to the Englishman, "that you are one of the officers from the English frigate anchored at Tyar. I have heard that peace has been declared between our two nations, and I rejoice."

Channing made a suitable reply, and gazed with interest at the stranger, who was a handsome man of less than twenty-five years of age, dressed in a rough suit of blue jean, and wearing a wide-rimmed hat of plaited straw. His face was tanned a rich brown by the Eastern sun; and rough and coarse as was his attire, his address and manner showed him to be a man of education and refinement.

He seemed somewhat discomposed when Channing, in a very natural manner, asked him the name of his ship, and answered—

"L'Aigle Noir, Monsieur, and my name is Armand Le Mescam."

"I have heard her name mentioned by our master," said the Marine officer, with a smile. "He has had the honour of serving in many engagements against your country's ships in these seas, in which our ships have not always secured a victory."

The Frenchman bowed and smiled, and then, feeling no doubt that he could do so with safety to himself, and that even if the cause of his presence on the island were known to the *Tritons* people that he would suffer no molestation, invited Channing to walk to his house and take a glass of wine.

"Ah!" said Channing, with a laugh; "then you have got wine as well as money from the wreck of L' Aigle Noir."

The Frenchman's face darkened, and he stopped short.

"You know then, Monsieur, the reason of my remaining on this island?"

"I have heard," answered Channing frankly; and then, noticing the agitation expressed on the Frenchman's face, he added, "but that does not concern me, nor indeed any one else on board the *Triton*—not now, at any rate, since France and England are at peace."

Monsieur Le Mescam seemed greatly relieved at hearing this, and in another minute, chatting gaily to his visitor, led the way into his house. The building was but little better than an ordinary native dwelling, but it was furnished with rude couches and seats made from the wreckage of the privateer, and scattered about were many articles, such as weapons, crockery, cooking utensils, clothing, &c. Two or three native servants, who were lounging about, at once presented themselves to their master, and one of them, bringing a small keg, filled two silver cups with wine, and Channing and his host, bowing politely to each other, drank.

For some little time the two men conversed pleasantly, and then the Frenchman, who so far had avoided all allusion to the treasure, offered to conduct his guest a part of the way back to the native village. That he had not presented Channing to his wife did not surprise the latter, who imagined that she could scarcely be clothed in a befitting manner to meet a stranger, and he therefore did not even let his host know that he was aware of his wife being with him on the island.

Drinking a parting cup of wine together, the two men set out, the Frenchman leading the way past a number of sheds built of bamboos, and covered with atap thatch. As they reached the last of these buildings, which stood almost at the water's edge, they came upon a woman who was sitting, with her back turned to them, under the shade of the overhanging thatched eaves, nursing a child.

In a moment she rose to her feet and faced them, and rough and coarsely clad as she was, Channing was struck by her great beauty and her sad and mournful face.

For a moment the Frenchman hesitated, and with a quick "Sit you there, Adela, I shall return shortly," was turning away again with Channing, when they heard the woman's voice calling in French, "Adrian, come back!" and then in another moment she added in English, as she saw Channing walking on, "And you, sir, in Heaven's name, do not leave me! I am an Englishwoman."

In an instant Channing turned, and quick as lightning the Frenchman, whose face was dark with passion, barred his way—"Monsieur, as an honourable man, will not attempt to speak to my wife when I request him not to do so."

"And I beg of you, sir, as my fellow-countryman, not to desert me. I am indeed an Englishwoman. My father's ship was captured, plundered, and then sunk by a French privateer, within sight of Malacca. Both he and my mother are dead, and I was forced to marry that man there," and she pointed scornfully through her tears to Le Mescam. "His captain, who I thought had some honour, promised to set me ashore at Manila, but when we reached there I was kept on board, and, ill and scarce able to speak, was married to Lieutenant Le Mescam, against my will, by a Spanish priest. Oh, sir, for the sake of my father, who was an English sailor, help me!"

Channing sprang towards her. "Madam, I am an Englishman, and there is a King's ship not four miles away. You, sir"—and he turned to the Frenchman, whose handsome face was now distorted with passion—"shall answer for your cowardly conduct, or I very much mistake the character of the gallant officer under whom I have the honour to serve. Ha!" And with sudden fury he seized Le Mescam's right arm, the hand of which had grasped a pistol in the bosom of his coat. "You cowardly, treacherous hound!" and wrenching the weapon from his grasp, he struck the Frenchman in the face with it, and sent him spinning backward upon the sand, where he lay apparently stunned.

Then Charming turned to the woman, who, trembling in every limb, was leaning against the side of the house. "Madam, I shall return to the ship at once. Will you come with me now, or shall I go on first? That our captain will send a boat for you within an hour you may rely on. He will take quick action in such a matter as this. If you fear to remain alone, I shall with pleasure escort you on board now."

"No, no," she pleaded; "he," and she pointed to the prone figure of the Frenchman, "would never hurt me; and I cannot leave him like this—I cannot forget that, wicked and cruel as he has been to me, he is the father of my child. Return, sir, I pray you, to your ship, and if you can help me to escape from my unhappy position, do so. Were it not for the money that my husband is employed in getting from the sunken privateer, my lot would not have been so hard, for he would have returned with the other survivors to Batchian; and from there, by the weight of my poor father's name, I could easily have escaped to Macassar, where my mother's relatives live."

"Do not fear then, Madam," said Channing kindly, "I shall leave you now, but rest assured that a few hours hence you shall be among your own countrymen once more." Then as two native women appeared, as if searching for their mistress, he raised his hat and walked quickly away.

Armand Le Mescam, with the bitterest rage depicted on his swarthy features, rose to his feet, and instead of returning to his house went slowly along towards one of his storehouses, without even glancing at his wife, who stood watching him from where Channing had left her. In a few moments she saw his figure vanishing among the palms, but not so quickly but that she perceived he carried a musket.

His intention was easy to divine, and with a despairing look in her eyes, she began to run after him, carrying the infant in her arms.

Private Watts, meanwhile, had very much enjoyed himself with the natives, who, by reason of the Polynesian strain in their blood, were a merry, demonstrative, joyous people, unlike most of the Malayan race, who are much the reverse, especially towards strangers. For some time he had been watching the native boys throwing darts at a target, and his attempts to emulate their skill aroused much childish merriment. Suddenly the lengthening shadows of the surrounding palms recalled him to the fact that it was getting late, so bidding goodbye to his entertainers, he shouldered his fowling-piece and set off to meet his master, taking the same path as that by which Lieutenant Channing had left him. Half an hour's walk brought him to a spot where the path lay between the thick forest jungle on one side and the open beach on the other, with here and there jagged clumps of broken coral rock covered with a dense growth of vines and creepers.

Three or four hundred yards away he could see the tall figure of Lieutenant Channing walking quickly along the path; and so, sitting down upon a little strip of grassy sward that skirted the beach side of the track, the soldier awaited his master.

With the approach of sunset the wind had fallen, and though a mile or two away the thundering surges leapt with loud and resounding clamour upon the barrier reef, only the gentlest ripple disturbed the placid water of the sheltered lagoon. Overhead the broad leaves of the coco-palms, towering above the darker green of the surrounding vegetation, drooped languidly to the calm of the coming night, and great crested grey and purple-plumaged pigeons lit with crooning note upon their perches to rest.

As he lay there, lazily enjoying the beauty of the scene, the soldier heard the loud, hoarse note and whistling and clapping of a hornbill, and, turning his head, he saw the huge-beaked, ugly bird, rising in alarm from one of the vine-covered boulders of coral which stood between the path and high-water mark not thirty yards away, and at the same moment he caught a gleam of something bright that seemed to move amid the dense green tangle that covered the rock; and then a man's head and shoulders appeared for a second in full view. His back was turned to Watts, who now saw, with a vague feeling of wonder, that he was kneeling, and peering cautiously out upon the path below. Further along Watts could see his master, now within a hundred feet of the boulder, and walking very quickly. Then an exclamation of horror broke from him as the kneeling man slowly rose, and pointed his musket full at Channing; but ere the treacherous hand could pull the trigger, the Marine had levelled his piece and fired; without a cry the man spun round, and then pitched headlong to the ground at Channing's feet.

"My God, sir!" panted Watts, as a few seconds later he stood beside his master, who was gazing with stupefied amazement at the huddled-up figure of Armand Le Mescam, who lay with his face turned upward, and a dark stream trickling from his mouth, "I was only just in time. He had you covered at ten paces when I fired."

Le Mescam never spoke again. The shot had struck him in the back and passed through his chest. As the two men bent over him, a woman carrying a child burst through the jungle near them, sank exhausted on her knees beside the dead man, and then fainted.

There was much excitement when the last boat returned to the *Triton* pulling as her crew had never pulled before. Then there was a rush of pig-tailed bluejackets to the gangway, as a murmuring whisper ran along the decks that the "soger officer was comin' aboard holdin' a woman in his arms," and the news was instantly conveyed to the captain, who was that evening dining with his officers, with the result that as the cutter ran up alongside, Captain Reay, the master, and half a dozen other officers were standing on the main deck.

"By Heavens, gentlemen, it's true!" cried Captain Reay to the others. "Here, show more light at the gangway!"

And then amid a babble of excitement, Lieutenant Channing, pale, hatless, and excited, ascended the gangway, carrying in his arms a woman whose white face and dark hair stood clearly revealed under the blaze of lights held aloft by the seamen. As he touched the deck, the sleeping babe in her arms awoke, and uttered a wailing cry.

"Take her to my cabin, Channing," said Reay, without waiting to question him. "Here! give me the youngster, quick! Sentry, pass the word for the doctor."

The moment the officers had disappeared a buzz of talk hummed, and Private Watts was besieged with questions. "Give us a tot, an' I'll tell ye all about it, afore I'm sent for by the captain," was his prompt answer; and then swallowing the generous draught provided him, he told his story in as few words as possible.

A big, bony sergeant slapped him on the shoulder, "Mon, ye'll hae your stripes for this."

"Ay, that he will," said a hairy-chested boatswain. "Well, it's a uncommon curious ewent: this 'ere young covey goes a-shootin', and bags a Frenchman, and the soger officer brings a hangel and a cherrybim aboard."

The officers of the Triton sat long over their wine that night, and Lieutenant Channing was the recipient of much merry badinage; but there was behind it all a sincere feeling of joy that he had escaped such a treacherous death. Private Watts being sent for, was excused by the Scotch sergeant, who gravely reported that he was bad in the legs, whereat the officers laughed, and straightway made up a purse of guineas for him. Suddenly, as Captain Reay entered, the babble ceased.

"Gentlemen, let Mr. Channing turn in; he wants rest. The lady and her baby are now sound asleep. She has told me her strange story. To-morrow, Mr. West, you can take a boat's crew, and bring aboard a large sum of money concealed in a spot of which I shall give you an exact description. It belongs to this lady undoubtedly, now that Watts's lucky shot has settled her ruffianly husband."

Two days after, the frigate had cleared her harbour of refuge, and was bowling along on her course for Ternate when Captain Reay sent for Lieutenant Channing to come to his cabin.

"Channing," he said, taking his hand with a smile, "it is my happy lot to give you what I know will prove a joyful surprise. This lady"—and he bowed to Mrs. Le Mescam, who was sitting looking at him with a bright expectancy in her dark eyes—"is your own cousin, Adela Channing. There, I'll leave you now. She has much to tell you, poor girl; I have decided to go straight to the Admiral at Singapore instead of touching at Ternate, and if old Cardew is worth his salt he'll give you leave to take her to Calcutta."

Of course, Channing and Adela fell in love with each other, and he duly married the lady, and when they reached England he received the news of the inheritance that had fallen to him by John Channing's death.

Ex-Sergeant Watts, of the Marines, followed his master when he retired from the Service, and was for long the especial guardian of the "cherubim," as Adela Channing's eldest boy had been named by the *Triton's* people— until other sons and daughters appeared to claim his devotion.

PROCTOR THE DRUNKARD

Proctor, the ex-second mate of the island-trading brig *Bandolier*, crawled out from under the shelter of the overhanging rock where he had passed the night, and brushing off the thick coating of dust which covered his clothes from head to foot, walked quickly through the leafy avenues of Sydney Domain, leading to the city.

Sleeping under a rock in a public park is not a nice thing to do, but Proctor had been forced to do it for many weeks past. He didn't like it at first, but soon got used to it. It was better than having to ask old Mother Jennings for a bed at the dirty lodging-house, and being refused—with unnecessary remarks upon his financial position. The Sailors' Home was right enough; he could get a free bed there for the asking, and some tucker as well. But then at the Home he had to listen to prayers and religious advice, and he hated both, upon an empty stomach. No, he thought, the Domain was a lot better; every dirty "Jack Dog" at the Home knew he had been kicked out of sundry ships before he piled up the *Bandolier*, and they liked to comment audibly on their knowledge of the fact while he was eating his dinner among them—it's a way which A.B.'s have of "rubbing it in" to an officer down on his beam ends. Drunkard? Yes, of course he was, and everybody knew it. Why, even that sour-faced old devil of a door-keeper at the Home put a tract on his bed every evening. Curse him and his "Drunkard, beware!" and every other rotten tract on intemperance. Well, he had been sober for a week now—hadn't any money to get drunk with. If he had he certainly would get drunk, as quickly as he possibly could. Might as well get drunk as try to get a ship now. Why, every wharf-loafer knew him.

A hot feeling came to his cheeks and stayed there as he walked through the streets, for he seemed to hear every one laugh and mutter at him as he passed, "That's the boozy mate of the *Bandolier*. Ran her ashore in the Islands when he was drunk and drowned most of the hands."

Proctor was twenty-five when he began to drink. He had just been made master, and his good luck in making such quick passages set him off. Not that he then drank at sea; it was only when he came on shore and met so many of the passengers he had carried between Sydney and New Zealand that he went in for it. Then came a warning from the manager of the steamship company. That made him a bit careful—and vexed. And ill-luck made him meet a brother captain that night, and of course they had "a time" together, and Proctor was driven down in a cab to the ship and helped up the gangway by a wharfinger and a deck hand. The next morning he was asked to resign, and from that day his career was damned. From the command of a crack steamship to that of a tramp collier was a big come-down; but Proctor was glad to get the collier after a month's idleness. For nearly a year all went well. He had had a lesson, and did not drink now, not even on shore. A woman who had stood to him in his first disgrace had promised to marry him when the year was out, and that kept him straight. Then one day he received a cold intimation from his owners that he "had better look out for another ship," his services were no longer wanted. "Why?" he asked. Well, they said, they would be candid, they had heard he was a drinking man, and they would run no risks. Six months of shamefaced and enforced idleness followed; and then Proctor was partly promised a barque. Another man named Rothesay was working hard to get her, but Proctor beat him by a hair's breadth. He made two or three trips to California and back, and then, almost on the eve of his marriage, met Rothesay, who was now in command of a small island-trading steamer. Proctor liked Rothesay, and thought him a good fellow; Rothesay hated Proctor most fervently, hated him because he was in command of the ship he wanted himself, and hated him because he was to marry Nell Levison. Proctor did not know this (Nell Levison did), or he would have either knocked the handsome black-bearded, ever-smiling Captain Rothesay down, or told him to drink by himself. But he was no match for Rothesay's cunning, and readily swallowed his enemy's smiling professions of regard and good wishes for his married happiness. They drank together again and again, and, at eleven o'clock that night, just as the theatres were coming out, Rothesay suddenly left him, and Proctor found himself staggering across the street. A policeman took him to his hotel, where Proctor sank into a heavy, deadly stupor. He awoke at noon. Two letters were lying on his table. One, from the owners of his barque, asked him to call on them at ten o'clock that morning, the other was from Nell Levison. The latter was short but plain: "I shall never marry a drunkard. I never wish to see you again. *I saw you last night.*" He dressed and went to the owners' office. The senior partner did not shake hands, but coldly bade him be seated. And in another minute Proctor learnt that it was known he had been seen drunk in the street, and that he could "look for another ship." He went out dazed and stupid.

For three days he kept up his courage, and then wrote to the owners of the barque and asked them to overlook the matter. He had served them well, he urged, and surely they would not ruin him for life. And Rothesay, to whom he showed the letter, said it was one of which no man need be ashamed. He would take it himself, he added, for he felt he was in some degree to blame for that fatal night. Take it he did, for he felt certain that it would not alter the decision of Messrs. Macpherson & Donald—he knew them too well for that. Then he came back to Proctor with a gloomy face, and shook his head. The wretched man knew what that meant, and asked him no questions. Rothesay, sneak and traitor as he was, felt some shame in his heart when, an hour later, Proctor held out his hand, thanked him, and bade him good-bye. "I'm clearing out," he said.

Then for six years Proctor was seen no more in Sydney. He went steadily to the devil elsewhere—mostly in the South Sea Islands, where he was dismissed from one vessel after another, first as skipper, then as mate, then as second mate. One day in a Fiji hotel he met a man—a stranger—who knew Rothesay well.

"What is he doing now?" asked Proctor.

"Don't know exactly. He's no friend of mine, although I was mate with him for two years. He married a girl that was engaged to another man—a poor devil of a chap named Proctor—married her a week after Proctor got the run from his ship for being drunk. And every one says that it was Rothesay who made him drunk, as he was mad to get the girl. And I have no doubt it's true. Rothesay is the two ends and bight of a damned sneak."

Proctor nodded, but said nothing.

He drank now whenever he could get at liquor, ashore or afloat. Sometimes he would steal it. Yet somehow he always managed to get another ship. He knew the islands well, and provided he could be kept sober there was not a better man to be found in the Pacific labour trade. And the "trade"—i.e., the recruiting of native labourers for the Fijian and Queensland sugar plantations from among the New Hebrides and Solomon Groups—was a dangerous pursuit. But Proctor was always a lucky man. He had come down to a second mate's berth now on the brig *Bandolier*; but then he was "recruiter" as well, and with big wages, incurred more risks than any other man on the ship. Perhaps he had grown careless of his life, which was lonely enough, for though not a morose man, he never talked with his shipmates. So for two years or more he cruised in the *Bandolier* among the woolly-haired, naked cannibals of the Solomon Group and thereabout, landing at places where no other recruiter would get out of his boat, and taking a box of trade goods with him, sit calmly down on the beach surrounded by savages who might without a moment's warning riddle him with spears or club him from behind. But Proctor knew no fear, although his armed boat's crew and the crew of the covering boat would call to him to get aboard again and shove off. Other labour ships there were cruising on the same ground who lost men often enough by spear or bullet or poisoned arrow, and went back to Fiji or Queensland with perhaps not a score of "recruits," but Proctor never lost a single man, and always filled the crazy old *Bandolier* with a black and savage cargo. Then, once in port again, his enemy seized him, and for a week at a time he would lie drunk in the local hells, till the captain sought him out and brought him on board again. Going back to the recruiting grounds with an empty ship and with no danger to apprehend from a sudden rush of naked figures, the captain gave him as much liquor as he wanted, else Proctor would have stolen it. And one night he was drunk on his watch, ran the *Bandolier* upon a reef, and all hands perished but himself and six others. One boat was saved, and then followed long days of hunger and thirst and bitter agony upon the sea under a blazing sun, but Proctor brought the boat and crew safely to the Queensland coast. A month later he was in Sydney penniless, and again "looking for a ship." But no one would have him now; his story was too well known.

And so for weeks past he had slept in the park at night, and wandered down about the wharves during the day. Sometimes he earned a few shillings, most of which went in cheap rum.

Half an hour's walk through the long shady avenue of Moreton Bay figs, and then he emerged suddenly into the noise and rattle of the city. Four coppers was all the money he possessed, and unless he could earn a shilling or two during the day on the wharves he would have to starve on the morrow. He stopped outside the *Herald* office presently, and pushing his way through a number of half-starved outcasts like himself, he read down the "Wanted" column of the paper. And suddenly hope sprang up in his heart as he saw this—

WANTED, *for the Solomon Islands Labour trade, four able Seamen used to the work. High wages to competent men. Apply to Harkniss & Co., George Street.*

Ten minutes later he was at Harkness & Company's office waiting to see the manager. Ten o'clock, the clerks said, would be time enough to come. Proctor said he would wait. He feared that there would be other applicants, and was determined to see the manager before any one else. But he need not have been so anxious. Men such as Harkness & Company wanted were hard to get, and the firm were not disposed to be particular as to their character or antecedents, so long as they could do the "work" and hold their tongues afterward. Ten o'clock came, and at half-past ten Proctor and two other men went out of the office each with a £1 note in his pocket, and with orders to proceed to Melbourne by steamer, and there join the barque *Kate Rennie*.

Before the steamer left for Melbourne, Proctor had parted with half of his pound for another man's discharge. He did not want to be known as Proctor of the *Bandolier* if he could help it. So he was now Peter Jensen; and Peter Jensen, a hard-up Norwegian A.B., was promoted—on paper—to John Proctor, master. At Melbourne they found the barque ready for sea, and they were at once taken to the shipping office to meet the captain and sign articles, and Proctor's heart beat fiercely with a savage joy when he heard the voice of the man who had stolen Nell Levison from him! So Rothesay was the captain of the *Kate Rennie!* And the Solomon Islands was a good place to pay off one's old scores.

The *Kate Rennie* sailed the next day. As soon as the tug cast off, the crew were mustered on the main-deck, and the watches and boats' crew picked. Peter Jensen, A.B., was standing furthest away when the captain's eye fell on him.

"What's your name?" he asked, and then in an instant his face paled— he recognised the man.

Jensen made no answer. His eyes were fixed in a dull stare upon the features of a little boy of six, who had come up from the cabin and had caught hold of Rothesay's hand. For Nell Levison's face was before him again. Then with an effort he withdrew his gaze from the child and looked down at the deck.

"You can have him, Mr. Williams," said Rothesay curtly to the mate.

From that day till the barque made the Solomon Islands, Rothesay watched the man he had injured, but Jensen, A.B., gave no sign. He did his work well, and spoke to no one except when spoken to. And when the boy Allan Rothesay came on deck and prattled to the crew, Jensen alone took no notice of him. But whenever he heard the child speak, the memory of the woman he had lost came back to him, and he longed for his revenge.

One night, as the barque was slipping quietly through the water, and the misty mountain heights of Bougainville Island showed ghostly grey under myriad stars, Rothesay came on deck an hour or two before the dawn. Jensen was at the wheel, and the captain walked aft, seated himself near him, and lit a cigar. Williams, the mate, was at the break of the poop, and out of earshot.

Presently Rothesay walked over to the wheel and stood beside the steersman, glancing first at the compass, and then aloft at the white swelling canvas. The barque was close-hauled and the course "full and by."

"Is she coming up at all?" said Rothesay quietly, speaking in a low voice.

"No, sir," answered Jensen steadily, but looking straight before him; "she did come up a point or so a little while back, but fell off again; but the wind keeps pretty steady, sir."

Rothesay stood by him irresolutely, debating within himself. Then he walked up to the mate.

"Mr. Williams, send another man to the wheel, and tell Jensen to come below. I want to speak to him about Bougainville; he knows the place well, I have been told. And as neither you nor I do, I may get something out of him worth knowing."

"Ay, ay, sir," answered the Welsh mate. "But he's mighty close over it, anyway. I've hardly heard him open his mouth yet."

A minute or two passed, and Jensen was standing at the cabin-door, cap in hand.

"Come in," said Rothesay, turning up the cabin lamp, and then he said quietly, "Sit down, Proctor; I want to talk to you quietly. You see, I know you."

The seaman stood silent a moment with drooping eyes. "My name is Jensen, sir," he said sullenly.

"Very well, just as you like. But I sent for you to tell you that I had not forgotten our former friendship, and—and I want to prove it, if you will let me."

"Thank you, sir," was the reply, and the man's eyes met Rothesay's for one second, and Rothesay saw that they burned with a strange, red gleam; "but you can do nothing for me. I am no longer Proctor, the disgraced and drunken captain, but Jensen, A.B. And," with sudden fury, "I want to be left to myself."

"Proctor," and Rothesay rose to his feet, and placed his hands on the table, "listen to me. You may think that I have treated you badly. My wife died two years ago, and I— —"

Proctor waved his hand impatiently. "Let it pass if you have wronged me. But, because I got drunk and lost my ship, I don't see how you are to blame for it."

A look of relief came into Rothesay's face. Surely the man had not heard whom he had married, and there was nothing to fear after all.

For a minute or so neither spoke, then Proctor picked up his cap.

"Proctor," said Rothesay, with a smile, "take a glass of grog with me for the sake of old times, won't you!"

"No, thank you, sir," he replied calmly, and then without another word he walked out of the cabin, and presently Rothesay heard him take the wheel again from the man who had relieved him.

Two days later the *Kate Rennie* sailed round the north cape of Bougainville, and then bore up for a large village on the east coast named Numa Numa, which Rothesay hoped to make at daylight on the following morning.

At midnight Jensen came to the wheel again. The night was bright with the light of shining stars, and the sea, although the breeze was brisk, was smooth as a mountain lake, only the *rip, ripy rip* of the barque's cutwater and the bubbling sounds of her eddying wake broke the silence of the night. Ten miles away the verdure-clad peaks and spurs of lofty Bougainville stood clearly out, silhouetted against the sea-rim on the starboard hand. The wind was fair abeam and the ship as steady as a church, and Proctor scarce glanced at the compass at all. The course given to him was W.S.W., which, at the rate the ship was slipping through the water, would bring her within two miles of the land by the time he was relieved. Then she would have to go about and make another "short leg," and, after that, she could lay right up to Numa Numa village.

Late in the day Rothesay had lowered one of the ship's boats, whose timbers had opened under the rays of the torrid sun, and was keeping her towing astern till she became watertight. Presently Proctor heard a voice calling him.

"Peter, I say, Peter, you got a match?"

Looking astern, he saw that the native who was steering the boat had hauled her up close up under the stern.

"Yes," he answered, taking a box of matches out of his pocket and throwing them to the native sailor. "Are you tired of steering that boat, Tommy?"

"No, not yet; but I wanted to smoke. When four bell strike I come aboard, Mr. Williams say."

Two bells struck, and then Proctor heard Williams, who was sitting down at the break of the poop, say, "Hallo, young shaver, what do you want on deck?"

"Oh, Mr. Williams, it is so hot below, and my father said I could come on deck. See, I've got my rug and pillow."

"All right, sonny," said the mate good-naturedly; "here, lie down here on the skylight."

The child lay down and seemed to sleep, but Proctor could see that his eyes were wide open and watched the stars.

Four bells struck, and Proctor was relieved by a white seaman, and another native came to relieve the man who was steering the boat, which was now hauled up under the counter. Just then, as the mate called out, "Ready about," Proctor touched the child on the arm.

"Allan, would you like to come in the boat with me?"

The boy laughed with delight. "Oh, yes, Peter, I would like it."

Proctor turned to the native who was waiting to relieve the man who was steering the boat. "You can go for'ard, Jimmy, I'll take the boat for you."

The native grinned. "All right, Peter, I no like boat," and in another moment Proctor had passed the child down into the boat, into the arms of the native sailor whose place he was taking, and quickly followed. As she drifted astern, the *Kate Rennie* went about, the towline tautened out, and a delighted laugh broke from the boy as he sat beside Proctor and saw the white canvas of the barque looming up before him.

"Hush!" said Proctor, and his hand trembled as he grasped the steer-oar. Then he drew the child to his bosom and caressed him almost fiercely.

For half an hour the barque slipped along, and Proctor sat and steered and smoked and watched the child, who now slumbered at his feet. Then the stars darkened over, a black cloud arose to the eastward, the wind died away, and the mate's voice hailed him to come alongside, as a heavy squall was coming on. "And you'll have trouble with the captain for taking his boy in that boat," added Williams.

"Ay, ay, sir," answered Proctor, as he looked at the cloud to windward, which was now quickly changing to a dullish grey; and then he sprang forward and cut the tow-line with his sheath-knife.

Five minutes passed. Then came a cry of agony from the barque, as Rothesay, who had rushed on deck at Williams's call, placed his hand on the tow-line and began to haul it in.

"Oh, my God, Williams, the line has parted. Boat ahoy, there, where are you?"

And then with a droning hum the squall smote the *Kate Rennie* with savage fury, and nearly threw her over on her beam ends; and Proctor the Drunkard slewed the boat round and let her fly before the hissing squall towards the dimmed outline of Bougainville.

For two days the *Kate Rennie* cruised off the northern end of Bougainville, searching for the missing boat. Then Rothesay beat back to Numa Numa and anchored, and carefully examined the coast with his boats. But no trace or Proctor nor the child was ever found. Whether the boat was dashed to pieces upon the reef or had been blown past the north end of the island and thence out upon that wide expanse of ocean that lies between the Solomons and New Guinea was never known, and the fete of Proctor the Drunkard and his innocent victim will for ever remain one of the many mysteries of the Western Pacific till the sea gives up its dead.

A PONAPEAN CONVENANCE

"Here also, as at Yap, the youngest wives and sisters of the chiefs visited the frigate.... Somewhat shocking at first to our feelings as Christians.... Yet to have declined what was regarded by these simple and amiable people as the very highest token of their regard for the officers of the expedition, would have been bitterly resented.... And, after all, our duties to our King and Queen were paramount... the foundation of friendly relations with the people of this Archipelago!... The engaging manners and modest demeanour of these native ladies were most commendable. That this embarrassing custom was practised to do us especial honour we had ample proof."

Chester, the trader, laid down the book and looked curiously at the title, "A Journal of the Expedition under Don Felipe Tompson, through the Caroline Islands." It was in Spanish, and had been lent him by one of the Jesuit Fathers in Ponapé.

"Ninety years haven't worked much difference in some of the native customs," thought he to himself. "What a sensation Don Felipe would have made lecturing at St. James's Hall on these pleasantly curious customs! I must ask Tulpé about these queer little functions. She's chock-full of island lore, and perhaps I'll make a book myself some day."

"Huh!" said Tulpe, Chester's native wife, whipping off her muslin gown and tossing it aside, as she lay back and cooled her heated face and bared bosom with a fan, "'tis hot, Kesta, and the sun was balanced in the middle of the sky when we left Jakoits in the boat, and now 'tis all but night; and wind there was none, so we used not the sail."

"Foolish creature," said Chester, again taking up his book, "and merely to see this new white missionary woman thou wilt let the sun bake thy hands and feet black."

Handsome, black-browed Tulpé flashed her white, even teeth as she smiled.

"Nay, but listen, Kesta. Such a woman as this one never have I seen. Her skin is white and gleaming as the inside of the pearl-shell. How comes it, my white man, that such a fair woman as this marrieth so mean-looking a man?

Was she a slave? Were she a woman of Ponapé, and of good blood, Nanakin the Great would take her to wife."

"Aye," said Chester lazily; "and whence came she and her husband?"

"From Kusaie (Strong's Island), where for two years have they lived, so that now the woman speaketh our tongue as well as thee."

"Ha!" said the trader quickly; "what are their names?"

She told him, and Chester suddenly felt uncomfortable.

Two years before, when spending a few idle months in Honolulu, he had met that white woman. She was waiting to be married to the Rev. Obadiah Yowlman, a hard-faced, earnest-minded, little Yankee missionary, who was coming up from the Carolines in the *Planet*. There had been some rather heavy love-passages between her and Chester. He preserved his mental equilibrium—she lost hers. The passionate outburst of the "little she missionary," as he called her when he bade her goodbye, he regarded as the natural and consistent corollary of moonlit nights beneath the waving palms on white Hawaiian beaches. When he returned to Ponapé he simply forgot all about her—and Tulpé never asked him inconsiderate questions about other women whom he might have met during the six months he was away from her. He had come back—that was all she cared for.

"I wonder how Tulpe would take it if she knew?" he thought. "She might turn out a bit of a tiger."

"What are thy thoughts, Kesta?" And Tulpé came over to him and leant upon his shoulder. "Is it in thy mind to see and talk with the new missionary and his wife?"

"No," said Chester promptly; "sit thou here, wood-pigeon, and tell me of the customs I read of here."

She sat down beside him, and leant her dark head against his knee, fanning herself the while she answered his questions.

"As it was then, Kesta, so is it now. And if it were to advantage thee I should do likewise. For is it not the duty of a woman to let all men see how great is her love for her husband? And if a great chief or king of thy land came here, would I not obey thee?"

Chester laughed. "No great chiefs of my land come here—only ship-captains and missionaries."

She turned and looked up into his face silently for a few moments, then rose.

"I know thy meaning now. But surely this mean-faced missionary is not to be compared to thee! Kesta, 'tis the fair-faced woman that is in thy mind. Be it as you will. Yet I knew not that the customs of thy land were like unto ours."

"What the devil is she driving at!" thought Chester, utterly failing to grasp her meaning.

Early next morning Tulpe was gone.

"Deny it not, white woman. If thou dost not love my husband, how came it that yesterday thou asked his name of me? See now, I deal fairly with thee. For three days will I stay *here* although thy husband is but as a hog in my eyes, for he is poor and mean-looking, while mine is— —, well, thou shalt see him; and for three days shalt thou stay in *my* house with my husband. So get thee away, then—the boat waits."

Pretty Mrs. Yowlman fled to her room and, wondering whether Chester knew, began to cry, while Tulpé sat down, and, rolling a cigarette, resignedly awaited the appearance of the Rev, Obadiah Yowlman.

An hour afterwards the Rev. gentleman came in with Chester, who had walked across the island on discovering Tulpé's absence.

"No, thank you," he said to the missionary; "I won't stay now.... Some other time I will do myself the pleasure of calling upon Mrs. Yowlman, and yourself... You must excuse my wife having called upon you twice. She is deeply imbued with the native customs and observances, and I—er— sincerely trust she has given no offence."

Then took he Tulpé's hand and led her, wondering, back to his home. And Tulpé thought he and the white woman were both fools.

IN THE KING'S SERVICE, SOME EPISODES IN THE LIFE OF A BEACH-COMBER

I

The white cloud mantle that had enwrapped the wooded summit of Lijibal was slowly lifting and fading before the red arrow-rays of the tropic sun—it was nearly dawn in Lêla Harbour. A vast swarm of sooty terns, with flapping wing and sharp, croaking note, slid out from the mountain forest and fled seaward, and low down upon the land-locked depths of Lela a soft mist still hovered, so that, were it not for the deadened throbbing beat and lapping murmur of the flowing tide, one might have thought, as he looked across from land to land, that the high green walls of verdure in whose bosom the waters of Lela lay encompassed were but the portals to some deep and shadowy mountain valley in a land of utter silence, untenanted by man.

But as the blood-redness of the sun paled and paled, and then changed into burnished gold, the topmost branches of the dew-laden trees quivered and trembled, and then swayed softly to the sea-breeze; the fleecy vapours that hid the waters of the harbour vanished, and the dark bases of the mountains stood out in purest green. Away out seawards, towards the hiss and boil of the tumbling surf, tiny strips of gleaming sandy beach showed out in every nook and bay. And soon the yellow sunlight flashed through the gloomy shadows of the forest, the sleeping pigeons and the green and scarlet-hued parrakeets awoke to life amid the sheltering boughs, and the soft, crooning note of one was answered back by the sharp scream of the other. Along the mountain sides there was a hurried rustling and trampling among the thick carpet of fallen leaves, and a wild boar burst his way through the undergrowth to bury in his lair till night came again; for almost with the first call of the birds sounded the hum and murmur of voices, and the brown people of Léla stepped out from their houses of thatch, and greeted each other as they hurried seaward for their morning bathe—the men among the swirl and wash of the breaking surf, and the women and children along the sandy beach in front of the village.

Out upon the point of black and jagged reef that stretched northward from the entrance to the harbour was the figure of a young boy who bathed by himself. He was the son of the one white man on Strong's Island, whose isolated dwelling lay almost within hail of him.

The father of the boy was one of those mysterious wanderers who, in the days of sixty years or so ago, were common enough on many of the islands of the North Pacific. Without any material means, save a bag of silver dollars, he had, accompanied by his son, landed at Lêla Harbour on Strong's Island from a passing ship, and Charlik, the king of the island, although at first resenting the intrusion of a poor white man among his people, had consented to let him remain on being told by the captain of the ship that the stranger was a skilful cooper, and could also build a boat. It so happened that many of the casks in which the king stored his coconut-oil were leaking, and no one on the island could repair them; and the white man soon gave the native king proof of his craft by producing from his bag some of a cooper's tools, and going into the great oil shed that was close by. Here, with some hundreds of natives watching him keenly, he worked for half an hour, while his half-caste son sat upon the beach utterly unnoticed by any one, and regarded with unfavourable looks by the island children, from the mere fact of their having learned that his mother had been a native of a strange island—that to them was sufficient cause for suspicion, if not hostility.

Presently the king himself, attended by his mother, came to the oil shed, looked in, and called out to the white man to cease his work.

"Look you, white man," he said in English. "You can stop. Mend and make my casks for me, and some day build me a boat; but send away the son of the woman from the south lands. We of Kusaie (Strong's Island) will have no strangers here."

The white man's answer was quick and to the point. He would not send his child away; either the boy remained with him on shore or they both returned to the ship and sought out some other island.

"Good," said Charlik with cold assent, and turning to his people he commanded them to provide a house for the white man and his boy, and bring them food and mats for their immediate necessities.

An hour or two afterwards, as the ship that had landed him at Lêla sailed slowly past the white line of surf which fringed the northern side of the island, the captain, looking shoreward from his deck, saw the white man and his boy walking along the beach towards a lonely native house on the farthest point. Behind them followed a number of half-nude natives, carrying mats and baskets of food. Only once did the man turn his face towards the ship, and the captain and mate, catching his glance, waved their hands to him in mute farewell. A quick upward and outward motion of his hand was the only response to their signal, and then he walked steadily along without looking seaward again.

"Queer fellow that, Matthews," said the captain to his mate. "I wonder how the deuce he got to the Bonins and where he came from. He's not a runaway convict, anyway—you can see that by the look in his eye. Seems a decent, quiet sort of a man, too. What d'ye think he is yourself?"

"Runaway man-o'war's man," said Matthews, looking up aloft. "What the devil would he come aboard us at night-time in a fairly civilised place like the Bonin Islands as soon as he heard that the *Juno*, frigate, was lying at anchor ten miles away from us there. And, besides that, you can see he's a sailor, although he didn't want to show it."

"Aye," said the captain, "likely enough that's what he is. Perhaps he's one of the seven that ran away from Sir Thomas Staine's ship in the South Pacific some years ago."

And Mr. Matthews, the mate of the barque *Oliver Cromwell* was perfectly correct in his surmise, for the strange white man who had stolen aboard the ship so quietly in the Bonin Islands was a deserter from his Majesty William IV.'s ship *Tagus*. For nearly seven years he had wandered from one island to another, haunted by the fear of recapture and death since the day when, in a mad fit of passion, he had, while ashore with a watering party, driven his cutlass through the body of a brutal petty officer who had threatened, for some trifling dereliction of duty, to get him "a couple of dozen."

Horror-stricken at the result of his deadly blow, he had fled into the dense jungle of the island, and here for many days the wretched man lived in hiding till he was found by a party of natives, who fed and brought him back to life, for he was all but dead from hunger and exposure. For nearly a year he lived among these people, adapting himself to their mode of life, and gaining a certain amount of respect; for in addition to being a naturally hard-working man, he had no taste for the gross looseness of life that characterised nine out of every ten white men who in those days lived among the wild people of the North Pacific Islands.

Two years passed by. Brandon—for that was his name—realised in all its bitterness that he could never return to England again, as recognition and capture, dared he ever show himself there, would be almost certain: for, in addition to his great stature and marked physiognomy, he was fatally marked for identification by a great scar received in honourable fight from the cutlass of the captain of a Portuguese slaver on the coast of Africa. And so, in sheer despair of his future, he resolved to cast aside for ever all hope of again seeing his native land and all that was dear to him, and live out his life among the lonely islands of the wide Pacific.

Perhaps, as he looked out, at long, long intervals of years, at the sails of some ship that passed within sight of the island, he may have thought of the bright-faced girl in the little Cornish village who had promised to be his wife when he came home again in the *Tagus*; but in his rude, honest way he would only sigh and say to himself—

"Poor Rose, she's forgotten me by now; I hope so, anyhow."

So time went by, slowly at first, then quicker, for the young native woman whom he had married a year before had aroused in him a sort of unspoken affection for her artless and childlike innocence, and this deepened when her first child was born; and sometimes, as he worked at his old trade of boat-building—learned before he joined the King's service—he would feel almost content.

As yet no fear of a King's ship had crossed his mind. In those days ten years would go by, and save for some passing merchantman bound to China by the Outer Route, which would sweep past miles away before the strong trade wind, no ship had he seen. And here, on this forgotten island, he might have lived and died, but that one day a sandal-wooding brigantine was becalmed about four miles away from the island, and Brandon determined to board her, and endeavour to obtain a few tools and other necessaries from her captain.

With half-a-dozen of his most trusted native friends he stepped into a canoe, and reached the brigantine just as night began to fall. The master of the vessel received him kindly enough, and gave him the few articles he desired, and then, suddenly turning to him, said—

"I want another man; will you come? I'm bound to Singapore with sandal-wood."

"No, thank you, sir. I can't leave here. I've got a wife and child."

The seaman laughed with good-humoured contempt, and sought to persuade him to come, but Brandon only shook his head solemnly. "I can't do that, sir. These here people has treated me well, and I can't play them a dirty trick like that."

After some little bargaining the natives who had come with Brandon agreed to return to the shore and bring off some turtle to the ship. It was still a dead calm, and likely to continue so all night, and Brandon, shaking the captain's hand, got into the canoe and headed for the island.

As they ran the bow of the canoe upon the beach Brandon called loudly to his wife to come out of the house and see what he had brought from the ship, and was instantly struck with alarm at hearing no answer to his call. Running quickly over the few hundred yards that separated his house from the beach, he lifted up the door of thatch and saw that the house was empty—his wife and child were gone.

In a moment the whole village was awake, and, carrying lighted torches, parties of men and women ran along the path to seek the missing woman, but sought in vain. The island was small and had but one village, and Brandon, puzzled at his wife's mysterious disappearance, was about to lead another party himself in another direction to that previously taken, when a woman who lived at a house at the extreme end of the village, suddenly remembered that she had seen Brandon's wife, carrying her child in her arms, walking quickly by in the direction of a point of land that ran far out from the shore on the lee side of the island.

In an instant he surmised that, fearing he might go away in the ship, she had determined to swim out to him. The moment he voiced his thought to the natives around him, the men darted back to the beach, and several canoes were at once launched, and in the first was Brandon.

There were four canoes in all, and as that of the white man gained the open sea, the crew urged him not to steer directly for the brigantine, "for," said they, "the current is so strong that Mâhia, thy wife, who is but a poor swimmer and knows not its strength, hath been swept round far beyond the point—and, besides, she hath the child."

For nearly half an hour the canoes paddled out swiftly, but noiselessly, the men calling out loudly at brief intervals, and every now and then Brandon himself would call.

"Mâhia! Mâhia! Call to us so that we may find thee!"

But no answer came back over the dark waters. At last the four canoes approached each other, and the natives and Brandon had a hurried consultation.

"Paranta," said the steersman of the nearest canoe, "let us to the ship. It may be that she is there."

The man who sat next to the speaker muttered in low tones, "How can that be, Kariri? Either the child hath wearied her arm and she hath sunk, or—the sharks."

Plunging his paddle deeply into the water, Brandon, brought the head of the canoe round for the ship, the faint outlines of whose canvas was just showing ghostly white half a mile away through the thin morning haze which mantled the still unruffled surface of the ocean.

Urged swiftly along by the six men who paddled, the white man's canoe was soon within hailing distance of the brigantine, and at the same moment the first puff of the coming breeze stirred and then quickly lifted the misty veil which encompassed her.

"Ship ahoy!" hailed Brandon. "Did a woman and child swim off to you during the night?"

Almost ere the answering "No" was given, there was a loud cry from one of the other canoes which had approached the vessel on the other side, and the "No" from the brigantine was changed into—

"Yes, she's here; close to on the port side. Look sharp, she's sinking," and then came the sound of tackle as the crew lowered a boat that hung on the ship's quarter.

With a low, excited cry the crew of Brandon's canoe struck their bright red paddles into the water with lightning strokes, and the little craft swept swiftly round the stern of the brigantine before the just lowered boat had way on her.

There, scarce a hundred yards away, they saw Mâhia swimming slowly and painfully along towards the ship, to the man whom she thought had deserted her. With one arm she supported the tiny figure of the child, and Brandon, with a wild fear in his heart, saw that she was too exhausted to hold it many seconds longer.

"Quick! Quick, man, for the love of God!" came in loud, hoarse tones from the captain of the brigantine, who stood on the rail holding to the main rigging, and drawing a pistol from his belt he sent its bullet within a few feet of the feeble swimmer.

Only another ten yards, when, as if aware of the awful fate that awaited her, Mâhia half raised herself, and with dying strength held the child out almost clear of the water. And then, as her panting bosom wailed out her husband's name for the last time, there pealed out upon the ocean a shriek of mortal agony, and he saw her drop the infant and disappear in a swirl of eddying foam. Ere that awful cry had ceased to vibrate through the morning air, a native had sprung from the canoe and seized the drowning child, and the agonised father, looking down into the blue depths, saw a running streak of bubbling white five fathoms beneath. Again the native dived, and followed the wavering track of white, and presently, not fifty feet away, they saw him rise with the woman on his arm, her long black hair twining around his brawny neck and shoulders.

"By God, he's saved her!" cried the mate, as both his boat and Brandon's canoe reached the native simultaneously, and they reached out their hands to take hold of the motionless figure.

"Paranta, turn thy eyes away," said a native, and flinging his arms around the white man, he forced his face away as the diver and his burden were lifted into the boat.

A shuddering sob stirred the frame of the mate or the brigantine when he saw that only the upper half of the woman's body was left.

II

With the captain of the sandal-wooder, the broken-hearted wanderer, had taken passage, and one day, as he watched the movements of his child as it frolicked with the rough seamen of the brigantine, the haunting fear of discovery returned to him in all its first force of three years before. A kindly remark made by the rough but good-natured skipper led him to reveal his story, and the seaman's face fell when the deserter asked him if he thought it possible he could ever return to England with safety.

"No, I don't. You *might* but I can tell you that a man with a figure like you—6 ft. 1 in. if you're an inch, and with a cut across the face—wouldn't miss being found out. And look here, 'tisn't even safe for you to come to Singapore. There's many a King's ship around these parts, and the chances are that some of the company of any one of 'em would recognise you—and you know what that means. If I were in your place I would try and get away in an American whaler. Once in America you'll be safe enough. The best I can do for you is to put you ashore at the Bonin Islands. There's bound to be whalers in there next season, making up northwards to the coast of Japan and Tchantar Bay."

One day they sailed slowly into a little land-locked harbour in the Bonin Islands, and Brandon, grasping the kind-hearted skipper's hand, bade him goodbye, and went ashore. Here, among the strange hybrid population of natives, half-bloods, runaways from whale-ships, and Portuguese, he found employment at boat-building, and for another three years lived contentedly enough, working hard, and saving what little money he could. Then came the *Oliver Cromwell* and reported that an English frigate which was at anchor a few miles away at another harbour would be at his then refuge on the following day.

Without saying a word of farewell to his rough and wild associates, he had taken his bag of honestly-earned money, and going on board the barque at night, besought the master to give him and the boy a passage away to any island in the Caroline or Marshall Groups at which the vessel could conveniently land them.

At noon next morning the barque was under way, and as she rounded the point the lofty spars of the frigate showed up scarce a mile distant, and Brandon, with a pistol in the bosom of his shirt, sat and trembled till the *Oliver Cromwell* was well away from her, and the frigate's white sails had become hull down.

For week after week the barque sailed past many a palm-shaded isle, with its belt of gleaming beach within the fringe of beating surf, and the brown people came out from their dwellings of thatch and shouted and bawled to the men on the passing ship; but at none of these would the captain land the deserter, for the natives were reputed to be savage and treacherous to the last degree.

At last the green peaks of Kusaie which shadowed the deep waters of Lêla Harbour were sighted; and here once more the wandering man sought to hide himself from the world.

III

The sun was high now, and the boy Harry, now a strong, sturdy-limbed youngster of seven, as he splashed about, called loudly to his father to come and bathe too.

"Come, father," he called. "See, the sun is between the big and little peaks, and to-day it is that you and I go to Utwé in the new boat."

At the sound of the boy's voice Brandon came to the door of his hut, and stroking his bearded chin, smiled and shook his head.

"Aye, aye, Harry. Come in, boy, and eat something, and then let us away to the king's boat-shed. To-day the people of Utwé shall see the new boat, and Charlik goes with us."

"Father," asked the boy, as he ate his food, "when shall we go away from this place? Kanka, the priest, said to me yesterday that by and by the king would build us a new house in the village—when you had finished another boat."

Brandon shook his head. He had found Charlik a hard master during the time he had lived on the island; for although both he and the boy were well treated in some respects, the savage and avaricious chief kept him constantly at work, and Brandon was beginning to weary of his existence.

Just as the trade wind began to whiten the tops of the long, sweeping ocean rollers, the new boat built by the king's white man slid out from the wooded shores of Lêla, and, under a great mat sail, sped down the coast towards the native village called Utwé.

Seated beside Brandon was the grim-faced Charlik, who was in high good humour at the speed shown by the boat, and promised to build him a new house within a few weeks. For nearly two hours the boat spun southward along the line of thundering breakers on the eastern shore, till Brandon hauled to the wind and ran inside the narrow passage to Utwé Harbour. And there, right before them, lay at anchor the very frigate he had so narrowly escaped at the Bonins!

Before the astonished king could prevent him the deserter had run the boat ashore on a shelving patch of reef, and seizing his boy in his arms, sprang out and made for the shore.

He would escape yet, he thought, as he sprang from ledge to ledge of coral rock, until he gained the beach. In the thick forest jungle he would at least be safe from pursuit by the ship's people.

Taking the boy by the hand, he set out at a run past the line of native houses which dotted the beach, and to all inquiries as to his haste he made no answer. Suddenly, as he turned into a path that led mountain-wards, he found his way blocked by an officer and a party of blue-jackets.

"Halt!" cried the officer, covering him with a fowling-piece. "Who are you, and why are you running like this?"

"That is my business, sir," he said. Then the officer sprang at him.

"Surrender, you villain! I know you—you are one of the men we want."

He turned like lightning, and, with the boy in his arms, sped back again towards the beach in the hope of getting a canoe and gaining the opposite shore of the island. But his pursuers were gaining on him fast, and when the beach was reached at last he turned and faced them, for every canoe was gone.

The officer motioned to his men to stand back.

"Brandon, there is no chance for you. Do not add another crime to that which you have already committed."

"No, sir; no. I shall do no more harm to any one in the King's service, but I will never be taken alive."

He pressed the muzzle of his pistol to his heart, pulled the trigger, and fell dead at their feet.

OXLEY, THE PRIVATEERSMAN

I

All day long the *Indiana*, Tom de Wolfs island trading brig, had tried to make Tucopia Island, an isolated spot between Vanikoro and the New Hebrides, but the strong westerly current was too much for her with such a failing breeze; and Packenham, the skipper, had agreed with Denison, his supercargo, to let Tucopia "slide" till the brig was coming south again from the Marshalls.

"Poor old Oxley won't like seeing us keep away," said Denison. "I promised him that we would be sure to give him a call this time on our way up. Poor old chap! I wish we could send him a case of grog ashore to cheer him up. But a thirty miles' pull dead to windward and against such a current is rather too much of a job even for a boat's crew of natives."

But about midnight the breeze freshened from the eastward, and by daylight the smooth, shapely cone of the green little island stood up clear and sharply defined from its surrounding narrow belt of palm-covered shore in a sunlit sea of sparkling blue, and Denison told the captain to get the boat ready.

"Ten miles or so isn't much—we can sail there and back in the boat."

Tucopia was a long way out of the *Indiana's*, usual cruising ground; but a year or so before a French barque had gone ashore there, and Denison had bought the wreck from her captain on behalf of Mr. Tom De Wolf. And as he had no white man on board to spare, he had handed his purchase over to the care of Oxley, the one European on the island.

"Strip her, Jack, and then set a light to her hull—there's a lot of good metal bolts in it. You shall have half of whatever we get out of the sale of her gear."

And so old Jack Oxley, who had settled on Tucopia because forty-five years before he had married a Tucopian girl, when he was a wandering boat-steerer in the colonial whaling fleet, and was now too shaky to go to sea, shook Denison's hand gratefully, and was well satisfied at the prospect of making a few hundred pounds so easily.

A quiet, blue-eyed, white-haired, stooping old man with a soft voice and pleasant smile, he had bade Denison goodbye and said with his tremulous laugh, "Don't be surprised if when you come back you find my old hull has broken up before that of the wreck. Eighty-seven is a good age, Mr. Denison. However, I'll take things easy. I'll let some of my boys" (his "boys" were sons of over forty years of age) "do all the bullocking{*} part of the work."

A colonial expression denoting heavy labour—i.e., to work like bullocks in a team.

When Denison reached the landing-place he was met by a number of the old whaler's whitey-brown descendants, who told him that Jack was dead—had died three months ago, they said. And there was a letter for the supercargo and captain, they added, which the old man had written when he knew he was dying. Denison took the letter and read it at once.

"Dear Mr. Denison,—Tom and Sam will give you all particulars about the gear and metal from the wreck.... You asked me one day if I would write you something about the privateer I sailed in, and some of the fights in which I was engaged. You and Captain Packenham might like to read it some day when time hangs heavy. Sam will give you the yarn.... Goodbye. I fear we shall not meet again.—Yours very truly, John Oxley."

A few days later, as the *Indiana* was sailing northward from Tucopia, Denison took out old Oxley's yarn. It was written in a round schoolboy hand on the blank pages of a venerable account-book.

"Old as I am now I have never forgotten the exultant feeling that filled my bosom one dull gray morning in February, 1805, when I, John Oxley, put my weak hands to the capstan bars to help weigh anchor on board the *Port-au-Prince* at Gravesend, and the strange, wild thrill that tingled my boyish blood at the rough, merry chorus of the seamen while the anchor came underfoot and the hands sprang aloft to make sail. For I was country-born and country-bred, and though even in our little town of Aylesbury, where my father was a farmer, we were used to hearing tales of the sea and to the sight of those who had fought the king's battles by land and sea, I had never until that morning caught sight of the ocean.

"Two weeks before I, foolish lad that I was, had been enticed by two village comrades into a poaching venture, and although I took no actual part therein—being only stationed as a watch on the outskirts of Colstone Wood—I was seized by two of Sir John Latham's keepers and taken away to the county gaol. I will not here attempt to describe the days of misery and shame that followed, and the grief and anguish of my parents; for although Sir John and the other county magistrates before whom I was brought believed my tale when I weepingly told them that I had no intention of poaching (and, indeed, I did not actually know that my two companions were bent upon so dangerous an enterprise) and my punishment was but light, yet the disgrace was too much for me to bear. So ere the sting of the whipping I received had died away I had made up my mind to run away to London and get some honest employment, and trust to time for my father's forgiveness. My sister Judith—Heaven bless her loving heart—to whom alone I made known my purpose, sought with tender words and endearing caresses to overcome my resolution; but, finding her pleading was of no avail, she made heart to dry her tears, and, giving me half a guinea, which a month before had been given to her by Lady Latham, she folded me in her arms, and, kissing me a last goodbye, as I stood with her at midnight behind my father's barn, bade me God speed.

"'Goodbye, John,' she whispered, ''twill surely break mother's heart, I fear, when she knows you have gone.'

"So, whispering back a promise that I would find some one in London to write to her for me and tell her how I fared, I gently took poor Judith's loving arms from around my neck, and ran as hard as I could across the field into the high road; for every moment my courage was failing me, and when I reached a hedge and lay down to rest awhile, my mother's face rose before me, and I thought I heard her tender voice crying, 'My boy, my boy! Has he gone without a last kiss from me?' Twice did I rise up with tears running down my cheeks and resolve to go back and at least receive her farewell kiss and blessing, but my boyish pride came to my aid, and with a choking sob I lay down again and waited for the morning.

"It took me some days to reach London, for it is a long journey from Aylesbury, and then for nearly a week I endured much hardship and misery, for my starved and dejected appearance was such that no one would give me employment of any sort, and my half-guinea became exhausted in buying food. But weak and wretched as I was, my courage to go on in the course I had taken was still unshaken; and, although it was a bitter winter, and I all but perished with the cold, I managed to always obtain some sort of shelter at night-time.

"I do not know, even now, in what part of London those my first wanderings led me; but at last, one morning, weak, footsore, and faint from hunger I came in sight of the shipping on the Thames, and for the moment forgot my woes in the strangeness of the sight. Seating myself on a great log of mahogany that some strange-looking, black-whiskered seaman had just rolled up from a ship lying in the dock, I remained gazing in a sort of dulled amazement at the bustle and, to my mind, confusion that seemed to prevail around me.

"For nearly half an hour I remained thus watching the hurrying to and fro of those about me; for there was an Indiaman just about to leave the dock, and many hundreds of people had come down to bid farewell to those on board, among whom were about a hundred or so of soldiers. Hungry and weary as I felt, the sight of these soldiers, and the inspiriting sounds of drum and fife music played upon the quarter-deck of the Indiaman, made me stand upon the log so that I might obtain a better view. Just then I heard a voice beside me exclaim—

"'Well, my lad, I suppose you would like to be one of them, with a red coat on your back and a musket on your shoulder, eh?'

"The suddenness of the address nearly caused me to fall off the log, and the speaker put out his hand to save me. He was an old, white-haired gentleman of between sixty and seventy, and kindness and benevolence seemed to irradiate his countenance.

"'Indeed, sir, I should,' I answered as I slipped down off the log and made him a bow, as was my duty to such a gentleman, and trying to speak bravely, 'I should like to be a soldier, sir.'

"He looked at me for a moment, and then put his hand on my shoulder.

"'Who are you, my lad, and how came you-down among the docks? You are a country lad, I can see. Have you been dishonest, or done anything wrong?'

"There was so much kindliness in his tones as he asked me this that I could not tell him naught but the whole truth, and although his face was very grave at the finish, his kind manner did not change, as putting his hand in his pocket he pulled out his purse and gave me a guinea and urged me to return to my parents.

"'Nay, sir,' I said, and I began to cry as I spoke, 'I cannot return home, and with your pardon, sir, neither can I take this money,' and then my courage returning somewhat, I added; 'but I would like to get honest work, sir.'

"'Come with me, then,' said he, 'and I will see what can be done. But first you must have some food.'

"With that he bade me follow him, and in a few minutes we were opposite a coffee-house frequented by people engaged at the docks. Pushing me in front of him, he told the landlord of the place to give me all the food I could eat, and said he would return for me in the evening.

"'Certainly, Mr. Bent,' said the landlord, who, by the way he bowed and scraped, seemed to be much impressed by the condescension of the old gentleman in entering such a humble place, and then, bowing my kind friend out, he took me to a table and bade a young woman attendant give me a good meal.

"'You are in luck, my lad,' he said to me, 'for that is Mr. Robert Bent, one of the richest gentlemen in London, and a great shipowner.'

"I remained at the coffee-house all day, and in the evening a hackney coach drove up, and the old gentleman, accompanied by a younger man of very commanding presence, came into the room where I was seated anxiously awaiting him.

"'Well, my lad,' said he, 'here you are. Now, I must tell you that I know Sir John Latham well, and, indeed, have just left him, for he is now in London. He has confirmed your story to me, and says that your father is a good, honest man, who, although he loves you very much, would rather that you did not return to Aylesbury with the memory of your disgrace still fresh in his mind. So this is what I now offer you. This gentleman here is Captain Duck, the master of a ship of mine which is leaving Gravesend in a day or two for the South Seas. He is willing to take you with him and try to make a man and a seaman of you. What do you say to it?'

"What else could I say but thank him warmly for his kindness, and promise I would try hard to do my duty and win my father's forgiveness?

"'Very good,' said he; 'and now I will leave you in the care of Captain Duck. He will buy you all that is necessary for the voyage, and I shall write to your father by Sir John Latham and tell him you are well bestowed with my good friend here. So goodbye, my lad, and do your duty like a man.'

"Then he shook my hand, and turning to his companion said —

"'Goodbye, Duck. Remember that whales as well as prizes must be sought after you double Cape Horn, and that I rely upon your good judgment not to engage an enemy's ship if you think she is better armed than the *Port-au-Prince*. But if you meet my other ship, the *Lucy*, and with her can take away some rich prizes from the Spaniards—why, well and good. I should be very pleased if you send me a prize home before you go into the Pacific.'

"So away he went in the coach, and in half an hour more, with my heart bounding with excitement, I set out with Captain Duck to join the *Port-au-Prince*, lying at Gravesend."

II

"For the first week or so I was very sea-sick and unable to leave my hammock, but after that I began to recover. Captain Duck, who was a most humane and considerate gentleman, sent frequent inquiries after me, and told the officers that I was to be allowed plenty of time to gain my strength. These inquiries were always made by a lad who was under the captain's immediate protection. His name was William Mariner, and being of an adventurous disposition he had gained his parents' consent to make the voyage. Of all those that sailed with us he and I only survived to reach England and tell the story of that fateful venture, and I have heard that Mr. Mariner wrote a book giving an account of the awful calamity that befel our ship, but that few people credited the strange story of his adventures.{*}

This was "Mariner's Tonga Islands," published by John Murray, Albemarle Street, London, in 1818. Seventeen of the privateer's crew escaped the massacre.

"Before going any further I will tell in a few words the nature of our mission to such far-off seas. The *Port-au-Prince* had a double commission. She was what was termed a private ship-of-war, or privateer, and England being then at war with Spain, she had been fitted out to cruise within certain latitudes in the Atlantic for prizes. If not very successful she was to double Cape Horn and proceed to the South Seas in search of whales, unless she met the *Lucy*, when they were to try the coast of South America for prizes. She was very well armed, and her crew were all men who had seen much service in the king's ships; many of them were old South-Seamen, expert in the whale-fishery. There was, besides Captain Duck, a regular whaling-master, William Brown. This gentleman was of a very quarrelsome temper, and long before we were out of the Channel began to show it, greatly to our misery. Captain Duck, on the other hand, was always very good to the men. He was a brave and gallant seaman, very stern and exacting when duty demanded it, but always full of good feeling and humanity to those under his command. He had formerly commanded a privateer in the Mediterranean, and had taken many rich prizes, and his owner, who thought very highly of him, had fitted out the *Port-au-Prince*, specially for him to command.

"In about a month I was looked upon as being quite a smart boy, and Captain Duck would often smile encouragingly at me, and to show his appreciation of my good conduct permitted young Mr. Mariner, who was a brave and handsome lad, to bring me into his cabin occasionally, and instruct me in reading and writing.

"We had a very stormy passage to the River Plate, where we began to look out for prizes, but without success; so, after waiting off the coast many weeks, and seeing nothing but two large ships of war, which were too heavily armed for us to engage, we stood southward to double Cape Horn. This was accomplished on the 18th of June, and three days later we sailed northward into the Pacific.

"Ten days after doubling the Cape we fell in with a South Sea whaler—I think her name was the *Vincent*, Captain Patrick Joy—and on that day there came about a collision between Captain Duck and Mr. Brown, the whaling-master. 'Twas this quarrel, arising out of the obstinacy and pride of Mr. Brown, which caused our future dreadful disaster, as will be seen later on. The *Vincent* signalled that she wanted us to send a boat; and highly pleased I was when young Mr. Mariner spoke to the gunner and asked leave for me to go in the boat with himself and Captain Duck. As soon as we got on board our captain was taken below by the master of the ship, but only remained a few minutes. When he returned on deck he seemed much pleased, and, ordering us back into the boat, was just about to descend himself when a harpooner belonging to the *Vincent* begged permission to speak to him.

"'Why, Turner, is it you, indeed?' and Captain Duck shook the man's hand warmly, and asked him how he had fared since he had last seen him.

"'Well, sir, I thank you,' answered the harpooner; 'but will you have me on board your ship, sir? You know me well, sir, and Captain Joy says he is willing to let me go and serve under my old captain again. Indeed, sir,' he added, 'I have it set in my mind that I shall again have the honour to board some more Spanish prizes with you; and I would rather kill a murdering Spaniard or Portugal than a honest whale. I am with you, sir, heart and soul, and will be proud to serve under you again; and Captain Joy won't stand in my way.'

"This being corroborated by Mr. Joy, Captain Duck told the man to put his things into the boat, and in a few minutes we were rowing back to the *Port-au-Prince*. Presently I heard our captain telling young Mr. Mariner that he had heard from Captain Joy that there were two Spanish ships lying at Conception, and he had resolved to go thither and cut them out— especially as one had thirty-three thousand dollars on board. As soon as we were on board, the harpooner from the *Vincent* told us that the news about the two ships was correct, and that we would have no trouble in cutting them out; for he knew the place well, and there were no guns mounted there. He also told us something about himself, which I here set down as showing his adventurous nature.

"Five years before he had sailed from London in a South Seaman, the *Sweet Dolly*, which had made a very successful voyage, for the ship was filled with whale oil in less than a year. The *Sweet Dolly*, on her return to England, fell in with the *Vincent*, and Turner, giving her captain instructions to pay certain money to his sweetheart, who lived in Bristol, shipped on board the *Vincent*. She, too, was very successful, and was going home a full ship when she met the *Port-au-Prince*. 'And now, lads,' said he to us, 'I will make another haul, for we are sure to take these two ships at Conception, and more besides; and I shall take my lass to church in a carriage.' Little did he know how soon he was to meet his fate!

"And now as to the quarrel I have spoken of between our good captain and Mr. Brown, the whaling-master. It seems that as soon as the matter of the two Spanish ships at Conception was mentioned to Mr. Brown he became very obstinate—and then, with many intemperate expressions and oaths, flatly refused to give up the good prospects of a whaling voyage for the sake of capturing a dozen prizes. Upon this Captain Duck reminded him that he, being only whaling-master, had nought to do with the matter; that it was his duty to aid in making the voyage a success, but that if they failed to get any prizes in the course of a month or so, then he (Captain Duck) would make all possible haste to get upon the whaling ground. Instead of receiving this in a sensible manner, Mr. Brown only became the more rude, and the upshot of it was that Captain Duck lost his temper, and, seizing a cutlass, presented it at Mr. Brown's breast.

"'Go to your cabin, sir, and remain there,' he said. 'I will deal quickly with the man who dares use mutinous language to me.' And then he ordered Mr. Tobias Williams, our officer of marines, to keep Mr. Brown in close custody. He seemed very much excited and angry—and very justly so; but half an hour afterwards, when Mr. Brown sent for him to express his sorrow for his rudeness, he forgave him most readily, and drank wine with him, saying that 'twas a pity that two shipmates should quarrel when in but a little time one might lose the number of his mess by a Spanish bullet.

"A week later we arrived off Quinquina, an island in Conception Bay, and anchored at nightfall. About midnight the boats were manned and armed, and proceeded towards Conception, pulling with muffled oars. I was in the boat with Mr. James Parker, the first lieutenant, who had with him twenty-six seamen and marines. The other boats were commanded by

Mr. Brown, the whaling-master, Mr. Williams, the officer of marines, and Mr. Peter Russel, the second lieutenant. The night was dark, but calm, which latter was unfortunate, as the *Port-au-Prince* could not follow the boats and cover the cutting-out party, as had been intended by Captain Duck. After an hour's rowing we got up unobserved to the first ship, and Mr. Parker, followed by Turner and the rest of his boat's crew, succeeded in getting on board and capturing the crew without alarming the other ships, which lay about a quarter of a mile away. After cutting her cables she was taken in tow by Mr. Russel's boat, and the other three set out for the second ship. We had just got within half a cable's length of her when Turner, again assuring Mr. Parker that there were no batteries on shore, took out one of his pistols to look at the priming. He was steering at the time, and by some woeful mishap the pistol went off.

"'Never mind, lads,' said Mr. Parker; 'I'll lay you alongside in another minute or two.' And with that we gave a cheer and bent to the oars.

"But before we had gone a hundred yards we knew that we were discovered from the shore, for two batteries immediately opened out upon us. However, we soon got aboard and captured the ship; but we were so close to the batteries that by the time we had cut her cables the ship was hulled in twenty places. Some of us were then sent back to the boats to tow her out of fire. I was in the boat with Turner, who was cheering the men to greater exertions in towing, when I heard a dreadful sound and felt something splash over me that I knew was not salt water, and saw Turner fall upon his face. Almost at the same moment another heavy shot struck the boat amidships at the water-line, and she at once began to fill, but the other boat came alongside and picked us up, including poor Turner.

"Finding that the calm still continued, and that many of our party were wounded, Mr. Parker called to us in the boat to come round on the port side, where the remaining boat was lying.

"'We'll stick to her a bit yet,' he called out, and then he sent some of our men up aloft to loose and set some sails. As soon as this was done he ordered every one back into the boats, and went to the helm himself, telling us that if a breeze sprang up and the sails wanted trimming he would call for us to come up again.

"All this time the ship was being hulled repeatedly, and we were in great concern—not for ourselves, as we were now all but out of danger—but for our gallant Mr. Parker, who seemed bent on getting away with the prize. The first thing we did after our boat was under shelter was to get a light and look at poor Turner; and the sight was a terrible one to me. The shot had carried away his lower jaw, his left arm as far as the elbow (for he was stooping when he looked at the priming of his pistol), and his right hand. The fleshy part of his thigh was also gone. The poor fellow could not do more than mutely look his dreadful anguish, and yet I could see he was perfectly conscious of all that was going on around him.

"For nearly a quarter of an hour we continued like this, feeling every shot that struck the ship. Every now and then one of us would clamber up the side to see after Mr. Parker, who would angrily order him back to his boat. At last Mr. Cresswell, our gunner, called out that the prize was sinking, and we saw that she was beginning to feel the effect of the water that was pouring into her, for she had been struck in many places between wind and water. At the same time Mr. Parker called out for four hands to come on deck as he had found the treasure, which was in the main cabin, packed in boxes. These were quickly taken out and placed in the boats, and then Mr. Parker liberated the crew of the prize, and ordered them into one of her boats to save themselves. We then shoved off and pulled after the first prize, but were met by Mr. Russel, who had had to abandon her on account of the calm and the close fire of another battery.

"'Never mind,' said Mr. Parker, with a laugh, 'if we can't bring them to Captain Duck the Spaniards won't get further use of them. I have set fire to mine.'

"'And I to mine,' said Mr. Russel.

"So this was our first engagement, and little did I relish it. We got back to the *Port-au-Prince* at daylight, and just as we came alongside we saw the first of the prizes blow up. Our first care was to lift the mutilated but still breathing body of poor Turner carefully on deck. Unable to utter more than a dreadful groaning sound, his eyes seemed filled with a longing to speak to Captain Duck, who bent over him with a pitying face.

"'Poor fellow,' said the captain to Mr. Russel, 'he wants to say something and cannot.' Then bending over him again, he asked him if the order he had on board in his (Captain Duck's) care was to be sent to Bristol. A feeble nod of the head was his answer, and in a few minutes he was gone. I was glad to learn afterwards that when he joined the *Port-au-Prince* he had an order on the owners of the *Vincent* for quite a large sum of money, and this he had given to Captain Duck, telling him that he wished it to be sent to a young woman named Mary Agnew, whose address in Bristol he wrote on the back and whom he had hoped to marry when he returned from this last voyage. Our captain afterwards sent the order home by the *Clinton*, South Seaman. (I learned afterwards from Mr. Bent that the poor woman received it safely.)

"On the following day we sailed into Conception Bay to give the batteries a taste of our metal. We went close in and then hove in stays and sent four or five shots right into the battery, but their guns were too heavy for us to do more, and with two men wounded we stood out of range again. After this we disguised the ship like an American, and went boldly into Coquimbo Roads. Here we were boarded by a party of gaily dressed gentlemen who came to trade with the supposed American. They brought with them nearly $3,000, and were deeply mortified to learn that the ship was an English privateer and they were our prisoners. One of them, however—Don Mario—took the matter very jocosely, and ate and drank and made merry, telling Mr. Mariner and Captain Duck that his entertainment was well paid for. Later on in the day more merchants came off, carrying much money, all of which they surrendered. Meanwhile four boats, well manned and armed, had gone ashore and captured some warehouses about a mile from the town. From these we obtained a great quantity of wine and some pigs of copper. Finding that the town was too well defended to be taken, we ransomed our prisoners, and Captain Duck having presented Don Mario with a cheese, in token of the good temper he had shown under his misfortune, we set sail again.

"It would take too long to tell of all that befel us during the next ten weeks or so, except that we harried every Spanish settlement along the coast, fired at every fort we saw, and took many prizes. As we were too shorthanded to man these, we took out all their stores, arms, and powder, and sank them right under the guns of a Spanish frigate at Arica, firing at her meanwhile with much merriment. While we were thus engaged a boat came alongside with six Englishmen in her. She belonged to the *Minerva*, a London South Seaman, bound to Port Jackson, and those in her were Captain Obed Cottle, his first and second mates, and three seamen. The remainder of the *Minerva's* crew, they stated, had mutinied, and after some bloodshed had permitted these six to leave in one of the boats. When they left the *Minerva* the mutineers ran up a black flag and announced their intention of turning the ship into a pirate. Captain Duck made them welcome, and they proved useful additions to our ship's company.

"On the 20th of September we fell in with our looked-for consort the *Lucy*, privateer of London, Captain Ferguson, belonging to the same owner as did the *Port-au-Prince*, and this gentleman and our good captain agreed to go shares in such plunder as the ships got in company. The following day, therefore, we anchored off Chinca and took that place, but were but poorly rewarded, as there were only two hundred dollars in the Governor's house. However, there was some excellent wine, of which we took twenty hogsheads on board, and we told the Governor to keep his money.

"And now comes the story of our fight with a very big ship, of which I have so often told you, Mr. Denison. On the 6th of October, the *Lucy* being-ahead (and both our ships off Paita), she took a king's tender laden with provisions, so the prisoners told Captain Ferguson, for the Spanish frigate *Astraea* then lying at anchor in Paita Roads. It had been our intent to capture the town, but the frigate's presence there put that out of the question for the time being. But we were willing to fight her outside, away from the batteries, and word to that effect was sent ashore, challenging her to come out and tackle us. She carried sixty guns, and was commanded by a Frenchman of great bravery. As soon as he received Captain Duck's challenge he got under way, and sailed out to meet the *Lucy* and *Port-au-Prince*. In half an hour we commenced a close action with the Spanish ship, and almost at the first shot I was stunned by a splinter which nearly put out my left eye. But young Mr. Mariner told me all that followed after I was carried below.

"The frigate's decks were crowded with men, for in addition to the ship's company she had on board nearly three hundred soldiers, who kept up a continuous but ineffective musketry fire. They and the Spanish sailors cursed us continually as they fired, and our crew returned the compliment, for many of our men could swear very well in Spanish. After fighting us for about an hour she bore up for the land, we sticking close to her and meaning to board; but at two o'clock our mizzen topmast was shot away, and falling athwart of our mainyard prevented us from bracing about. Then before we could get clear of this, the Spaniard came to the wind and sent a broadside that shot away our mizzen and main topmast and fore topsail yards, and played sad havoc with our braces and bowlines. In this condition, and being now almost under the guns of the forts, we had to discontinue the fight, and with the *Lucy*, haul off. The *Astraea*, too, had suffered much, and was glad to get back into Paita as quick as she could. We had several men badly wounded, among whom was our captain; and one poor boy, named Tommy Leach, was cut in halves by grape-shot. We made a second attempt to capture her two days later, but were again beaten off.

"Next morning Mr. Brown and Captain Duck had more angry words. And then two parties began to form, one in favour of whaling, and the other in favour of taking prizes. However, Captain Duck said he would go first to the Galapagos and refit before anything else was done. We anchored at James Island on the 16th, and found there three ships, the *Britannia* and *British Tar* of London, and the American ship *Neutrality*. From Captain Folger, of the *Neutrality*, which had just arrived from Paita, we learnt that the *Astraea* had had her fore-topmast shot away, thirty hands killed, and one hundred and twenty wounded. Monsieur de Vaudrieul, her commander, told Captain Folger that his cowardly Spanish officers wished him to strike before he fired the last broadside at our ship, and only that we could not board him he would have done so.

"We returned to the coast after this, and captured many prizes. One of these, the Spanish brig *Santa Isidora* was placed in charge of Mr. Parker, who, with ten hands, was ordered to take her to Port Jackson. Then the same week—the *Lucy* having parted company with us—we took the corbeta *Santa Anna*. She was a fine, new vessel and a fast sailer, and well armed. She had a prize crew put on board under the command of a gentleman adventurer of our company, Mr. Chas. Maclaren, who was ordered to follow Mr. Parker's prize to Port Jackson. Whether they ever reached this place I cannot say. I know I never heard of the corbeta again, but did hear that the *Santa Isidora* was captured by the natives of the Paumotu Islands and all hands massacred.

"During the time that we lay at the Galapagos, our kind and brave captain continued to get worse from his wound (he had been struck by a falling spar during an engagement with the *Astraea*, which had injured him internally), and at last it was evident to us all that his days were numbered. And then, too, his ardent and courageous spirit fretted greatly because of some news we had heard from the *O'Caen*, an armed American whaler, which on the 7th of August anchored near us. This was that a Spanish sloop-of-war was at anchor at a little port on the mainland, only a few days' sail from our anchorage. She was on her way to Callao from the northern ports of North America and Mexico, and carried tribute from the different Governors on those coasts. Much of this tribute was in furs, sealskins, and other valuable commodities, and she also had on board 170,000 dollars in money. Her crew were all very sick, and she was leaking badly, having been ashore at San Diego. The captain of this vessel had sent for assistance to Acapulco by a small trading vessel, and the master of the *O'Caen* said we could take her easily. She would have proved a rich prize to us, and our captain fretted greatly at his illness, for he was quite unable to do more than speak in a whisper.

"Four days afterwards I was sent to watch by his bedside by the gunner, and scarcely had I seated myself by him when he put his hand on mine, and I saw he was trying to speak. I was about to leave him to call assistance, but he held my hand with his dying strength.

"'John,' he said, in a little, thin voice, 'quick, listen to me.... Tell Mr. Brown... make for the Spanish sloop. But I fear he is a shuffler.... but... a rich prize..., God bless you, my lad.'

"And with this the grip of his hand relaxed, and his eyes closed in death. For some minutes I permitted my tears to flow uninterruptedly, then went on deck and reported our dear captain's end to the gunner, as well as his last words. Mr. Brown was then on shore, but soon came off; and that evening our worthy and lamented commander was borne to his lonely grave on the island, amid tears of unfeigned grief by every one present.

"At daylight next morning Mr. Brown, upon whom the command now devolved, ordered us with very unwarrantable and harsh language to get the ship ready for sea.

"'Sir,' said the gunner, 'to-day is Sunday, and the men are not yet over the loss of the captain.'

"But this only brought forth a very violent explosion from Mr. Brown, who called him a mutineer, and added that he intended to sail that day for the whaling ground; that the Spanish sloop might rot at her moorings for all he cared; and finally that he was master now, and would brook no interference.

"So amid the gloomy looks and muttered discontent of the men the anchor was weighed, and the *Port-au-Prince* stood out of the harbour to meet with her final and terrible disaster."

III

"It was on Saturday, the 20th of November, 1806, that we anchored at one of the Haapai Islands, in the Tonga Group, or as people now call them, the Friendly Islands. The town was named Lifuka, and it was a very beautiful place to look at, for the houses of the natives were embowered in palm groves of the loveliest verdure, and a very white beach ran from one end of the island to the other.

"Our voyage from the Galapagos had in no wise been a fortunate one; for we had taken but two whales, and the crew were in a highly mutinous state. Our new captain had grossly insulted the officer of marines from the first, and said that he and his men were a set of lazy, skulking dogs. Now ours had always been a very happy ship's company when Captain Duck was alive, and the marines we had on board had become as good seamen as any other of our people, so that this speech rankled deeply in their minds and bore bitter fruit, as will presently be shown.

"No sooner had we dropped anchor than a great number of natives came on board. They were an extraordinarily fine built race, and, indeed, although we had some very big and powerful men in the ship's company, no one of them was anything like in stature and haughty carriage to these naked, brown-skinned savages. Mr. Brown invited some of the chiefs into the cabin, and, with young Mr. Mariner, entertained them. Although they knew he was the commander they paid him little deference, but seemed to be greatly taken with Mr. Mariner, embracing him with every demonstration of affection, as if he were some long lost friend.

"In a few hours their numbers had increased to such an extent that one of our crew, a native of the Sandwich Islands (who had joined the ship at the Galapagos) ventured to tell Mr. Brown that he thought they had hostile intentions. He had, he said, heard them use the word *mate*, which in his islands meant to kill; and this and other expressions which much resembled those used in his own country led him to think that some mischief was intended. Instead of listening to poor Hula—for so he was named—Mr. Brown ordered him on deck, and threatened to flog him, so that the poor fellow came back quite dejected.

"'Jack,' said he to me—I was a favourite of his—'Captain he fool. You get cutlass and pistol and keep close alongside Hula. I think Kanaka men want to take ship and kill all white man.'

"I was, indeed, by this time quite terrified at the number of savages on board, and made haste to obey the poor man's warning; whereupon Mr. Brown, who just then came on deck, swore violently at me for a fool, and ordered me to lay aside my arms. 'The natives,' said he, 'mean us no harm, and I will not affront them by letting any of you timid fools carry arms in their presence.'

"The following day was Sunday, and the crew came aft in a body, and asked permission for half of the ship's company to go ashore. To this request Mr. Brown refused to accede, called them lazy, mutinous dogs, and swore he would flog the first man who attempted to leave the ship. No sooner had he said this than one Jim Kelly, the ship's armourer, stepped out in front, and brandishing a Mexican dagger swore he would run it through the first man that sought to stay him. His example was followed by William Clay, Jabez Martin, David Jones, William Baker, James Hoag, and Tom Woods, the carpenter, who, drawing their cutlasses, said they would stand to him. Then twelve others followed, and with defiant exclamations went over the side into canoes, many of them taking their clothes with them.

"In the meantime there came on board a young native chief of immense stature, named Vaka-ta-Bula, who inquired for Mr. Mariner. He seemed very pleased to see the young gentleman, and petted and fondled him as the other natives had done previously. This apparent friendliness seemed to quite overcome all sense of danger in Mr. Brown's mind; for, to the fear of the rest of the officers and crew, he ordered all our axes, boarding-pikes, cutlasses, and firearms to be taken below, and then signified his intention of accompanying Vaka-ta-Bula on shore to the native village. However, at the earnest entreaty of Mr. Dixon, the second in command, he consented to put off his visit till the following morning.

"At nine o'clock in the morning I was sent aloft by the sailmaker to help unbend the foretopsail, which was to be repaired, and looking down saw the decks were rapidly filling with natives. Mr. Brown had already gone ashore with the chief Vaka-ta-Bula, Mr. Mariner was in the cabin writing, and the rest of the officers were engaged in various work on deck. Just then I saw Mr. Dixon jump up on one of the carron-ades, and make signs to the natives that no more were to come on board. Suddenly, a tall native, who stood behind him, dashed out his brains with a club; and then in an instant a dreadful cry resounded through the ship, and all those of her crew on deck were attacked and savagely slaughtered. Horrified at the terrible butchery

I saw going on below, I thought at first to leap overboard and attempt to swim to the shore, but before I could collect my thoughts I was seized by several natives and dragged to the deck.

"Just then—so I was afterwards told—young Mr. Mariner came on deck, and, seeing that every soul of the ship's company on deck lay wallowing in their blood, ran down-the scuttle into the gunroom, where, with the cooper, he rapidly devised some means or escape from the general slaughter. But the hideous yells and dreadful clamour of the savages as they rushed below to seek out and murder those of the crew still alive so appalled them that they fled to the magazine, and resolved to blow up the ship rather than meet with such a fate.

"Fired with this resolution, Mr. Mariner ran back to the gunroom for a flint and steel, but before he could secure those articles he was seized by a number of savages; and at that moment I was also dragged down into the cabin, where the first sight that met our eyes was Vaka-ta-Bula, holding Captain Duck's bloodstained sword in his hand. He was surrounded by many other chiefs and, greatly to our relief, he went up to Mr. Mariner and embraced him. Then, in broken English, he said that Mr. Brown and many of those who had gone on shore were already killed; that now that he had possession of the ship he was satisfied, and was inclined to spare those on board who yet remained alive. Then he asked us how many were left.

"'Three,' said the young gentleman, pointing to himself, the cooper, and myself.

"'Good,' said Vaka-ta-Bula, handing the bloodied sword to a native; 'three no too many.' Then he told us we must follow him ashore, and motioned us to go on deck.

"A very shocking sight there met our view. Upon the quarter-deck lay twenty-five bodies, all perfectly naked, and placed closely together side by side. Only one or two could we recognise, for the poor fellows' heads had been battered out of all human semblance by blows from the heavy native clubs, and from their still warm bodies ran a dreadful stream of red that flooded the quarter-deck and poured along the covering-board to the deck below. But even worse than this was the appearance of a short, squat old native whose head was covered with what had a few minutes before been snow-white hair, but was now dyed deep with the life-blood of our unfortunate companions.

"Over his left shoulder was thrown poor Mr. Dixon's jacket, and his frightful appearance was increased by his being—save for this one garment—absolutely naked, and holding across his huge and ensanguined thighs a heavy ironwood club, bespattered with blood and brains. So terrifying an object was he that we could scarce believe him human till he opened his horrid mouth, and with a dreadful laugh pointed to the mutilated bodies of our shipmates. I saw no more then, for I swooned.

"When I came to I found myself in a house in the village, but my companions were not visible; and, indeed, I never saw them again, for I was taken away the next day to another island, where, although I was kindly treated, I remained a prisoner for two long weary months, knowing nothing of what befell those of my shipmates who had been spared from the general massacre.

"About ten weeks afterwards, when the shock of that dreadful slaughter which I had witnessed had somewhat worn off, I began to take an interest in my surroundings. My first object was to try and learn something about young Mr. Mariner; but the natives seemed to evade my inquiries, and at first would tell me nothing. But after a time the chief with whom I lived, whose name was Fatafehe, told me that Finau, the native king who had planned and carried out the cutting off of the *Port-au-Prince* had taken a great liking to the young gentleman, who was now high in favour with him and the *matabuli* or leading men. And later on I was told that thirteen of my surviving comrades had taken service with Finau, and were then engaged with him in preparing for an expedition intended to conquer the large neighbouring island of Tongatabu. Seven of the privateer's carronades and two eighteen-pounder guns which formed part of the armament were worked by the thirteen Englishmen; and about seven months afterwards I heard that at the storming of Nukualofa, the great fortress on Tonga-tabu, Finau achieved a great victory, and made much of his white artillerymen, giving them houses and land and wives, and making them of equal rank with his *matubuliu*. The tale of the terrible slaughter at the taking of this fort was something dreadful even to hear, and yet I have heard that young Mariner said in his book that Finau was by no means a bloodthirsty man. I can only speak of the man as I heard of him—but Mr. Mariner, who lived with him for some three or four years, no doubt knew this savage chieftain well, and was competent to speak as he did of him.

"For ten months I lived with the chief Fatafehe in the Haapai Group, and then from there I was removed to the larger island of Vavau. Here I spent a year before I could make my escape, which by a kind Providence I was at last enabled to effect by swimming off on board the ship *Chalice*, of Nantucket, as she lay at anchor in Niafu Harbour.

"Her captain treated me very kindly, and put me on the ship's books, and then, Mr. Denison, began my career as a whaleman.

"It was quite another year ere I succeeded in reaching England, where I made haste to tell my story to Mr. Robert Bent; but he had already heard of the disaster that had overtaken his ship. He behaved very generously to me, and gave me twenty guineas to carry me home to my native place, and told me—as I still desired to follow a seaman's life—to come to him when I wanted a ship.

"My parents and my dear sister Judith had for about six months mourned me as dead, and ours was truly a happy and wonderful reunion, and the first night I spent at home we all knelt down together and thanked God for my deliverance.

"Mr. Mariner, I am glad to say, escaped from those dreadful islands three years later, and reached England in safety. And so I come to the end of this tale of a very strange and calamitous voyage, brought about mainly through the obstinacy of the whaling-master of the *Port-au-Prince*."

"And now, Mr. Denison and Captain Packenham, as I think we shall never meet again, I want you to be good to my boys, Tom and Sam, and warn them both against the drink. It is kind, generous gentlemen like you who, meaning no harm, send so many half-caste lads to hell."

THE ESCAPEE

One hot, steaming morning, a young man, named Harry Monk, was riding along a desolate stretch of seashore on the coast of North Queensland, looking for strayed cattle. He had slept, the previous evening, on the grassy summit of a headland which overlooked the surrounding low-lying country for many miles, and at dawn had been awakened by the lowing of cattle at no great distance from his lonely camping-place, and knew that he would probably discover the beasts he sought somewhere along the banks of a tidal creek five miles distant. Although the sun was not yet high the heat was intense, and his horse, even at a walking pace, was already bathed in sweat. The country to his right was grim, brown, forbidding, and treeless, save for an occasional clump of sandal-wood, and devoid of animal life except the ever-hovering crows and a wandering fish-eagle or two. To the left lay the long, long line of dark, coarse-sanded beach, upon which the surf broke with violence as the waves sped shoreward from the Great Barrier Reef, five leagues away.

The track along which the man was riding was soft and spongy sand, permeated with crab-holes; and at last, taking pity on his labouring horse, he dismounted, and led him. Half a mile distant, and right ahead, a grey sandstone bluff rose sheer from the water's edge to a height of fifty feet, its sides clothed with verdure of a sickly green. At the back of this headland, Monk knew that he would find water in some native wells, and could spell for an hour or so before starting on his quest along the banks of the tidal creek.

It was with a feeling of intense relief that he at last gained the bluff, and led his sweltering horse under an acacia-tree, which afforded them both a welcome shade from the still-increasing heat of the tropic sun. Here for ten minutes he rested. Then, taking off the saddle, Monk took his horse through the scrub towards the native wells, after first satisfying himself that there were no natives about, for the wild blacks upon that part of the coast of North Queensland were savage and treacherous cannibals, and he knew full well the danger he was running in thus venturing out alone so far from the station of which he was overseer. As yet, he had seen neither the tracks by day nor the fires by night of any myalls (wild blacks), but for all that he was very cautious; and so as he emerged from the scrub, holding his bridle and carrying his billy-can, he kept his Winchester rifle ready, for above the native wells were a mass of rugged sandstone boulders, thrown together in the wildest confusion and covered with straggling vines and creepers—just the sort of place to hide the black, snaky bodies of crouching niggers, waiting to launch their murderous spears into the white man as he stooped to drink. For a minute or so he stood and watched the boulders keenly, then he dropped his rifle with a laugh and stroked his horse's nose.

"What a fool I am, Euchre! As if you wouldn't have smelt a myall long before I could even see him! Stand there, old boy, and you'll soon have a drink."

He soon clambered down to the bottom of the ravine, and found to his joy that two of the three wells contained water, sweet, pure, and limpid. After satisfying his own thirst he thrice filled his billy-can and gave his patient horse a drink, then, leaving him to crop the scanty herbage that grew about the wells, he climbed to the top of the bluff and sat down to rest under a lofty ledge of rock.

Taking out his pipe and tobacco he began to smoke. Below him the surf beat unceasingly against the base of the bluff and sent long swirls of yellow foam high upon the desolate beach beyond.

An hour had passed, and then, rising and descending to the wells, he filled his canvas water-bag. Then, giving Euchre another drink, he saddled up again and led him through the scrub to the summit of the bluff. Here for a moment he stood to enjoy the first breaths of the sea breeze which had sprung up during his rest, and to scan the coast to the southward, which was rather high and well-wooded. Suddenly he uttered an exclamation of astonishment, and, springing into his saddle, rode down the steep descent at a breakneck pace—a white man was running for his life along the beach towards the bluff, pursued by six blacks. Un-slinging his Winchester as he galloped over the sand he gave a loud cry of encouragement to the man. But neither the man nor his pursuers heard it. Dropping his reins, but urging his horse along with the spur, Monk levelled his rifle at the foremost native, fired, and missed, and then he saw the white man fall on his hands and knees with a spear sticking in his back. But ere the black had time to poise another spear the overseer's rifle cracked again and the savage spun round and fell, and the other five at once sprang towards the short thick scrub that lined the beach at high-water mark. Then Monk, steadying himself in the saddle, set his teeth and fired again and again, and two of the naked ebony figures went down upon the sand.

"The other four won't trouble me any more," he muttered, as he rode back to the wounded man; "and I'm no native police-officer to shoot black fellows for the pleasure of it, though I'd like to revenge poor Cotter and his murdered children "—a settler and his family had been murdered a few weeks previously.

The wounded man was lying on his left side, unable to rise, and Monk, jumping off his horse, saw that the long, slender spear had gone clean through his right shoulder, the sharp point protruding in front for quite a foot.

The man was breathing hard in his agony, and Monk, before attempting to draw the spear, placed the nozzle of his water-bag to his lips. He drank eagerly, and then said—

"Now, comrade, pull the cursed thing out."

Taking a firm grip around the shaft of the weapon, the overseer succeeded in drawing it, and then began to staunch the flow of blood by plugging the holes with strips of his handkerchief, when the man stayed his hand, and said calmly—

"Let it bleed awhile, my friend; it will do good. So; that will do. Ah, you are a brave fellow!"

Supported on Monk's arm, the stranger, who was a powerfully-built, black-bearded man, dressed in garments which were a marvel of rags and patches, walked slowly with him to the foot of the bluff and sat down under the shade of a tree.

"My good friend," he said, with a smile, "you were just in time. Now, tell me, what are you going to do with me?"

"Carry you up this bluff, and then put you on my horse and take you to Willeroo Station as soon as the heat of the sun has passed. 'Tis only thirty miles."

He shook his head. "I was never on the back of a horse in my life, and I am weak. I have not had food for nearly two days, and no water since last night. Ah, heaven! give me that water-bag again."

He drank deeply, and Monk pondered as to what had best be done. He soon made up his mind. He would carry him to the top of the bluff, leave him food and water and his Winchester, and then ride as hard as he could to the station for assistance. But, to his astonishment, the man implored him not to do so.

"See, my friend. You have saved my life and I am grateful. But I shall be doubly grateful to you if you do not bring assistance—I want none. This spear-wound—bah! it is nothing. But I do want food."

His words, few as they were, rang with earnest entreaty, and then it flashed through Monk's brain who the man was. He was Kellerman, the notorious escapee from New Caledonia, for whom the North Queensland police had been seeking for the past six months, after his breaking out of Cooktown gaol. For the moment Monk said nothing; but, with sudden sympathy, he lit his pipe and handed it to his companion. "Take a smoke, old man, and we'll see presently what is best to be done."

The story of Kellerman's escape from that hell upon earth, the prison of He Nou, in New Caledonia, was well known to Monk, and had filled him with pity, for the man before him was the only survivor of a party of five escapees who had landed at Cape Flattery; the others were killed and eaten by the blacks. Kellerman, who was a man of powerful physique, had succeeded in reaching a beche-de-mer station on the coast, where for six or eight months he worked steadily and made a little money. From there he went to a newly-discovered alluvial goldfield north of Cooktown with a prospecting party, who all spoke well of him as "a plucky, energetic fellow, and a good mate." Then, one day, two mounted troopers rode into camp; and Kellerman, with despair in his eyes, was taken in handcuffs to Cooktown. He was at once identified by a French warder from Noumea, and was placed in prison to await transhipment to the terrors of Noumea again. On the third night he escaped, swam the alligator-infested Endeavour River, and hid in the dense coastal scrubs. What horrors the man had gone through since then Monk could well imagine as he looked at his gaunt frame and hollow, starved-like eyes. The overseer made up his mind.

Carelessly picking up his rifle he strolled over to where his horse was standing, and placed the weapon on the ground. Then he came back, and, sitting on a rock in front of the convict, he leant his chin on his hand and looked him in the face.

"I'll tell you what I will do," he said quietly, "I shall take you to a place on the top of this bluff, make you a damper and a billy of tea, give you my blanket, and stay with you till daylight. Then I shall ride to Willeroo Station and return early the next morning with more provisions and some clothing and a razor—your beard is too long. And perhaps, too, I can get you a horse and saddle. Then, as soon as you are better, you can travel towards New South Wales. You speak English well, and New South Wales is the best place for you."

The Frenchman sprang to his feet, his face blanched to a deathly white, and his limbs trembled.

"Why do you — — who are you? Ah, my God — you know me!"

"Yes, I know you; sit down. You are Kellerman, but I will not betray you."

"You will not betray me?"

The anguished ring in his voice went to the overseer's heart, and rising he placed his hand on the convict's arm. "Sit down. I will give you a proof that I harbour no evil intentions to you." Then he walked away to where his Winchester lay, picked it up, and returning placed it in the convict's hands.

"In that rifle there are left twelve cartridges. I have thirty more in my saddle-pouch. They and the rifle are yours to defend yourself from the blacks on your way down the coast. If you use it against white men you will be a murderer."

Kellerman clutched the weapon convulsively for a moment, and his eyes flashed. Then he thought a moment.

"I promise you that I will not use it against a white man — even to save myself."

In less than an hour Monk had fixed the wounded man comfortably under the overhanging ledge of rock, boiled him some tea, and made him a damper, of which he ate ravenously. His wound troubled him but little, and as he lay on the overseer's blanket he talked freely of his past life. His earlier life had been spent in England and America. Then came the Franco-German war, and from America he had returned to France to take part in the struggle, and when the dark days of the Commune fell upon Paris, Kellerman was one of its warmest adherents, and paid the penalty with worse than death — he was sentenced to transportation for life. His only relatives were a brother and a sister, both of whom were little more than children when he was transported.

Monk listened with deep interest, and then bade him try and sleep. The Frenchman at once laid his head upon his pillow of leaves and was soon slumbering. At dawn Monk rose and saddled his horse; then, making some fresh tea, he was about to bid his companion goodbye till the following morning when Kellerman asked him if he had a pencil and paper with him.

The overseer pulled out an old pocket-book which he used when out mustering cattle to note down the brands of any strange cattle on Willeroo run.

"Before you go, my friend, I want you to write down something in that book," said the convict. "Do you know a little creek about fifteen miles from here?"

"Yes, I do; there is a lot of heavy timber on it, pretty fer up."

"Exactly. Now, there is gold in the headwaters of that creek, and it has not yet been prospected by anybody, except myself. And if I had had a dish with me I could have washed out ten, twenty, aye, thirty ounces a day. It is easy to get. I lived on the headwaters of that creek for six weeks. Then the water dried up, but still I got gold. But thirst drove me away, and knowing these native wells were here I made up my mind to come and camp on this hill till rain fell; and, but for you, I would now be being eaten in a blacks' camp. Now, write as I tell you. You must work that creek, my friend, and send me some share of all the gold you get. If I am dead you must seek out my brother and sister. No, no; to-morrow may never come; write now."

Then he gave Monk explicit directions as to the locality of a particularly rich "pocket," which the overseer wrote carefully down.

The sun had just risen when Monk, bidding the convict goodbye, turned to lead his horse down the hill. Suddenly he stopped, and, walking back, he carefully put out the fire.

"You need have no fear from blacks," he said, "but there is a detachment of native police at Willa Willa, thirty-five miles from here, inland. Possibly they *may* be out on patrol now, and if so, might come to the wells to water their horses. Therefore it is best to take precautions, though you are safe out of sight up here."

"Thanks, my good friend," said the Frenchman, with a sigh, as he laid his head upon his pillow again.

Once more filling his water-bag at the wells, the overseer mounted, and, pushing through the scrub, soon emerged upon the open beach, and struck into a canter. Suddenly he pulled up sharply—a number of horse tracks were visible on the hard, dark sand, just above water-mark, and leading round the back of the bluff. Turning his horse's head he followed cautiously.

"It must be Jackson and his black troopers," he muttered; "and, by heavens, they have gone through the back scrub to get to the top of the bluff!"

For some minutes he hesitated as to the best course to pursue, when suddenly he heard a voice from the summit above him, "Surrender in the Queen's name!" There was a moment's silence, then he heard a laugh.

"*Peste!* I could shoot you all if I cared to, Mr. Officer, but, being a fool, I will not break a promise to a friend." Then the sharp crack of a rifle rang out.

Spurring his horse through the scrub, Monk dashed over the rough ground and up the hill. In front of the cave were a sub-inspector of black police, a white sergeant, and eight black troopers. They were looking at Kellerman, who lay on the ground with a bullet through his heart—dead.

"Confound the fellow!" grumbled the sergeant; "if I'd ha' known he meant to play us a trick like that I'd ha' rushed in on him. I wonder how he managed it? I could only see his head."

"Leant on the muzzle and touched the trigger with his naked toe, you fool!" replied his superior officer, sharply.

Twelve months afterward Monk left North Queensland a rich man, and went to Europe, and spent quite a time in France, prosecuting certain inquiries. When he returned to Australia he brought with him a French wife; and all that his Australian lady friends could discover about her was that her maiden name was Kellerman.

EMA, THE HALF-BLOOD

I

For nearly ten miles on each side of old Jack Swain's trading station on Drummond's Island,{*} the beach trended away in a sweeping curve, unbroken in its monotony except where some dark specks on the bright yellow sand denoted the canoes of a little native village, carried down to the beach in readiness for the evening's flying-fish catching.

* One of the lately annexed Gilbert Group in the South Pacific.*

Perhaps of all the thousands of islands that stud the bosom of the North Pacific, from the Paumotus to the Pelews, the Kingsmill and Gilbert Islands are the most uninviting and monotonous in appearance.

The long, endless lines of palms, stretching from one end of an island to the other, present no change or variation in their appearance till, as is often the case, the narrow belt of land on which they so luxuriously thrive becomes, perhaps, but fifty yards in width, and the thick matted undergrowth of creepers that prevail in the wider parts of the island gives place to a barren expanse of wind-swept sand, which yet, however, supports some scattered thousand-rooted palms against the sweeping gusts from the westward in the rainy season, and the steady strain of the southeast trades for the rest of the year.

In such spots as these, where the wild surf on the windward side of the island sometimes leaps over the short, black reef, shelving out abruptly from the shore, and sweeps through the scanty groves of palm and pandanus trees, and, in a frothy, roaring flood, pours across the narrow landbelt into the smooth waters of the lagoon, a permanent channel is made, dry at low water, but running with a swift current when the tide is at flood.

Within an hour's walk from the old trader's house there were many such places, for although Drummond's Island—or Taputeauea, as its wild people call it—is full forty miles in length, it is for the most part so narrow that one

176 | Rodman The Boatsteerer

can, in a few minutes, walk across from the ceaseless roar and tumult of the surf on the ocean reef to the smooth, sandy inner beach of the lagoon.

Unlike other islands of the group, Drummond's is not circular in its formation, but is merely a long, narrow palm-clad strip of sand, protected from the sea on its leeward side, not by land, but by a continuous sweep of reef, contracted to the shore at the northern end, and widening out to a distance of ten or more miles at its southern extremity. Within this reef the water is placid as a mill-pond.

The day had been very hot, and as the fierce yellow sun blazed westward into the tumbling blue of the sailless ocean, a girl came out from the thick undergrowth fringing the weather-bank of the island, and, walking quietly over the loose slabs of coral covering the shore, made her way towards a narrow channel through which the flowing tide was swiftly sweeping.

Just where the incoming swell of the foaming little breakers from the outer reef plashed up against the sides of the rocky channel, stood a huge coral boulder, and here the girl stopped, and clambering up its rough and jagged face sat down and began to roll a cigarette.

The name of the girl was Ema. She was the half-caste daughter of the old trader. She had come to bathe, but meant to wait awhile and see if some of the native girls from the nearest village, who might be passing along to her father's store, to buy goods or sell native produce, would join her. So, lighting her cigarette with a piece of burning coconut husk that she brought with, her, she spread the towel she carried upon the rock and waited, looking sometimes at the opposite side of the channel to where the path from the village led, and sometimes out to sea.

Somewhat short in stature, the old trader's daughter looked younger than she was, for she was about twenty—and twenty is an age in those tropic climes which puts a girl a long way out of girlhood.

No one would ever say that little Ema Swain was beautiful. She certainly was not. Her freckled face and large mouth "put her out of court," as Captain Peters would sometimes say to his mate. (Captain Peters frequently came to Drummond's, and he and Etna's father would get drunk on such occasions with uniform regularity.) But wait till you spoke to her, and then let her eyes meet yours, and you would forget all about the big mouth and the freckles; and when she smiled it was with such an innocent sweetness that made a man somehow turn away with a feeling in his heart that no coarse passion had ever ruffled her gentle bosom.

And her eyes. Ah! so different from those of most Polynesian half-blooded girls. Theirs, indeed, in most cases, are beautiful eyes; but there is ever in them a bold and daring challenge to a man they like that gives the pall of monotony to the brightness of a glance.

Nearly every white man who had ever seen Ema and heard the magical tones of her voice, or her sweet innocent laugh, was fascinated when she turned upon him those soft orbs that, beneath the long dark lashes, looked like diamonds floating in fluid crystal.

I said "nearly every white man," for sometimes men came to Jack Swain's house whose talk and manner, and unmistakable looks at her, made the girl's slight figure quiver and tremble with fear, and she would hide herself away in another room lest her father and brother might guess the terror that filled her tender bosom. For white-headed Jack was a passionate old fellow, and would have quickly invited any one who tried to harm the girl "to come outside"; Jim, her black-haired, morose and silent brother, would have driven a knife between the offender's ribs.

But the girl's merry, loving disposition would never let her tell her brother nor her father how she dreaded these visits of some of the rough traders from the other islands of the group to the house. Besides that, neither of them noticed Ema; for Jim always got as drunk as his father on such occasions of island harmony and foregathering of kindred spirits.

So for the past ten years the girl had grown up amongst these savage surroundings—a fierce, turbulent, native race, delighting in deeds of bloodshed, and only tolerating the presence of her father among them because of his fair dealing and indomitable courage. In those far back, olden days, when the low sandy islands of the Equatorial Pacific were almost unknown (save to the few wandering white men who had cast their lives among their wild and ferocious inhabitants, and the crews of the American whaling fleet), no one but such a man as he would have dared to dwell alone among the intractable and warlike people of Drummond's Island.

But old Swain had lived for nearly forty years among the islands of the South Seas, roaming from one end of the Pacific to the other, and his bold nature was not one to be daunted. There was money to be made in those times in the oil trade; yet sometimes, when he lay upon his couch smoking his pipe, some vague idea would flit through his mind of going back to the world again and ending his days in civilisation.

But with the coming morning such thoughts would vanish. How could he, a man of sixty, he thought, give up the life he had led for forty years, and take to the ways of white men in some great city? And then there were

Jim and Ema. Why, they would be worse off than he, poor things. Neither of them could read or write; no more could he—but then he knew something of the ways of white people, and they didn't. What would they do if he took them to the States, and he died there? No! it wouldn't do. They would all stay together. Jim would look after Em if he died. Yes, Jim would. He was a good boy, and very fond of Em. A good boy! Yes, of course he was, although he was a bit excitable when he came across any grog. He hadn't always been like that, though. Perhaps he learnt it aboard that man-o'-war.

And then the old trader, as he lay back on his rough couch, watching the curling smoke wreaths from his pipe ascend to the thatched roof, recalled to memory one day six years before, when the American cruiser *Saginaw* had anchored off the village of Utiroa, where Swain then lived, and a group of the officers from the war-ship had stood talking to him on the beach.

Beside him were his son and daughter; the boy staring curiously, but not rudely, at the uniformed officers, the girl, timid and shrinking, holding her father's hand.

"How old is your son?" the commander of the cruiser had asked him kindly; "and why don't you let him see something of the world? Such a fine young lad as he ought not to waste his life down here among these God-forsaken lagoons." And before the trader could frame a reply the boy had stepped out and answered for himself.

"I wan' to go away, sir. I has been two or three voyages in a whaler, sir, but I would like to go in a man-o'-war."

The grey-bearded captain laughed good-naturedly, but the kindly light in his eyes deepened as the girl, with an alarmed look, took her brother by the hand and sought to draw him back.

"Well, we'll talk about it presently, my lad. I don't think this little sister of yours would thank me for taking you away."

And, half an hour afterwards, as the rest of the officers strolled about the native village, the captain and old Jack did talk the matter over, and the end of it was that the stalwart young half-caste was entered on the ship's books, and at sunset Ema and her father saw the cruiser spread her canvas, and then sail away to the westward.

In five years or so Jim would be free to return home again, unless he preferred to remain in the service altogether.

Three years passed, and then, one day, a Hawaiian trading schooner swept round the north end of the island, her white sails bellying out to the lusty trades. A boat was lowered and pulled ashore, and the first man that jumped out of her on to the beach was Jim Swain.

Half-way between his father's house and the beach the old man met him.

"Well, I be darned! Why, Jim, what hez brought you back?"

"Got tired of it, dad," he answered, in his quiet way, but without meeting his father's eye. And then he added, "The fac' is, dad, I bolted from the *Saginaw* at Valparaiso. Now, don' ask me no more 'bout it."

"Right you are, my boy," said the trader, placidly; "but you'll have to get out o' the way if another cruiser comes along. But that isn't likely to happen for many a year. Come along and see Em. She'll jes' go dancin' mad when she sees you."

For the next twelve months the father and daughter lived at Utiroa, and Jim voyaged to and fro among the islands of the group, returning every few months, and again sailing away on a fresh cruise; but never once had the old man asked him any further questions as to his reasons for deserting from the *Saginaw*. But Em, gentle-hearted Em, knew.

One bright morning there came in sight a lofty-sparred ship, with snow-white canvas, sailing at a distance of two miles from the shore along the reef, from the south end of the island, and Ema Swain rousing her brother from his mid-day slumber, with terror in her eyes, pointed seaward.

Taking his father's glass from the bracket on the wall in the sitting-room, the half-caste walked out of the house to a spot where he could obtain a clear view of the ship. For a minute or so he gazed steadily, then lowered the glass.

"A man-o'-war, Em, right enough; but I don' think she's an American. I'll wait a bit until she gets closer."

"No, no, Jim! What you run such risk for? You go, Jim." And then, in her trembling fear, their mother's tongue came to her aid, and the agitated girl dragged him back into the house, imploring him in the native language to yield to her wishes.

In another two hours they were sailing down the lagoon in the old trader's whaleboat towards a place of safety, for Utiroa was, they knew, the only spot where a man-of-war would anchor.

But long before they reached the village for which they were bound they saw the great ship slowly change her course and bear away to the westward, and leave the low, sandy island astern.

A long, steady look at her told the sailor eye of Jim Swain that he had nothing to fear, even had she kept on and anchored at Utiroa.

"All right, Em," he said, with a low laugh, "we had no need to be scared; she's a Britisher. That's the *Tagus*. I see her 'bout a year ago at Samoa." And then he hauled the boat to the wind and beat back to his father's place.

And so time went by, and the haunting fear of discovery that for the first year or so after his return to the island had so often made the young half-caste start up in his sleep with a wild alarm in his heart when the cry of "Te Kaibuke!"{*} resounded from village to village, slowly died away.

* "*A ship!*"

II

Nearly an hour had passed since the girl had left her father's house, and now, as the sun dipped into the ocean, the flowing tide swept through the narrow channel in little waves of seething foam, and Ema, with one last look at the path on the opposite side, descended to the beach, and throwing off her loose bodice of blue print and her short skirt, tied around her waist a native waist-girdle of yellow grass, and stepped into the cold waters of the channel.

For some few minutes she laved herself, singing softly the while to herself as is customary with many Polynesian native women when bathing, when suddenly, through the humming drone of the beating surf on the windward reef, she heard the sound or voices.

"Ah!" she said to herself, "now I will wait and startle these girls from Tabeâue as they come along." And so she sank low down in the water, so that only her dark head showed above the surface.

But amid the sound of native voices she heard the unfamiliar tones of white men, and in an instant she sprang to the shore, and, seizing her clothes, fled to the shelter of the boulder.

In a minute she had dressed herself, and was peering out through the fast-gathering darkness at a group of figures she could just discern on the opposite side of the channel. They had halted, and the girl could hear the natives in the party discussing means as to getting the white men across, for the water was now deep, and the current was swirling through the narrow pass with great velocity.

There were in the party some eight or ten natives and nearly as many white men; and these latter, the girl could see, were in uniform, and carried arms; for presently one of them, who stood a little apart from the others, struck a light and lit a cheroot, and she caught the gleam of musket-barrels in the hands of those who were grouped in the rear.

Wondering how it came about that armed white men were searching through the island at such an hour, the girl was about to call out to the natives—some of whom she recognised—not to attempt the passage without a canoe, when she heard the sound of oars, and looking across the darkening waters of the lagoon she saw a boat, filled with men, pulling rapidly along in the direction of Utiroa.

When just abreast of the passage they ceased rowing, and a figure stood in the stern, and hailed the shore party.

"Are you there, Mr. Fenton?"

"Yes," answered the man who had struck the light. "Come in here, Adams, and take us across. There is a channel here, and though I guess it is not very deep, the current is running like a mill-race."

Still crouching behind the coral boulder the girl saw the boat row in to the shore, a little distance further down, so as to escape the swirling eddies of the passage.

As the man-o'-war cutter—for such was the boat—touched the rocks, a lantern was held up, and by its light the girl saw a short, stout man step out on to the beach and walk up to the officer in charge of the shore party.

"Ah, Adams, is that you? Well, this is a devil of a place. We have crossed at least half a dozen of these cursed gutters, and thought to have crossed this one too, without trouble, but the tide is coming in fast. However, it's the last one—at least so this infernal hang-dog looking native guide tells me. So the sooner we get across in the cutter and get this man-hunting business over the better I'll like it."

"Aye, aye, sir!" answered the man he had addressed as Adams. "It won't take us much longer, I guess. Not a canoe has passed us going down the coast, so we are pretty sure to catch him at home."

"That is what this truculent scoundrel says," and the officer nodded in the direction of a native who had seated himself on the ground only a few yards distant from the rock behind which the girl was hidden. "He tells me that young Swain came home about a week ago from Maiana"—another island of the group—"and the old man induced him to stay at home and help him rig a new boat he has just built."

"We'll catch him, sir," answered Adams, confidently.

Rodman The Boatsteerer | 183

Clutching the side of the rough boulder in an agony of terror, the girl saw the two men turn away, and, followed by the rest of the shore party, natives and all, walk down to the boat. Then, standing upright, she watched them get in and the cutter shove off.

That they were in search of her brother she was now only too certain, and dreading that the boat would land the shore party again on her side of the channel and she be discovered and prevented from giving the alarm, she sprang over the loose slabs of coral that strewed the shore between the water and the coconut palms, and fled along the night-enshrouded path towards her father's house.

Ere she had gained the level ground the clattering sound made by the displaced coral stones reached the ears of those in the boat, which was instantly headed for shore, and the officer, with eight or ten bluejackets, leapt out and, led by the native guides, followed in swift pursuit.

III

Within the trader's house the father and son sat smoking in silence, waiting for the girl's return. A coconut-oil lamp, placed in the centre of a table, showed that the evening meal was in readiness.

"Em's a powerful long time, Jim," said the old man, rising from his seat, and, going to the door, he looked through the serried vista of the palm trunks which showed white and ghostly in the darkness.

"Aye," said Jim, "she is. I'll give her a call."

Just beside the doorway lay a huge conch shell, such as is used by the people of the Equatorial islands either as a summons to assemble or a call to one person only, and the stalwart young half-caste, taking it up, placed the perforated end to his lips and blew a loud, booming note.

A wild clamour of alarm answered the call, and a swarm of noddies and terns, roosting in countless thousands among a thicket of pandanus palms near by, slid from their perches, and with frightened croak and flapping wing whirled and circled around the trader's house, then vanished in the darkness ere the echoes of the conch had died away.

"That'll bring her, Jim," said the old man, turning to the lamp and pricking up the wick with his knife.

Silent Jim nodded.

"Yes, she's comin' now. I can hear her runnin'."

They heard her footsteps over the dead palm branches which strewed the path, and in a few seconds more, with a gasping sob of terror, the girl sprang into the room and almost fell at her brother's feet as she clasped her arms around his neck.

"Ha!" and old Swain, seizing a loaded musket from a number that stood in a corner of the room, stepped to the door. "Jus' what I thought would happen one of these days. Some o' them flash native bucks from the south end has been frightenin' o' her. Quick, Em, who was it?"

For a moment or so the exhausted girl strove to speak in vain, but at last she found her voice.

"No, father, no. But Jim, Jim, it is you they want! Come, Jim, quick, quick! They very close now."

"What in thunder are you talkin' 'bout, Em? An' who wants Jim?" And then, turning to his son, he asked, "Have you been a-thumpin' any o' those south-end natives lately, Jim?"

"No, no," said the girl, rising to her feet, and endeavouring to speak calmly; "you don' know, father. But Jim must go, an' you an' me mus' stay here. Quick, quick, for God's sake, dear, go out at the back an' cross to the windwar' side. Plenty place there for you to hide, Jim, for two or tree day."

A savage light came into the half-caste's eyes, as with an abrupt yet tender gesture he placed his huge brown hand on his sister's curly head; then, without a word, he seized a musket and cutlass, and with a farewell wave of his hand to the wondering old man, opened the door at the back of the house and disappeared among the pandanus thicket.

Leaning his musket against the wall, the old man poured some water into a cup and, putting his arm round the trembling figure of the girl, placed it to her lips.

"Here, take a drink, Em, an' then tell me what all this here means. What's the boy been a doin', an' who's after him?"

With shaking fingers the girl raised the cup to her lips and drank; then, with terror-filled eyes, she placed her hand upon his knee.

"Listen."

"Thar's nothin' outside, Em. What in the worl' has scared ye so, gal?"

"Don' you ask now, father. I carn' tell you now. Jes' you listen; don' you hear people a comin'? Don' you hear people a talkin'?" she answered.

For half a minute they waited and listened, but no sound broke upon the stillness of the island night save the ceaseless hum of the surf, and the quick panting breaths of the girl.

"'Taint nothing, Em, on'y the surf a poundin' on the reef."

"P'raps they're all a comin' in the boat. Dad, there's a lot o' man-o'-war men comin' for Jim. I was bathin', and I heerd 'em talkin'. They'll kill him, dad, if they gets him. Niban, that native that Jim gave a beatin' to onst, was showin' 'em the way here—an' I runned and runned——"

A half-stifled shriek escaped her as she sprang to her feet.

There was a sudden rush of booted feet and the clank of steel. Then a voice rang out—

"Keep your men close up to the back of the house, Adams."

Forcing his trembling daughter down upon her seat, the trader, placing his pipe in his mouth, lit it, and advanced to the open door, to meet, face to face, an officer in the uniform of the American navy.

"Stand back, sir!" and the officer pointed a pistol at the trader's breast; but as the light of the lamp fell upon the old man's wrinkled features and snow-white hair, he lowered his weapon to his side.

"What might your business be, sir, and why are you and your men a-comin' inter my house at night time, an' pointin' a pistol at me?"

Then, still eyeing the officer, he stepped backward, and placed his arm protectingly around his daughter's shoulder.

"Stay outside till I call you, Williams," said the officer, turning to a leading seaman, who, with drawn cutlass, had followed him inside.

Then he came into the room.

"Who else have you here with you?" he began, when he stopped suddenly in his speech, and raised his cap. "This girl is your daughter, I suppose?"

"My daughter, sir. But what is your business, I ask again? What may you want here, anyway?"

The angry light in the old man's eyes, and the sharp tone of his voice, called the officer to his duty.

"I am sorry to be here, Mr. Swain; but be good enough to ask your daughter to leave us alone for a minute or two. My business is such that I can tell it better to you alone."

At a sign from her father the girl rose from her seat and reluctantly walked into her room. The officer watched her retreating figure disappear, then he turned sharply round on his heel.

"I am a lieutenant on the United States ship *Adirondack* and my business is to arrest a man named James Swain, a deserter from the *Saginaw* and a murderer as well."

Even in the dim light of the rude lamp the officer saw the rugged bronze of the old trader's face pale to a deathly whiteness, and he leant one hand upon the table to steady himself.

"That's a kinder surprise to me, sir. An' I doesn't believe it, nohow. A deserter my boy Jim might be; but I won't allow he's murdered any one. Maybe you mean he killed a man in a fair fight?"

Rodman The Boatsteerer | 187

"I cannot talk this over with you, old man. My orders are to arrest James Swain. He is here, I know; and although it is a painful duty for me to fulfil, you must stand aside and let that duty be done."

"You can look for him, sir; but I can tell you that you won't diskiver him here."

"We shall see about that." And the officer, walking to the door, called out, "Come in, Williams, and search the place. Use no violence, but if the man we want, or any other person in the house, resists, make short work of it."

With a dozen men at his heels, Williams entered the house, and the officer, taking his stand at the back door, leant against it, pistol in hand.

There were but three rooms in the trader's house—the sitting-room, which was also used as a sleeping room by the old man and his son; the trade room, or store; and Ema Swain's bedroom. The first two were at once entered and searched, and in a few minutes Williams, the boatswain's mate, reported that the man they sought for was not there.

"There is but one more room, sir," said old Swain, quietly, from his seat at the table. "Ema, come out, and let these men look in your room." And he glanced defiantly at the officer.

Calmly and quietly she walked into the front room, and, sitting down beside her father, looked on. But although she was outwardly so calm, the girl's heart was beating nigh to bursting, for she had overheard Williams tell one of the bluejackets that some of Adams' men had, long before the main body approached, formed a complete line of guards on both sides of the house, extending from the inner lagoon beach right across the island, which, at this place, was not a quarter of a mile in width. And the girl knew that at the unguarded open ends on either side there was no chance of concealment, for there the coast rose steep-to from the sea, and was bare of verdure.

Presently the boatswain, with two or three bluejackets, re-entered the room.

"There's no place in the girl's room, sir, where a man could hide. He must have cleared out, sir, long before we reached her. I guess that that noise we heard crossing the channel was made by him. I think he's just doubled on us and made down for the south end of the island."

Pressing her father's hand warningly, the girl fixed her dark, dreamy eyes on the officer and spoke.

"Yes, that true. My brother he ran away long time before boat come up. Some one been tell him that 'Merican man-o'-war anchor down at south end. So he run away."

The officer, with an exclamation of disgust, put his pistol back in his belt.

"That lying scoundrel of a native has just fooled us nicely, Williams. Sound a call for Adams and his men to come back, and let us get back to the cutter. We'll have to begin the search again to-morrow."

The boatswain's mate had just stepped outside and placed his whistle to his lips, when the thundering report of a heavy musket-shot echoed through the air. Then silence for a few seconds, followed by the sharper sounds of the rifles of the American bluejackets.

Before any one could stay her Ema Swain darted through the guard of blue-jackets at the door, and disappeared in the direction of the sound of firing; and almost immediately afterwards the officer and his party followed.

But ere Lieutenant Fenton and his men had advanced more than a hundred yards or so into the gloomy shadows of the palm-grove, he called a halt, as the sound of voices came through the gloom.

"Is that you, Adams?" he called.

"Yes, sir," answered a voice from a little distance; "we've got him; he ran right into us; but before we could catch him he shot the native guide through the body."

In a few minutes Adams's party joined that of the officer, and then in silence, with their prisoner in their midst, they marched back to the trader's house.

"Bring the prisoner inside, Adams," said Lieutenant Fenton, briefly.

With hands handcuffed behind his back and a seaman on each side, Jim Swain was marched inside his father's house. A bullet had ploughed through his left cheek, and he was bleeding profusely.

"Stand aside, old man," and the officer held up a warning hand to old Jack. "It is folly for you to attempt to interfere."

And then a blue-jacket, almost as old as the trader himself, placed himself between father and son.

Taking a paper from his pocket the officer read it to himself, glancing every now and then at the prisoner.

"He's the man, sure enough," he muttered. "Poor devil!" Then turning to the man Adams, he asked—"Are you absolutely certain that this is the man, Adams?"

"Certain, sir. That is the man who murdered the boatswain of the *Saginaw*. I took particular notice of him when I served in her, because of his colour and size, and his sulky temper."

"Jim," broke in the old man's voice, quaveringly, "you haven't murdered any one, hev' you?"

The half-caste raised his dark, lowering face and looked at his father, and for a moment or so he breathed heavily.

"Yes, dad. I killed th' man. We had a muss in Valparaiso, an' I knifed him."

Old Swain covered his face with his hands and sank into a seat, and then Lieutenant Fenton walked over to him and placed a kindly hand on his shoulder. Then he withdrew it quickly.

"I have a hard duty, Swain, and the sooner it is over the better. I am ordered to arrest your son, James Swain, for the crime of murder and for deserting from his ship. He will be taken to San Francisco. Whatever you wish to say to him, do so now. In another ten minutes we must be on our way to the ship, and there will be no further opportunity for you to see him."

"Aye, aye, sir," said the old man, huskily, and rising he walked slowly over to his manacled son, and put his trembling hand on his arm.

"You will excuse me, sir, if I talk to him in the native lingo."

Fenton nodded, motioned to the seamen who stood beside the prisoner to move away, and then walked to the further end of the room.

"Jim," said the old trader, quickly, speaking in the native language, "what's to be done? I have only got to send a native along the beach with the shell{*} and we shall have you away from these people in no time."

{*} *The conch shell.*

"No, no, father, even if every one of them was killed it would do no good. An' they would never let me be taken away from them alive. It is no use, father, to try that. But"—and here he bent his head forward—"if I could free my hands I would make a dash—and be shot. I swear I shall never be hanged. Father, where is Em? I would like to see her before I go."

"She runned away, boy," said the old man, brokenly, and speaking in English; "runned away, jes' as soon as she heerd the firin'. She went to look for you, Jim. Heaven help the gal, Jim, when she comes back an' finds you gone."

For a little while longer they talked, and then Lieutenant Fenton came toward them, and Adams, at a sign from his superior, took the old trader by the arm, and with rough kindness forced him away from his son.

Suddenly, however, he dashed the seaman aside and sprang toward his son, but, strong and active as he was, he was no match for a man like Adams, who threw his arms around him and held him in a vice-like grip.

"That will do, mister," said old Jack, quietly. "I reckon I give in. Th' boy has got to go—an' thet's all about it, an' I ain't agoin' to try an' stop you from takin' him."

And then as the blue-jackets closed around him, Jim Swain turned.

"Goodbye, dad, and say goodbye to Em for me."

"Poor old man!" said Fenton to himself, as the party marched along the narrow, sandy track. "Hang me, if I wouldn't be pleased to see the fellow escape."

The four men who were left in charge of the boat had sprung to their arms the moment they heard the sound of the firing, and for some time they scanned the dark outline of the shore with intense anxiety.

"I guess it's all right," said one of them at last. "I only heard three or four shots. Hullo! here they come along the beach. Shove in."

Tramp, tramp, along the hard sand the landing party marched, and a seaman in the boat, picking up a lantern, held it up to guide them.

Two hundred yards behind was Ema Swain, striving hard to catch up with them and see her brother for the last time in this world, she thought.

IV

"Lift him in carefully," said Lieutenant Fenton, as the boat's bows touched the beach; "he seems pretty weak."

"Thank you, sir!" and the prisoner turned his dark eyes upon the officer. "I am nearly dropping. I got a hard hit in the chest with a musket butt from one of your men, sir."

A couple of men lifted him in, and then as soon as the rest of his people had taken their places the lieutenant followed.

"Push off, Gates."

As the heavy boat slid out from the shore into the still waters of the lagoon, the lieutenant glanced down at the manacled figure of his prisoner.

"Let him sit up, Adams, and take the irons off. He can't lie there like a trussed fowl; and see if one of you can't stop that bleeding."

Adams bent down, and unlocking the handcuffs lifted him up.

Then, quick as thought, Jim Swain, dashing him aside, sprang overboard and dived towards the shore.

"Quick! Show a light," said the officer, standing up in the stern, pistol in hand, waiting for the man to rise.

A long narrow streak of light showed his figure not ten feet away from the beach. In another minute he would touch the shore.

"Stop!" cried the officer. "Swim another yard and you are a dead man."

But the half-caste kept steadily on. Again Fenton's warning cry rang out, then he slowly raised his pistol and fired.

The shot told, for as the half-caste rose to his feet he staggered. And then he sped up the steep beach towards the thick scrub beyond.

As he panted along with the blood streaming from a bullet wound in his side, his sister's hand seized him by the arm.

"Jim, Jim!" she gasped, "only a little more, and we———"

And then half a dozen muskets flashed, and the two figures went down together and lay motionless on the bloodied sand.

Fenton jumped ashore and looked at them. "Both dead," he said, pityingly, to old Swain, who with a number of natives now stood beside him.

"Aye, sir," said the trader, brokenly, "both. An' now let me be with my dead."

But neither Ema nor Jim Swain died, though both were sorely wounded; and a month later they with their father sailed away to Samoa.

LEASSÉ

There were only a score or so of houses in Leassé village—curious saddle-backed structures, with steeply pitched roofs of gray and yellow thatch, rising to a sharp point fore and aft; and in all the twenty not more than one hundred natives—men, women, and children—dwelt. At the back of the village the dense mountain forest began, and all day long one might hear the booming notes of the gray wood-pigeons and the shrill cries of the green and golden parrakeets as they fed upon the rich purple berries of the *masa'oi* and the inflorescence of the coco-palms. In front, and between two jutting headlands of coral rock, with sides a-green with climbing masses of *tupa* vine, lay a curving beach of creamy sand; westward the sea, pale green a mile from the shore, and deeply blue beyond the clamouring reef, whose misty spume for ever rose and fell the livelong day, and showed ghostly white at night.

It was at night time that young Denison, ex-supercargo of the wrecked brig *Leonora* first saw the place and took a huge liking to it. And the memories of the seven happy months he spent there remains with him still, though he has grown grizzled and respectable now and goes trading no more.

A white moon stood high in a cloudless sky when he bade farewell to the good-natured ruffian with whom, until two months previously, he had had the distinction of serving as supercargo. The village wherein Captain Bully Hayes and his motley rum-drinking crew had established themselves was six miles from Leassé, on the shores of the Utwé Harbour, at the bottom of which lay the once shapely *Leonora*, with her broken fore-topmast just showing above the water. For reasons that need not here be mentioned, Denison and the captain had quarrelled, and so the former was deeply touched and said goodbye with a husky throat when the burly skipper placed one of his two remaining bottles of gin in his hand and said he was a "damned young fool to take things up so hotly." So, without a further word, he swallowed the lump in his throat and stepped out quickly, fearing that some of the crew (none of whom knew of his going) might meet him ere he gained the beach and mingle their tears—for they all loved him well—with the precious bottle of gin.

For nearly an hour he walked along the sandy shore of a narrow and winding strip of low-lying land, separated from the high and wooded mainland by a slumbering lagoon, deep in parts but shallow at the south end where it joined the barrier reef. Here Denison crossed, for the tide had ebbed, and, gaining the shelving beach on the other side, he saw before him Mout Leassé village, standing out clearly in the blazing moonlight against the black edge of the mountain forest, which, higher up, was wrapped in fleecy mist. It was near to dawn, but, being tired and sleepy, the ex-supercargo lay down on the soft warm sand, away from the falling dew of the pendulous palm leaves, and slept till it came.

An hour after daylight he was in the village and being hugged and embraced by the inhabitants in general and Kusis, the headman, and his wife and daughter in particular. I have already mentioned that Denison was very young then; he would not permit such a thing now.

Still, although three-and-twenty years have passed since then, Denison often wishes he could live those seven months in Leassé over again, and let this, his latter-day respectability, go hang; because to men like him respectability means tradesmen's bills, and a deranged liver, and a feeling that he will die on a bed with his boots off, and be pawed about by shabby ghouls smelling of gin. There, it is true, he had no boots to die in had his time come suddenly, but he did not feel the loss of them except when he went hunting wild pigs with Kusis in the mountains. And though he had no boots, he was well off in more important things—to wit, ten pounds of negro-head tobacco, lots of fishing-tackle, a Winchester rifle and plenty of ammunition, a shirt and trousers of dungaree, heaps to eat and drink, and the light heart of a boy. What more could a young fool wish for—in the North-west Pacific. But I want to tell something of how Denison lived in a place where every prospect pleased, and where (from a theological point of view) only man was vile.

At daylight he would awaken, and, lying on his bed of mats upon the cane-work floor, listen to the song of the surf on the barrier reef a mile away. If it sounded quick and clear it meant no fishing in the blue water beyond, for the surf would be heavy and the current strong; if it but gently murmured, he and Kusis and a dozen other brown-skinned men (Denison was as brown as any of them) would eat a hurried meal of fish and baked taro, and then carry their red-painted canoes down to the water, and, paddling out through the passage in the reef, fish for bonito with thick rods of *pua* wood and baitless hooks of irridescent pearl shell.

Then, as the sun came out hot and strong and the trade wind flecked the ocean swell with white, they would head back for shining Leassé beach, on which the women and girls awaited their return, some with baskets in their hands to carry home the fish, and some with gourds of water which, as the fishermen bent their bodies low, they poured upon them to wash away the stains of salty spray.

An hour of rest has passed, and then a fat-faced, smiling girl (Denison dreams of her sometimes, even now) comes to the house to make a bowl of kava for the white man and Kusis before they go hunting the wild pig in the mountain forest. There is no ceremony about this kava-drinking as there is in conventional Samoa; fat-faced Sipi simply sits cross-legged upon the matted floor and pounds the green root with a rounded piece of jade upon a hollowed stone.

The kava is drunk, and then Kusis takes off his cumbrous girdle of grass and replaces it by a narrow band of closely-woven banana fibre, stained black and yellow (there be fashions in these parts of the world) and reaches down his pig-spear from the cross-beams overhead, while Tulpé, his wife, ties cinnet sandals upon the white man's feet. Then, good man and true, Kusis takes his pipe from his mouth and gives his wife a draw ere he goes, and the two men step outside upon the hot, gravelly path, Denison carrying his Winchester and Kusis leading two sad-faced mongrel dogs. As they pass along the village street other men join them, some carrying spears and some heavy muskets, and also leading more sad-faced dogs. Black-haired, oval-faced women and girls come to the doors of the houses and look indolently at the hunters, but they neither speak nor smile, for it is not the nature of the Strong's Islanders to speak when there is no necessity for words. Once, fifty years ago, when they were numbered by thousands, and their villages but a mile apart along the coast, it was different; now they are a broken and fast-vanishing race.

As the hunters, walking in single file, disappear into the deep jungle shades, the women and girls resume their daily tasks. Some, who squat upon the floor, with thighs and knees together and feet turned outward and backward, face curious little looms and weave girdles from the shining fibre of the banana stalk; others, who sit cross-legged, plait mats or hats of pandanus leaf for their men folk; while outside, in the cook-sheds, the younger children make ready the earthen ovens of red-hot stones to cook the sunset meal. Scarcely a word is spoken, though sometimes the women sing softly together as they weave and stitch.

And so another hour has gone, and the coco-palms along the shore begin to throw long lines of shadows across the sloping beach. Then far off a musket-shot sounds, and the women cease their work and listen for the yelping of the hunters' dogs as they rush at their wounded prey, battling fiercely for his life upon the thick carpet of forest leaves.

By and by the huntsmen come back, their brown skins dripping with sweat and their naked legs stained with the bright red clay of the sodden mountain-paths. Two of them carry slung on a pole a gaunt, razorbacked boar, with hideous yellow tusks curving backward from his long and blood-stained snout.

Again the patient women come forth with gourds of water; they pour it over the heads and bodies of the men, who dry their skins with shreds of white beaten bark; two sturdy boys light wisps of dry coconut leaves and pass the flames over the body of the boar in lieu of scalding, and the melancholy dogs sit around in a circle on their haunches and indulge in false hopes. Presently, one by one, the men follow Denison and Kusis into the latter's house and sit down to smoke and talk, while Sipi the Fat pounds more kava for them to drink. Then mats are unrolled and every one lies down; and as they sleep the sun touches the sea-rim, swarms of snowy gulls and sooty terns fly shoreward with lazily flapping wing to roost, a gleam of torchlight shows here and there along the village paths, and the island night has come.

THE TROUBLE WITH JINABAN

Palmer, one of Tom de Wolf's traders on the Matelotas

Lagoon in the Western Carolines, was standing at his door, smoking his pipe and wondering what was best to be done. Behind him, in the big sitting-room, were his wife and some other native women, conversing in low tones and looking shudderingly at a basket made of green coconut leaves which stood in the centre of the matted floor.

Presently the trader turned and motioned one of the women to come to him.

"Take it away and bury it," he said, "'tis an ill thing for my wife to see."

The woman, whose eyes were red with weeping, stooped and lifted the basket; and then a young native lad, nude to the waist, stepped quickly over to the place where it had lain and sprinkled a handful of white sand over a broad patch of red which stained the mat.

Palmer, still smoking thoughtfully, watched the rest of the women follow her who carried the basket away into the grove of breadfruit-trees, and then sat down upon a bench outside his door.

The sun was blazing hot, and on the broad, glassy expanse of the slumbering atoll a dim, misty haze, like the last vanishing vapours of a sea fog in some cold northern clime, hovered low down upon the water; for early in the day the trade wind had died away in faint, warm gusts, and left the island and the still lagoon to swelter under the fierce rays of an all but equatorial sun. Five miles away, on the western side of the reef-encircled lagoon, a long, low and densely-wooded islet stood out, its white, dazzling line of beach and verdant palms seeming to quiver and sway to and fro in the blinding glare of the bright sunlight. Beyond lay the wide sweep of the blue Pacific, whose gentle undulations scarce seemed to have strength enough to rise and lave the weed-clad face of the barrier reef which, for thirty miles, stretched east and west in an unbroken, sweeping curve.

In Ailap village, where the trader lived, a strange unusual silence brooded over all; and though under the cool shades of the groves of breadfruit and orange-trees groups of brown-skinned people were sitting together, they only spoke in whispered tones, and looked every now and again at the figure of the white man standing at his door.

And as the people sat together in silence, Palmer, with his bearded chin resting on the palm of one hand, gazed steadily before him, seeming oblivious of their presence, for he was thinking deeply, and wondering what had best be done to rid the island of Jinaban.

Presently a young man, dressed like a seaman and wearing a wide-rimmed hat of pandanus leaf, came along the path that led from the village to the trader's house. He stopped for a moment at the gate as if in doubt whether to open it or not; and then catching sight of Palmer's figure he pushed it open quickly and walked towards him, and the trader, roused by the sound of approaching footsteps, raised his head and looked in some surprise at the new-comer, who was an utter stranger to him.

"Good morning," said the man to Palmer, and the moment he had spoken and lifted his hat, the trader saw that he was not a white man, for his dark complexion, wavy black hair and deep-set eyes proclaimed him to be of mixed blood. Nearly six feet in height, he yet walked and moved with that particularly easy and graceful manner so noticeable among the native races of Polynesia, and Palmer was quick to see from his stature and appearance generally that he was not a Caroline Island half-caste. And he noticed as well that the stranger had a firm, square-set jaw and a fearful raw-looking slash across his face that extended from ear to chin.

"Good morning," he answered. "Do you want to see me?"

"Yes," answered the man, in a slow, hesitating sort of manner. "I was the second mate of that schooner "—and he waved his hand with a backward sweep toward the lagoon, where a large white-painted vessel was being towed down to the passage by her boats, to anchor and wait for the land-breeze at night—"but last night I had a row with the skipper. He called me a half-bred Maori nigger, an' so——"

"And so you had a fight?"

"Yes, sir, we had a fight. But he couldn't stand up to me for more than a couple of rounds; an' sang out for the mate an' carpenter to come and help him, an' the three of 'em went for me: They got me down at last, and then the mate gave me a slash across the face with his knife. So, as I didn't want to get killed, I jumped overboard and swam ashore. I've been hiding in the village since."

Palmer looked steadily into the man's immovable face, and then said—

"You want a stitch or two put in that cut. Come inside and I'll do it for you. Your skipper was here at daylight this morning looking for you. He told me quite a different story; said that you gave him 'lip' and then struck him."

The half-caste laughed quietly. "He lied, sir. He's a regular bully, and he and the mate knock the men about something terrible. But he made a mistake when he started on me and called me a nigger. And if he tries to bring me aboard of that floating hell again I'll kill him, as sure as my name is Frank Porter."

The trader's face lightened up. "Are you Frank Porter, the man who saved the *Marion Renny* from being cut-off in the Solomon Islands?"

"Yes," answered the half-caste, "I am the man."

Palmer extended his hand. "You're welcome to my house, Frank Porter. And there's no fear of the captain coming ashore again to look for you. Now come inside, and let me dress that ugly slash for you."

"Thank you, Mr. Palmer. But I did not come to you for that. I came to see if you can give me a berth of some sort on your station. I'm a pretty handy man at almost anything."

The trader thought a moment; then he looked up quickly. "I cannot give you anything to do on the station—there is nothing *to* do. But I will give you five hundred dollars and a home in my house if you will help me to do one thing."

"What is that?"

"Put a bullet into a man here who has murdered thirty people within ten years. I cannot do it alone, I have tried and failed, and these people cannot help me. Come inside, and I'll tell you all about it."

The half-caste followed Palmer into his sitting-room, and the trader, getting needles and silk thread from his wife, stitched up the wound in the man's face. Then he gave him a glass of whiskey, and as they smoked their pipes, told him the story of Jinaban, the Outlaw.

Two years before, when Palmer first landed on the white beach of Matelotas Lagoon to settle down as a trader for turtle-shell, Jinaban was one of the three chiefs who ruled over the cluster of palm-clad islets—the two others were his half-brothers, Jelik and Rao. All three had met the white man as soon as he landed, and he and they had exchanged gifts and vows of friendship after the manner of the people of Las Matelotas.

But Jinaban, who was a man of violent temper, was bitterly aggrieved when Palmer decided to build his house and trading station in the village ruled over by his half-brother Jelik. He had long been anxious to secure a white trader for his own village, and bitter words passed between Jelik and Raô and himself. Palmer stood by and said nothing. He had taken an instinctive dislike to Jinaban, whose reputation as a man of a cruel and sanguinary nature had been known to him long before he had come to settle in the Carolines. But Palmer was not a man to be daunted by Jinaban's fierce looks and the bitter epithets he applied to his half-brothers, whom he accused of "stealing" the white man from him. He quietly announced his intention of standing to the agreement he had made with Jelik; and the next day that chief's people set about building a house for the trader. In a month the house was finished, and Palmer, who meant to try the lagoon for pearl shell, and thought that his stay on the island would be a long one, announced his intention of taking a wife, and asked Jelik for a young girl named Letanë. She was about seventeen, and her gentle, amiable disposition had attracted him from the first day he landed on the island. Calling the girl to him, Jelik questioned her as to her inclinations, and she at once, in the most innocent and charming manner, expressed her liking for the white man, but said that her uncle Jinaban, who had gained some idea of her feelings towards Palmer, had threatened to kill her if she dared to marry him; for he (Jinaban) had determined that the people of Ailap—Jelik's village—should not monopolise him altogether, and that a wife should be chosen from his (Jinaban's) village.

Jelik's face instantly become grave. He knew the rancour of Jinaban's feelings towards him, and dreaded to incur his further hatred, and soon acquainted Palmer with his fears. The trader laughed at them, and said that he would be dictated to by no man as regarded his choice of a wife, and, drawing the smiling Letanë to him, told the chief to make all haste with the wedding feast. The news of this soon reached Jinaban, who soon after made his appearance at Palmer's house accompanied by many old men of his clan and a young and beautiful girl named Sépé. Trembling with suppressed rage and excitement, he addressed the trader with all the eloquence he could command. He was, he said (and with truth), the greatest of the three brothers in rank and influence, but had yielded to the white man's desire to live in Ailap under the protection of his brother Jelik; but neither he (Jinaban) nor his people would put up with the additional insult of the trader espousing an Ailap girl. And then, pointing to the girl who accompanied him—a handsome creature about eighteen or twenty years of age—he earnestly besought Palmer to make her his wife. Before the trader could frame a reply Letanë, accompanied by a number of her young girl friends, walked into the room, and, sitting down beside him, put her hand on his shoulder, and, though her slender form trembled, gave her uncle and the girl Sépé a look of bold defiance.

Palmer rose to his feet, and placed his hand on the head of the girl, who rose with him. "It cannot be, Jinaban. This girl Letanë, who is of thine own kin, shall be my wife. But let not ill-blood come of it between thee and me or between thee and her; for I desire to live in friendship with thee."

Without a word Jinaban sprang to his feet, and, with a glance of bitter hatred at the trader and the girl who stood beside him, he walked out of the house, accompanied by his old men and the rejected Sépé, who, as she turned away, looked scornfully at her rival and spat on the ground.

In a few weeks the marriage took place, and Palmer made the customary presents to his wife's relatives. To Jinaban—who refused to attend the feasting and dancing that accompanied the ceremony—he sent a new fishing-net one hundred fathoms in length, a very valuable and much-esteemed gift, for the cost of such an article was considerable. To Jelik, his wife's guardian, he gave a magazine rifle and five hundred cartridges, and to Raô, the other brother, presents of cloth, tobacco, and hatchets.

That night, whilst Palmer slept with his bride, Jinaban came to the house of his brother Jelik. His black eyes gleamed red with anger.

"What right hast thou, my younger brother, to take from the white man that which I coveted most? Am not I the greater chief, and thy master? Give me that gun."

Jelik sprang to his feet. "Nay, why shouldst thou covet my one gift from the white man? Is not the net he gave thee worth twenty such guns as the one he hath given me?"

Jinaban leapt at his brother's throat, and for a minute or two they struggled fiercely; then Jelik fell with a groan, for Jinaban stabbed him in the throat twice. Then seizing the rifle and two bags of cartridges he sallied out into the village. Behind him, panting with rage, ran his murdered brother's wife, a young woman of twenty years of age. She carried an infant in her arms, and was running swiftly, clutching in her right hand a short dagger.

"Stand, thou coward, Jinaban!" she called, setting the child down in the path—"stand, thou coward, for though thou hast slain my husband thou shalt not rob me of that which was his—give me back the gun."

Jinaban laughed fiercely, and his white teeth flashed from his black-bearded lips; he slipped some cartridges into the rifle. He waited till the woman was within ten yards of him, then raised the weapon and shot her dead. And now, his tiger nature aroused to the full, he sprang into the middle of the village square of Ailap, and began firing at every person he saw, sparing neither age nor sex. His second brother, Raô, a courageous young man, seizing the only weapon available—a seaman's cutlass—rushed forth from his house and, calling upon Jinaban to lay down his weapon, advanced towards him. Pretending to consent—for a cartridge had jammed and the rifle would not work—Jinaban held out the butt to Raô in token of surrender; then the moment Raô grasped it, he sprang at his throat and bore him to the ground, and, tearing the cutlass from his hand, he plunged it through and through the prostrate man's body. Then, with a savage threat against the whole of the murdered men's families, he turned and fled towards the beach. Dragging a light canoe down into the water, he sprang into it, and pushed off just as Palmer appeared on the scene, and, raising his revolver, fired six shots at the escaping murderer. None of the shots, however, took effect, and Jinaban, with an oath of vengeance against the white man, paddled swiftly away and reached the low, densely wooded and uninhabited island on the western side of the lagoon.

This for two years had now been his lair. Paddling over at dead of night from time to time, he would stalk, rifle in hand, through the village, and, entering any house he pleased, demand food and tobacco. And such was the terror of his name and his chiefly prestige that no one dared refuse. Sometimes, moved by the lust for slaughter, he would command that the food he demanded should be carried before him and placed in his canoe. Then he would shoot the unfortunate bearer dead on the beach. Against his half-brother's families he manifested the most deadly hatred; and on one occasion, meeting a girl, a slave of Rao's widow, on a little islet some miles away from Ailap, he shot the poor child through her legs, breaking them both, and left her to perish of starvation. Palmer well knew that he was willingly supplied with food by the people of his own village, although they asserted their innocence of aiding him in any way, and expressed the utmost fear and horror of the outlaw. That his death would be a relief to them as well as to the people of Ailap was certainly true, but Palmer and his wife Letanë were well aware that none of Jinaban's own people would ever raise hand against him; and, indeed, the Ailap people, though they now had the strongest feelings of friendship for the white man, were so smitten with terror at the constantly recurring bloody deeds perpetrated by Jinaban, that they were too terrified to accompany the trader over to the outlaw's island and track him to his lair. Twice had Palmer crossed over in the darkness of night, and, Winchester in hand, carefully sought for traces of Jinaban's hiding-place, but without success. The interior of the island was a dense thicket of scrub which seemed to defy penetration. On the last occasion Palmer had hidden among a mass of broken and vine-covered coral boulders which covered the eastern shore. Here for a whole night and the following day he remained, keeping a keen watch upon the line of beach in the hope that he would see Jinaban carrying his canoe down to the water to make one of his murderous descents upon the Ailap village. His own canoe he had carefully concealed among the scrub, and as he had landed on a very dark night upon a ledge of rocks that stretched from the water's edge to the thicket, and carried the canoe up, he was sure that no trace of his landing would be visible to Jinaban. At dark on the following evening he gave up his quest and paddled slowly over to the village, sick at heart with fear for his wife Letanë, for the outlaw had made a threat that she should soon fall a victim to his implacable hatred.

Halfway across the lagoon he heard the sound of two shots, and by its sharp crack knew that one came from Jinaban's rifle—the rifle he had given to the slaughtered Jelik. Urging his canoe along the surface of the quiet water, Palmer soon reached the beach of Ailap village, and was horrified to learn that the man he had sought had just left after shooting a lad of fifteen—a cousin of Letanë—whom he had surprised while fishing in the lagoon. Cutting off the boy's head, Jinaban had boldly stalked through the village till he reached Palmer's house, through the open window of which he had thrown his gory trophy, and then made his escape.

The trader's wife, who at the time was sleeping in the big room of the house, surrounded by half a dozen natives armed with muskets, at once sprang up, and, seizing a rifle, started in pursuit, for she feared that Jinaban had learnt of Palmer's absence, and would wait for and shoot him as he crossed the lagoon. She managed to reach the beach in time to see the escaping murderer paddling along in his canoe close in shore. Kneeling down, she took careful aim and fired. A mocking laugh answered the shot.

That was the story that Palmer told the half-caste Maori, who listened to him attentively throughout.

For some minutes, however, after the trader had finished, he did not speak, and then at last said in his slow, methodical way—

"I will promise you that I'll get you Jinaban, dead or alive, before a week is out. And I don't want money. But I want you, please, to get some one of your natives here to come and tell me all they can about Jinaban's friends in the other village."

Palmer called to his wife. She came in, heavy-eyed and pale-faced, for the youth whose head she and her women had just buried was much attached to her, and her husband as well. At that moment the lad's relatives were searching the lagoon in the hope of finding the body, into which it had doubtless been thrown by the ruthless hand of Jinaban; and Letanë had just returned alone to the house.

In a very short time the half-caste learnt from Letanë that Sépé, who lived in Jinaban's village, was strongly suspected of receiving visits from the outlaw, and even of visiting the man himself; for on several occasions she had been absent from her mother's house for two or three days at a time. And as most of Jinaban's people were in secret sympathy with their outlawed chief, the girl's movements were never commented on by the inhabitants of her own village, for fear that the relatives of the murdered chiefs, Raô and Jelik, and other people of Ailap, would kill her. But in some way Sépé had betrayed herself, and Letanë was now having a strict watch kept upon the girl by two or three of her women attendants whom she had sent to reside in Ijeet, as Jinaban's village was called. Ostensibly they had gone to visit some relatives there. Sépé, however, was always on her guard, and so far the spies had learnt nothing fresh.

At Porter's request the trader's wife gave him a description of Sépé's appearance, and also described the exact position of the house in which she lived with her mother. Then the half-caste unfolded his plan to Palmer and his wife.

"And now," he said, "I must go. If I stay longer it may spoil our plans by making Jinaban's friend suspicious. Give me the bottle of gin, and I'll carry it so that every one can see it as I walk through the village. And you must get all your men out of the way by the time I come back. They might shoot me, but the women will be too frightened."

Palmer went to his trade room and returned with a large bottle of Hollands, which he gave to Porter, together with a box of revolver cartridges; these the half-caste carefully concealed in the bosom of his singlet. Then, shaking hands with the trader and his wife, he walked out of the house, down the steps, and along the path to the village.

"Parma," said Letanë to her husband, as they watched the seaman disappear among the coco-palms, "dost think this man will be true to us in this thing?"

"Aye," replied the trader, "sure am I of his good faith; for he it was who four years ago, single-handed, fought two hundred of the wild man-eaters of the Solomon Islands, when they captured the ship in which he sailed, and slew every man on board but himself. Twenty-and-three of those devils of *kai tagata* (cannibals) did he kill with his Winchester rifle from the fore-top of the ship, although he was slashed in the thigh with a deep knife wound, and was faint from loss of blood. And then when the rest had fled in their canoes he came down and steered the ship away from the land and sailed her in safety to a place called Rubiana where white men dwell."

"Ah-h-h!" and Letanë's dark eyes opened wide in admiration.

An hour later Frank Porter, with an half-emptied bottle of liquor placed before him on the matted floor, was sitting in a house in Jinaban's village, surrounded by a number of young men and women.

"Come," he said, with drunken hilarity, and speaking in the Ponapé dialect, which is understood by the people of Las Matelotas, "come, drink with me;" and pouring out some of the liquor he offered it with swaying hand to the man nearest him; "drink, I tell thee, for when this bottle is empty then shall I make the white man give me more."

"Bah!" said a tall, dark-skinned girl, whose head was encircled with a wreath of red and yellow flowers, and who stood with her rounded arms folded across her bare bosom, "thou dost but boast. How canst thou *make* Parma give thee liquor, if, as thou sayest, thou hast no money? Is he a child to be frightened by loud words—which are but born in the belly of *that*" and she laughed and pointed contemptuously at the bottle beside him.

The half-caste looked at her with drunken gravity.

"Who art thou, saucy fool?" he asked, "to so talk to me? Think ye that I fear any white man? See!" and staggering to his feet he came over to where she stood, "seest thou this bloodied cut across my face, which was given me by a white man, when I fought with, three but last night?"

The girl laughed mockingly. "How know I but that last night thou wert as drunk as thou art now, and fell on the ship's deck and so cut thy face, and now would make us think that——"

"Nay, Sépé," broke in a lad who sat near, "'tis true, for I was on the ship and saw this man fight with three others. He does not lie."

"Lie!" and the half-caste, drawing his knife from its sheath, flashed it before the assembled natives; "nay, no liar am I, neither a boaster; and by the gods of my mother's land I shall make this Parma give me more grog to drink before the night comes, else shall this knife eat into his heart. Come ye all, and see."

And in another minute, followed by the girl Sépe and a dozen or more men and women, he sallied out into the road, knife in hand, lurching up against a palm-tree every now and then, and steadying himself with a drunken oath.

Sitting or standing about Palmer's house were some scores of native women, who waited for him to awaken from his afternoon's sleep and open his store so that they might sell him the pearl-shell that the menfolk had that day taken from the lagoon. But the white man seemed to sleep long to-day, and when the people saw Letanë, his wife, coming from her evening bathe, they were glad, for they knew she would open her husband's store and buy from them whatever they had to sell. But suddenly, as she walked slowly along the shaded path, a man sprang out upon her and seized her by the wrist. It was the half-caste sailor.

"Back!" he shouted warningly to the women, as they rushed towards him, "back, I say, else do I plunge my knife into this woman's heart." And then, releasing his hold of Letanë's wrist, he swiftly clasped her round the waist, and swung her over his shoulder with an exulting laugh. "Tell ye the white man that his wife shall now be mine, for her beauty hath eaten away my heart," and he ran swiftly away with his struggling burden, who seemed too terrified even to call for assistance.

And then as the loud cries of alarm of the women sounded through the village, Palmer sprang out from his house, pistol in hand, and darted in pursuit. The half-caste, with a backward glance over his shoulder, saw him coming.

Dropping the woman, who seemed to have swooned, for she lay motionless upon the path, Porter awaited the white man, knife in hand, and laughed fiercely as Palmer, raising his pistol, fired at him thrice. In another instant they were struggling fiercely together, and a cry of terror broke from the watching women when they saw the trader fall as if stabbed or stunned, and the half-caste, leaping upon him, tear the pistol from his hand, and, with an exultant cry, wave it triumphantly in the air. Then he fled swiftly through the palm grove towards Ijeet.

When Palmer opened his eyes, Letanë and a number of terrified women were bending over him, all but Letanë herself imagining he had been stabbed.

"Nay," he said, putting his hand to his head, "I was but stunned. Help me into my house."

That night the whole population of Ailap came to his house and urged him to lead them to Ijeet and slay the coward sailor who had sought to take his life and steal from him his wife.

"Wait," he answered grimly, "wait, I pray thee, O my friends, and then shalt thou see that which shall gladden thy hearts and mine. And let none of ye raise his hand against the half-caste till I so bid him."

They wondered at this; but went away contented. Parma was a wise man, they thought, and knew what was best.

When the house was in darkness, and the trader and his wife lay on their couch of mats with their sleeping child between them, Palmer laughed to himself.

"Why dost thou laugh, Parma?" And Letanë turned her big eyes upon his face.

"Because this man Porter is both wise and brave; and in two days or less we shall sleep in peace, for Jinaban shall be dead."

Back from the clustering houses of Ijeet village the man who was "wise and brave" was sitting upon the bole of a fallen coco-palm with his arms clasped round the waist of the star-eyed Sépé, who listened to him half in fear, half in admiration.

"Nay," she said presently, in answer to something he had said, "no love have I for Jinaban; 'tis hate alone that hath led me to aid him, for he hath sworn to me that I shall yet see Letanë lie dead before me. And for that do I steal forth at night and take him food."

"Dost thou then love Parma?"

"As much as thou lovest his wife," the girl answered quickly, striking him petulantly on his knee.

The half-caste laughed. "Those were but the words of a man drunken with liquor. What care I for her? Thee alone do I love, for thy eyes have eaten up my heart. And see, when thou hast taken me to Jinaban, and he and I have killed this Parma, thou shalt run this knife of mine into the throat of Letanë. And our wedding feast shall wipe out the shame which she hath put upon thee."

The girl's eyes gleamed. "Are these true words or lies?"

"By my mother's bones, they be true words. Did not I flee to thy house and bring thee this pistol I wrenched from Parma's hand to show thee I am no boaster. And as for these three women of Ailap who spy upon thee—show me where they sleep and I will beat them with a heavy stick and drive them back to their mistress."

Sépé leant her head upon his shoulder and pressed his hand. "Nay, let them be; for now do I know thou lovest me. And to-night, when my mother sleeps, shall we take a canoe and go to Jinaban."

At dawn next morning Palmer was aroused from his sleep by a loud knocking at the door, and the clamour of many voices.

"Awake, awake, Parma!" cried a man's voice; "awake, for the big sailor man who tried to kill thee yesterday is crossing the lagoon, and is paddling swiftly towards thy house. Quick, quick and shoot him ere he can land."

In an instant the trader and every one of his household sprang from their couches, the door was thrown open, and Palmer, looking across the

Rodman The Boatsteerer | 209

lagoon, which was shining bright in the rays of the rising sun, saw about a quarter of a mile away, a canoe, which was being urged swiftly along by Frank Porter and a woman. She was heading directly for his house, and already Palmer's bodyguard were handling their muskets, and waiting for him to tell them to fire.

Taking his glass from its rack over the door he levelled it at the approaching canoe, and looked steadily for less than half a minute, and then he gave an exulting cry.

"Oh, my friends, this is a lucky day! Lay aside thy guns, and harm not the sailor; for in that canoe is Jinaban, bound hand and foot. And the fight that ye saw yesterday between this half-caste and me was but a cunning plan between us to get Jinaban into our hands; and no harm did he intend to my wife, for she too knew of our plan."

A murmur of joyful astonishment burst from the assembled natives, and in another moment they were running after Palmer down to the beach.

The instant the canoe touched the sand, Porter called out in English—

"Collar the girl, Mr. Palmer, and don't let her get near your wife. She means mischief."

Before she could rise from her seat on the low thwart, Sépé was seized by two of Palmer's people. Her dark, handsome face was distorted by passion, but she was too exhausted to speak, and suffered herself to be led away quietly. And then Jinaban, who lay stretched out on the outrigger platform of the canoe, with his hands and feet lashed to a stout pole of green wood, was lifted off.

A few hurried words passed between Palmer and the half-caste, and then the former directed his men to carry the prisoner up to the house. This was at once done, amidst the wildest excitement and clamour. The lashings that bound him to the pole were loosened a little by Palmer's directions, and then four men with loaded rifles were placed over him. Then, calling a native to him, Palmer told him to take a conch-shell, go from village to village, and summon all the people to the white man's house quickly.

"Tell them to come and see Jinaban die," he said sternly.

As soon as the prisoner had been disposed of for the time being, Palmer and Porter went into the dining-room, where Letanë had prepared a hurried breakfast for the half-caste.

"Where is Sépé?" he asked, as he sat down.

"Locked up in there," said Palmer, pointing to one of the store-rooms.

"Poor devil! Don't be too rough on her. I had to lay a stick across her back pretty often before she would help me to carry Jinaban down to the canoe. And I had to threaten to shoot her coming across the lagoon. She wouldn't paddle at first, and I think wanted to capsize the canoe and escape, until she looked round and saw my pistol pointed at her. Then she gave in. I wasn't goin' to let Mr. Jinaban drown after all my trouble. But"—his mouth was stuffed with cold meat and yam as he spoke—"I'm sorry I had to beat her. An' she's got the idea that your missus will kill her when I tell you all about her."

Washing down his breakfast with a copious drink of coffee, Porter lit his pipe, and then, in as few words as possible, told his story. And as he told it a loud, booming sound rang through the morning air, and the hurrying tramp of naked feet and excited voices of the gathering people every moment increased, and "Jinaban!" "Jinaban!" was called from house to house.

"As soon as the girl an' me got to the island," he said, "she told me to wait in the canoe. 'All right,' I said, and thinking it would be a good thing to do, I told her to take the revolver and box of cartridges with her, just to show them to Jinaban in proof of the story of the fight I had with you; I thought that if she told him I was armed he might smell a rat and shoot me from the scrub. An' I quite made up my mind to collar him alive if I could. The night was very dark, but the girl knew her way about pretty well, an', leaving me in the canoe, she ran along the beach and entered the *puka* scrub. About an hour went by, an' I was beginning to feel anxious, when she came back. 'Come on,' she said, 'Jinaban will talk with you.' I got out of the canoe and walked with her along the beach till we came to what looked like a tunnel in the thick undergrowth. 'Let me go first,' she said, stooping down, and telling me to hold on to her grass girdle, she led the way till we came out into an open spot, and there was Jinaban's house, and Jinaban sitting inside it, before a fire of coconut shells, handling your revolver and looking very pleased. He shook hands with me and, I could see at once, believed everything that Sépé had told him. Then we had a long talk and arranged matters nicely. I was to stay with him until the first dark, rainy night. Then we were to come over and hide ourselves in your boat-shed to wait until you opened your door the first thing in the morning. We were both to fire together, and bring you down easy. Then Sépé was to settle her account with your wife while Jinaban rallied the Ijeet people, in case the Ailap natives wanted to fight. After that he and I were to divide all the plunder in the house and station between us, take two of your whaleboats, and with some of his people make for some other island in the Carolines as quick as possible. And Sépé was to be Mrs. Frank Porter.

"Then, before he knew what was the matter with him, I hit him under the ear, and laid him out stiff; and after choking the girl a bit to keep her quiet, I tied him up safely."

Palmer set his teeth, but said nothing. Then the half-caste, having finished his pipe, rose.

"What are we going to do with him—hang him, or what?" he inquired, coolly.

"Stand him out there on the beach and let one of the Ailap people shoot him."

Jinaban was led forth from Palmer's house into the village square, and bound with his back to a coconut palm. On three sides of him were assembled nearly every man, woman, and child on Las Matelotas Lagoon. Not a sign of fear was visible in his dark, bearded face; only a look of implacable hatred settled upon it when Palmer, followed by the half-caste seaman and a servant boy, walked slowly down his verandah steps and stood in full view of the assemblage. He was unarmed, but the boy carried his rifle.

Raising his hand to command silence, the murmuring buzz of voices was instantly hushed, and the trader spoke. There, said he, was the cruel murderer who had so ruthlessly slain more than a score of men, women, and children—many of whom were of his own blood. Jinaban must die, and they must kill him. He himself, although he had good cause to slay him, would not. Let one of those whose kith and kin had been slain by this cruel man now take a just vengeance.

A young man stepped out from among the crowd, and Palmer, taking the rifle from the boy who held it, placed it in his hand. He was the brother of the girl whom Jinaban had shot through the legs and left to die of starvation and thirst.

Slowly the young native raised the rifle to his shoulder, glanced along the barrel, then grounded it on the sand.

"I cannot do it," he said, handing the weapon back. Jinaban heard and laughed.

"Just what I thought would happen," muttered Palmer to Porter. "We must hurry things along, even if we have to do it ourselves," and then, raising his voice, he called out—

"Ten silver dollars to the man who will shoot Jinaban."

No one moved, and a low murmur passed from lip to lip among the crowded natives. A minute passed.

"Oh, cowards!" said Palmer scornfully. "Twenty dollars!"

"Double it," said the half-caste in a low voice; "and be quick. I can see some of Jinaban's people looking ugly."

"Forty dollars, then, and ten tins of biscuit to him who will kill this dog. See, he mocks at us all."

A short, square-built man—a connection by marriage of the murderer's brother, Rao—sprang into the open, snatched the rifle from Palmer's hand, and levelled it at Jinaban. But as his eye met those of the dreaded outlaw his hand shook. He lowered the weapon, and turned to the white man.

"Parma," he said, giving back the rifle to Porter, "I cannot do it; for his eye hath killed my heart."

"Ha!" laughed Jinaban, and the group of Ijeet men swayed to and fro, and a savage light came into Palmer's eyes. He looked at Porter, who at that moment raised the rifle and fired, and a man who was approaching Jinaban, knife in hand, to cut his bonds, spun round and fell upon the sand with a broken back. In a moment the crowd of Ijeet men drew off.

"Back, back," cried the half-caste, fiercely, springing towards them and menacing them with the butt of his empty rifle, and then hurling it from him he leaped back and picked up something that stood leaning up against the wall of Palmer's boat-shed. It was a carpenter's broad-axe—a fearful looking weapon, with a stout handle and a blade fourteen inches across.

"Look," he cried. "This man must die. And all the men of Ailap are cowards, else would this murderer and devil now be dead, and his blood running out upon the sand. But, as for me who fear him not—see!"

He took two steps forward to Jinaban and swung the axe. It clove through the murderer's shaggy head and sank deep down into his chest.

Two days later Sépé, who had made her peace with Palmer's wife, met the sailor as he was walking down to the beach to bathe.

"Wilt thou keep thy promise and marry me?" she asked.

"No," answered the half-caste, pushing her aside roughly; "marriage with thee or any other woman is not to my mind. But go to the white man and he will give thee the forty dollars and ten tins of biscuit instead. Something thou dost deserve, but it shall not be me."